Gods of Outrageous Fortune

Book 1 in the Dodecarchy series

KL Skinner

In this dark and twisty thriller, Kim Anderson, an intelligent 30something, is kidnapped while running an errand for her boss and falls down a rabbit hole of crime and conspiracy. Her tortured, logical mind tries to put the pieces of the puzzle together as she realises she will have to become someone else to find out what's really going on. Her quest for answers takes her from London to Crete; a journey of self-discovery, as much as the pursuit of truth.

There is only one perfect life; its imperfections make it so.

For Shaun

First published 2021

ISBN: 978-1-9162902-1-1

A catalogue record for this book is available from the British Library.

Set in Goudy Old Style by Ken Boyter
Cover and book design, typeset by Ken Boyter www.kenboyter.co.uk
Cover illustration by Toby Rigby

Acknowledgments

Thanks to editor, Kate Miller, for your critical eye and encouragement throughout, Toby Rigby for the wonderful cover illustration and Ken Boyter, for the design and typesetting.

Thanks to the Hertford Writers' Circle (www.hertfordwriterscircle.org.uk) for being willing test subjects through many readings and thank you to others who have volunteered as readers and allowed me to use your names as characters. Whether goodies or baddies, I'm grateful to you all.

Sincere thanks to my friends at various universities, James, Helen, Vicky and Steven. Thank you for the science, both real and imaginary. Thanks also for pointing out the practicalities. Any implausible leaps are of my own making.

And thank you to Shaun for your patience. This has been a long time coming. I hope you find it worth the wait.

PART 1

Chapter 1

Well, I suppose it all depends on what you call scary. One person's thrill could be another person's horror. I don't much care for the rodents some people keep as pets and I hate amusement rides, but being dumped in the middle of nowhere, with no means of communication, sounds like a relaxing holiday to me.

I certainly wasn't frightened to begin with, but then I didn't know what the day had in store. Everything had seemed so normal. My alarm had gone off as normal, my husband had ignored it, and I ate breakfast and went to work as normal.

It was about mid-morning that I got a call from my manager, Andrew. He was delayed at a meeting and asked me to pick up his client from the train station. He hoped to be back at the office by the time I returned.

Andrew didn't usually ask me for such a favour, but I don't think the unusual circumstances occurred to him. They didn't occur to me. I was just helping him out.

The train station lies just outside the main drag of the town. Most towns are built around such places, but here, the station was built to service the town, which was originally a hamlet, too small to have its own station. The back of the railway line is farmland with a few wooded areas; a small reminder of the way the landscape used to look before the needs of the people took over.

Bulky looking barns and animal sheds are scattered here and there like misshapen dice on a games board. The farmers' houses appear luxurious by comparison. Most of them were built when farmers were an authority in the rural towns and their idea of a second job was mayor or town councillor. Now, many of the farm buildings are empty and abandoned and the unemployed workers will tell anyone who'll listen that it's because the powers that be don't care about local regeneration.

The beautiful station clock read twenty past nine, but then it's always read twenty past nine. It stopped on daylight saving time around 1965 and nobody bothered to correct it.

Nobody will correct it now because the iron lattice support it sits on is rusted to hell and any attempt to adjust the clock could send it crashing to the ground. Even the surround was pretty, once upon a time. They seemed to have a knack back then, of being able to make even the most functional, attractive. The simple white face now just gazes serenely down on the unobservant commuters below and patiently waits for their return, while the once bright blond of the brass surround slowly tarnishes in the weather.

The ugly and unforgiving digital display in the main entrance, however, said 11:17. Years ago we would have given someone the benefit of the doubt and called that a quarter past eleven. With the introduction of digital technology, you are sharply reminded that if you were expected at a quarter past eleven, you are now running two minutes late.

'Excuse me,' I called to the man behind the glass, interrupting him from a most important report on the sports pages. 'Is there another train due from London this morning?'

He tutted loudly over his teeth then lifted his head to see who had spoken.

My business dress has different effects on different people, I have found, and a smart blouse and skirt combo with high heeled shoes tends to be the most effective at persuading others that it would be in their best interests to give me what I want.

'Sorry, love,' he said, rising from his seat, 'ain't gonna be another fer at least an hour.' He hoisted his baggy trousers up towards his paunch, unsuccessfully. 'Could always wait in waitin' room,' he suggested, swaggering over to the glass. 'There's a vending machine in there.'

'Thank you, but no,' I replied, giving him only my second best smile. 'I'm waiting for someone, and it appears they're a little late.'

'Oy, oy,' he winked mischievously, 'private meetin', is it? I'm good at keeping secrets like that. Seen a lot as an attendant 'ere, I 'ave.'

I regretted my next words as soon as they left my mouth.

'A client, actually,' I said coldly.

Mr Attendant's eyebrows immediately shot up and his eyes widened almost to the size of his smile.

'Almost given up hope there was one of you round this neighbourhood,' he whispered, leaning on the counter. 'Wiv green eyes, too! I could be one of yours. Got some stashed away, wouldn't mind spending a bit on a classy bird like you.'

'Not unless you're into printing,' I called over my shoulder.

'That's one you could teach me,' he laughed.

I'd already made the decision to head back to the office when I saw a very handsome man leaning against the railing opposite the entrance. He was eyeing me carefully, as if weighing me up before coming to some sort of conclusion. I was about to give him a mouthful, but he spoke first.

'Excuse me,' he said politely, 'but are you from Brownlow Print?'

'Yes,' I said, relieved to have a reason to be standing outside a train station at that time of the day. 'Kim Anderson. Pleased to meet you.'

His handshake was firm and confident; here was a man used to being in control.

'David Peters. Pleased to meet you, too.' His blue eyes twinkled as he only half tried to suppress a smile. He was in his early thirties, I guessed, with dark hair cut short and slightly tousled. He was just a little taller than me. 'Do you have a car?'

'Oh, yes, of course. This way.'

'Do you mind if we stop at another office on the way?' he asked. 'I need to meet with a colleague and pick up some papers.'

I was happy to oblige. If we ran late, I could suggest lunch. That's so much easier to explain away.

Alarm bells should have started ringing then, but I honestly didn't think anything of it. Why would a guy who had supposedly travelled miles by train, need to stop at a local office for papers? The question never occurred to me.

Peters redirected me to the back of the town. I was driving towards the farms and, I realised later, the abandoned farm buildings. As I drove, Peters was chatting amiably about how the offices were tastefully converted in a minimalist style, and looking back now, I can't believe how I took it all in.

We drew up outside some kind of stable block and, parked to the side I saw the back end of what I thought was a SUV.

'Well, that's good,' I thought, 'at least there's someone else here.'

Unfortunately for me, I was right. There was.

I accompanied Peters to the main door, and like a true gentleman, he pushed it open and stepped back to let me in first.

I didn't get to see much of the interior; it was dark and became darker still when something was pulled down over my head. It smelt warm and moist and felt like sacking against my skin.

Immediately I started thrashing about, trying to hit anything, but Peters quickly had my arms behind my back and I felt the sharp pain of a plastic tie cutting into the flesh around my wrists.

I started kicking, but Peters' mate already had rope to hand and I soon found my ankles tied tightly. Everything seemed so well organised. This was a violent dance, choreographed in advance.

Peters had hold of my shoulders while his friend grabbed my legs, and I was carried back out into the open. My feet briefly touched the ground and I realised I'd lost a shoe. I heard a car door open and felt a shove in the middle of my back. I'd been pushed into the SUV and my mind raced as I tried in vain to identify what make it was. I wasn't even sure of the colour.

The hand in my back continued to push until my face was squashed against the cushions on the back seats and I could hardly breathe.

I kept my mouth shut and tried to breathe through my nose. I could hear a car and realised with dismay that it was mine. Peters was keeping me controlled while his friend drove my car out of sight. I remembered I'd left my handbag in the car.

Soon Peters released the pressure on my back and I heard a soft thud as my missing shoe landed on the car floor. I cursed silently. They were leaving no clues.

The doors slammed and the engine started. As we began to move, I started screaming. I cursed Peters and the driver, called for help and demanded to know where we were going.

Everything I yelled was ignored and even laughed at. The more I cursed and pleaded with Peters, the more amusing he found it.

I couldn't help wondering if this was some sort of ridiculous practical joke, but I was sure no-one I knew would take a joke this far.

I tried counting the seconds and attempted to time how long the journey took, but I was so nervous and my pulse was pounding so loudly in my ears, that I soon gave up and resigned myself to sitting it out and seeing what happened. I didn't have too long to wait.

As the car slowed, the sounds changed and there was a crunch of gravel under the tyres. This continued for a little while, before the road surface changed again to something soft and bumpy.

The car stopped and I started to yell again, but this time a leather-gloved hand was pushed against my throat, choking the rising tide of screams and I knew whoever this man was, he'd done this before and meant business. I simply nodded slowly to show I understood.

I felt Peters move beside me and the doors opened. Wherever we were, we'd arrived.

Peters bent down and silently my shoe was reconnected with my foot and the rope disappeared. For some strange reason, I felt pathetically grateful. It was a gesture of kindness in a cruel situation.

I was pulled from the car and made to walk a little way. The ground was soft earth and very uneven. I guessed it was the end of a farm track made rutted by the frequent passage of vehicles.

I counted the steps I took. There were about fifty. No

doubt Peters and the glove wearing man could have managed the distance in less, but I couldn't see where I was going.

We went through a doorway and veered left. I stumbled against some steps and realised I was expected to walk up a staircase. It twisted on its journey and I tripped and half fell as I was pushed forward. When we got to the top I was pulled to the right and through another doorway.

'I hope you like what we've done with the place,' joked Peters. 'You're going to be here a while.' A door slammed. My hands were sore, my wrists were bleeding and my neck ached. My head was still covered. I couldn't see anything and I wasn't able to do anything.

I let my knees bend and I dropped to the floor, feeling the rough, worn floorboards tear at my nylons. I couldn't believe what was happening to me. I started to cry. Suddenly, I stopped. I'd heard a brief noise. There was breathing. I knew I wasn't alone.

'Peters! Is that you, you bastard? Cut me loose!'

There was definitely movement behind me. I felt my arm being held in a firm, but not cruel, grip and I was lifted to my feet.

I recognised gloved hands. Panic started to rise. Who was this guy and what did he want with me? I heard a click and a moment later my hands were free.

Chapter 2

I didn't know if Peters had a weapon, but now that I knew Gloves did, I wouldn't forget that.

I touched my wrists and flinched. The right one was worse off; it had what felt like a two-inch cut from the base of my thumb.

Gloved hands pushed something soft and warm to the damaged skin. He'd given me his handkerchief.

'Thank you,' I said. I felt stupid but there wasn't anything else I could think of to say.

I cautiously lifted my hands and slowly brought them to my face. I was taking a risk, but hey, nothing ventured, nothing gained. I pinched the edge of the hood between my fingers and thumbs and gently started to lift. Of course, he stopped me. I expected him to, but he wasn't violent or mean, he simply held a gloved hand over mine until I let go of the hood. I stood there a moment, waiting for another reaction, but none came. I heard a door open and close, a click in the lock, but no footsteps.

Taking the bull by the horns, more out of bravado than bravery, I gripped the hood and pulled it off in one, swift movement. I was entirely alone.

I took a few minutes to look around me.

The house I'd been brought to had clearly been vacant for quite some time. The wallpaper was flowery and faded. Where there had been lavender and forget-me-nots climbing the walls, now there were only pale imitations. A small window to the side of the room had been closed off. I went over to take a closer look.

Crudely, nails had been hammered into the wooden frame, preventing it from being opened. Beyond the glass, shutters restricted most of the light except for a few persistent beams pushing their way through the gaps in the warped wood. Beneath the window was a cold radiator. Flecks of chipped paint decorated the floor, like upswept confetti.

There was no furniture to speak of, but clearly I had been expected and everything had obviously been very carefully planned. In the corner of the room a makeshift bed had been made, with a mattress on the floor, a pillow and a couple of blankets.

Next to the mattress was an old wooden kitchen chair, beneath which was a bucket. I foolishly wondered what it was for, until I realised I actually needed to go.

On top of the chair was an old washing up bowl, inside, a roll of toilet paper and a bar of soap.

'Nice B&B,' I thought sarcastically.

I screwed up the handkerchief and threw it in the bowl. Then something caught my eye.

It was difficult to see against the fabric, but the handkerchief was monogrammed. The embroidery was in white and almost invisible, but a smear of my blood had highlighted a corner. I picked up the handkerchief to take a closer look. I could just make out 'AB'.

If the handkerchief was monogrammed, what other markings might there be?

I glanced around the room. I couldn't think of anything, really, until I saw the hood lying discarded on the floor.

Picking it up, I shook it out to take a closer look and some small seeds scattered to the floor. I knelt and ran my fingers over them. Some were rough, some were smooth, and some were larger than the others and fairly flat. I recognised those as oats and there was hay amongst the seeds, too. I ran my fingers through my hair and found more.

When I opened out the hood, I recognised it as a horse's nosebag. Were there stables out here? There was some sort of logo on the bag. It had faded badly, but was red and circular with a horse's head in the centre.

'Where am I? And why am I here?'

I heard a click in the lock again. Oh my God! He was coming back!

I knew I had to remain calm. There was no point in acting rashly. I had to remember, this one had a knife.

'Are you hungry? We have a gourmet lunch for you.' Peters, the bastard! I had a special thank you for him.

I rushed over to the door and stood with my back to it just a foot in from the frame. As the door started to swing open, I stepped backwards into its path and sent it slamming shut in Peters' face. There was a crash as a tray went down, but I wasn't fast enough to run through before Peters blocked my way.

I faced him, shaking, terrified of what he might do. I hadn't stopped to consider whether he had a knife too.

'That was stupid,' yelled Peters as I felt a stinging slap to my right cheek. The shock of the blow sent me back two paces and down on to the floor. If a slap was coming I would have expected it from the other side. Most people are right-handed, aren't they?

Peters started walking menacingly towards me.

'I'm sorry, I'm sorry.' I held up my hands, but Peters didn't stop.

'You'll pay for that, you stupid bitch.' I thought he was going to kick the hell out of me, and I curled up into a ball instinctively.

'No! please, don't.' But there was a creak on the stairs and suddenly Peters' rage vanished as quickly as it had appeared.

I looked towards the noise but Gloves was staying carefully out of sight. All I could see were the remains of a sandwich and a shattered glass of water in the doorway.

'You'll get nothing more to eat from me,' snarled Peters. 'You don't deserve the good treatment you're getting. Remember who's in charge around here.'

'Oh, I know who's in charge,' I said. 'It's your mate out there. Who is he? Tell me! What do you want from me?' I was panicking and my voice was starting to crack. Usually I mask my fears with wisecracks, but none seemed appropriate at the moment.

Peters remained silent. I knew he was trying to dominate

my personality, I was sure I'd read somewhere that's what attackers try to do in these situations. They aim to damage your sense of self. I realised with a deepening sense of foreboding that this wasn't a joke and I couldn't make light of the situation.

Peters grabbed my arm and dragged me, half crawling, half walking, over to the mattress, where he dropped me.

When his hands went to his belt I feared the worst, but he pulled out a large plastic tie, the same kind he'd used on my wrists earlier. Taking a few steps back and keeping his eye on me, he retrieved the nosebag from the floor. Becoming deprived of one of the senses is usually the worst threat to frighten little children in fairy tales. Now it seemed as if every childhood nightmare had come back to haunt me.

'No, please don't,' I begged. 'Look, you've got the wrong person. There's been a mistake.'

Roughly, the hood was yanked down and I was in darkness once more.

'Please don't,' I begged again. 'I don't like the dark.'

Further speech was impeded as the hood was tightened. I could feel Peters twisting the cloth. I reached up and grasped his wrists, but this made no difference. He was determined to finish his task. When he could twist the hood no further, he applied the tie. I heard the fast clicking as he pulled it secure. My hands immediately went to the hood, finding the twisted tongue of cloth protruding from the tight mouth of the tie. I could barely get my thumbs under the hood and any attempt to loosen it was useless.

A sharp shove to the middle of my chest sent me back on to the mattress, where I lay still until I heard the door shut and I was alone once more.

'Is this it for me?' I wondered. 'Am I going to die here? Why haven't they killed me already?'

Presumably there was still more they wanted from me. They were going to try and break me down, even humiliate me if they had to. There had to be something else, something that made me useful to them, even if I was an inconvenient burden. But what? Nick and I had no money. We weren't quite on the breadline, but what savings we did have wouldn't have worried Bill Gates. They hadn't taken my rings. My wedding ring wouldn't have been worth much anyway, but my engagement ring had a good quality diamond and they'd ignored that.

I thought I was going to start crying again. My throat felt rough and my eyes were sore.

I don't know how long I lay in the darkness. I must have dozed because I awoke startled by a sound.

The door opened again. I lay very still and listened as hard as I could.

The footsteps were almost inaudible but the grip on my arm was unmistakable.

'Don't you ever take those gloves off?' I asked as he pulled me to my feet. 'Your hands must get awfully hot.'

I heard the dragging of a chair and a clinking sound as something was put on the floor.

Gloves pushed me on to the chair and I felt, rather than

heard, him move behind me.

I remembered he carried a knife and all too soon I heard the familiar click. One hand was placed on my forehead and my head was tilted back before the hood became loose again.

Suddenly I could move my head. He'd released me. I tentatively lifted my hands to the hood and I lifted it up over my face. I must have looked quite funny. I was wearing it like a hat. I rubbed my hands over my tear stained face and took a breath.

I could see a plate on the floor by my feet. Balanced on the plate was a glass of milk and two biscuits.

'Aww, how sweet of you,' I said. I was actually quite touched. 'Milk and cookies. You shouldn't have!'

Next to the plate was a blue wallet-style folder. I recognised it immediately. It was the kind I used in the office.

Every process had its own colour. Job orders from the customer I filed in blue wallets, invoices paid were in green wallets and authorised dispatch details were in pink wallets. The files were for printouts of data I held on my computer. I had to admit to my colleagues to being anal about paperwork. I kept copies of everything.

'Where the hell did you get that!' I yelled. I always kept the files in a locked drawer. Andrew had never been that interested in administration and left most of the paperwork to me. I dealt with practically everything and, most times, all he had to do was put his signature on a document.

'What are you doing with my order file?' I yelled again. 'That's confidential. You must have broken into my drawer!'

I half twisted in the chair to face the robber who'd rifled through my desk. This invasion was a personal affront. I didn't get far. As soon as I started to move my head, the gloved hand, familiar by now, gripped the back of my neck and the message it conveyed was clear.

I froze automatically. A thousand thoughts were rushing through my head all at once but one became prominent. There was only one way he could have known how important that file was to me.

'Are, are you who I think you are?' I stammered. 'Are you Andrew? Look, there's obviously been some mistake. This file is just for routine orders. You could have asked me for it. There's only minimal financial information in there.'

Unsurprisingly, he didn't reply. The grip on my neck remained as he lowered the hood.

The grip gradually lessened and a moment later I heard the door close and lock.

He'd left the hood loose and I pulled it off as soon as I could and sat staring at the file on the floor. I'd been left in this isolated room to get on with some work, but what work, I wasn't sure.

A line from a song repeated in my head.

Alone again, naturally.

Chapter 3

I refused to look at the file. I knew what was in it, for God's sake; I'd done all the paperwork. Andrew never even had to dirty his hands with it, I took care of everything. So, now what? Was I expected to go through it all again, was there something I'd missed? Had I made a financial mistake? With my head for figures, I thought that was unlikely. Why hadn't he just asked me?

Gloves didn't come back to the room that night. He had to know by now that he had the wrong employee. That must be it. I was the wrong person, this was an error and as soon as they realised that, I'd be released. I looked down at my hands. I couldn't make them stay still.

I had no idea what time it was. I don't usually wear a watch and now I cursed that oversight. For some strange reason I really needed to know the time, it was suddenly very important. I lay in the dark for ages just staring at the ceiling and wondering how on earth this could be happening to me.

This was the first time I had ever stayed away from my husband all night without him knowing where I was. Was he driving around looking for me? Had he called the police?

He must have called the police. Did my Dad know? All of a sudden, I desperately wanted to talk to Nick. I wanted to tell him not to worry, that everything was going to be alright and I'd be home soon. Or perhaps I wanted to hear him say those things to me. Nick would find me.

I curled up into a ball and pulled the blankets up over my head. I was hungry, cold and alone. I cried until I slept. Nick would find me.

There was an engine revving, doors slamming and voices shouting. I heaved a sigh and tried to ignore the noise. More banging. A car door slammed.

I rolled over to mutter to my husband.

'God, Nick. Can't you yell out the window at them or something?'

I reached out to his side of the bed and my hand banged against a hard surface, hurting my fingers. I squealed and opened my eyes. It was then that I realised my nightmare was continuing. I had hit my hand against the leg of the chair beside the mattress.

Voices were still shouting. I ran over to the window and tried to look out. The shutters were warped, but they still restricted what I could see.

I could make out a car. I thought it was the SUV. Anyway, I could see the colour, dark blue. The back doors were open and there were boxes on the ground next to it. I didn't know if this was the vehicle that brought me here, but I thought it safe to assume it was.

The boxes looked familiar. I could only see corners, but they looked like large plastic stackable boxes, the kind we used at work for the transport of large volumes of print to archive. Cardboard boxes of a similar size with our company logo were used to deliver print to the customer.

A figure was hauling the boxes into the back of the car and didn't seem to be too happy about the task. He was the one doing all the complaining and all the donkey work. His annoyance appeared to be directed at someone standing in the doorway, whom I couldn't see at all.

Four of these boxes were finally loaded in the car and as soon as he had slammed the doors shut, he hurried around to the driver's side. He seemed to walk with a shuffle and a lope and suddenly the car was racing away down the bumpy track and out of sight.

I hadn't been able to see him clearly, but one thing I was sure of. He wasn't Peters.

Another door slammed, presumably the front door, and I heard muffled voices. They were coming from below me.

I closed my eyes and tried to think. When I was brought here, which way did we turn? Yes, that was it. Left, it was left up the stairs and then right as the stairs turned twice and then right into this room. But that didn't make sense. If I stood with my back to the door, the window was on my left.

Surely the window would be looking out on to the back of the cottage, what would once have been the back garden. There wouldn't have been any access for a car.

There were only two possibilities I could think of. One: there was access for a car because the back entrance was made that way and any garden space was given up for vehicles. That would not be so unusual, especially if the cottage was part of a farm. Working vehicles would be parked out the back and the most used entrance would be the back door. Or, two: I had been smuggled in through the back door and my window looked out on to the front of the cottage. That would mean I'd been bundled up the back stairs without being brought through the cottage. That in turn suggested that the building was a lot bigger than I had first assumed. There couldn't be that many houses with space for a back stairs.

The room my kidnappers seemed to be using the most was below me. If I could assume that was the main room, then my theory about the larger cottage was the most likely.

Traditionally, the big main room would be at the front of the house and the smaller family rooms towards the back. If that was true, then there would be another two rooms downstairs: a smaller room and a kitchen, maybe even a scullery or utility room, as well.

If the upstairs rooms were based on the same layout, there would be a similar number of rooms up here. That would mean at least one more bedroom, maybe two, and a bathroom.

The voices below me stopped. I heard some more movement. I went to the door and listened carefully. There were footsteps on the stairs.

I ran back to the mattress and sat down like a good little girl to wait for whoever came.

Peters opened the door, and just for a moment, I was disappointed. He locked it behind him and pocketed the key.

He was carrying a bucket which was two thirds full and steaming.

'Good morning,' he said pleasantly, in a voice that made my skin crawl. 'Room service, I do hope it's not too early.' His sarcasm suggested that bringing me hot water was not his own idea.

'No, that's fine, thank you.'

He picked the soap out of the washing up bowl and dropped it in my lap, then proceeded to pour the hot water into the bowl. He pulled the bucket from under the chair and replaced it with the one he had just emptied.

'I can tell you've done this before,' I said. 'Such efficiency, I'm impressed!' Peters threw me a warning look.

'Please don't drop the chamber pot on your way out,' I added.

Without further warning, Peters reached out with his free hand and grabbed a handful of my hair, pulling me sharply towards him. He lent down and hissed in my ear.

'You're here for one reason only and after that, we will have no further use for you. We will then have to decide just what we are to do with you.'

Peters let go of me with a flick of his wrist and I unbalanced backwards on to the mattress.

That's always been a failing of mine; I open my mouth and stick both feet right in, covering my panic with badly thought out comments.

'What is it you want from me? I'm not an important person.' I was breathing hard and trying to remember the breathing patterns Nick had taught me.

By this time, I was fairly sure Peters didn't carry a weapon. If he'd had a knife too, I didn't think he would have been shy about using it. In fact, I felt fairly sure that if he did once have a knife, Gloves would have confiscated it.

It was becoming increasingly clear to me, Gloves was the brains and Peters was the brawn. If, as I suspected, Gloves had done this sort of thing before, it was entirely possible Peters had too. I was going to have to be a lot more careful in front of him.

I let out a sigh and sat with my knees up and my head down.

Peters picked up the blue wallet from the floor and flicked through the pages. He gave me a mean look before dropping it back on the floor. Perhaps I had already failed my task.

I stayed still on the mattress, not looking up until I heard the door close and lock.

I let out another long breath and tried to calm my heart. The police would be looking for me; Nick would find me.

I used the hot water and washed as best I could, but without clean clothes, I didn't feel much better.

I was attempting to dry myself with my blouse when a creak on the stairs told me someone was coming. Assuming it was Peters, I stayed where I was, but the door didn't open. I went to the door and put my ear against it to listen. Footsteps were walking away from me. He was going into the other room. I desperately tried to rack my brains to remember how many rooms I guessed this place had.

He didn't go far before stopping. I could hear movement and then footsteps getting progressively louder. He was coming to my room.

I still had my hands against the door when I heard the lock click. The handle moved slowly and the door only opened a fraction.

I grabbed hold of the handle with both hands and yanked it as hard as I could. If there was going to be an opportunity for me to escape, I had to take it, however slight.

He had obviously anticipated this, as the handle flew from my grasp and the door slammed. I banged my hands against the door.

'You've made a mistake! You have to release me.' I banged against the door again. 'You have to release me!'

I expected to hear footsteps going back downstairs but I heard nothing as I stood there waiting. By now, I believed it was Gloves on the other side of the door.

'You must know that you have the wrong person here. I'm not the person you need. Andrew?'

I waited and again, the door opened a fraction.

To my surprise, cloth appeared in the crack. I pulled it into the room and opened the folds to reveal a pair of men's joggers. Hardly the height of male fashion, but I was grateful just the same, and even more so when more items appeared. This must have been the movement I'd heard. He had been opening drawers, getting clothes for me.

'Are you in trouble, Andrew?' I whispered to the crack in the door. Yesterday, I couldn't imagine Andrew being involved in criminal activity. Had he spoken to Nick? He would have had to confess his mistake. Nick would come for me.

The door shut quickly, pulling away from beneath my fingers. The lock clicked once and rapid footsteps hurried down the stairs.

I laid out the clothes on my mattress and found that apart from the joggers, I'd also been given a tee shirt, what looked like a vest or undershirt, and a pair of boxer shorts.

Under normal circumstances, I wouldn't wear men's underwear, it's not my sort of thing. But these weren't normal circumstances and all the clothes, although old, were clean and a whole lot more appealing than what I was still wearing.

Once changed, I realised that one thing I hadn't been given was a pair of socks. The shoes I was wearing when brought here were heeled court shoes, not the most functional when planning an escape.

The room had no carpet and the floorboards weren't in the best of shape. I worried how my feet would survive exposed to a floor like this.

I am usually unable to sit still anyway, and spending the whole day on the mattress with nothing else to do was not my idea of a fun time.

Peters arrived with a mug of tea and buttered toast about twenty minutes after I was dressed. Neither of us spoke. I was being a lot more wary now and he was eyeing me suspiciously. I had no idea why that was, but he seemed to be as wary of me as I was of him.

I was sitting on the mattress with my head in my hands, when I glanced up and again saw the blue folder lying on the floor where Peters had left it. Gloves hadn't actually come into the room that morning and Peters had said nothing about it when he returned. I had been deliberately ignoring it but my curiosity was getting the better of me and finally I gave in and opened the folder.

It was certainly not as I had left it. The orders file was a universal folder with details of more than one company, but someone had gone through the file and changed the paperwork within. Now it only contained papers from one company. These were copies of receipts, payments and shipping orders for a company called Fireflight Healthcare.

be as wary of me as I was of him.

I was sitting on the mattress with my head in my hands, when I glanced up and again saw the pile of folders on the floor where Peters had left it. [illegible] hadn't actually come into the room that morning and Peters had said nothing about it when he returned. I had been deliberately ignoring it but my curiosity was getting the better of me and finally I got up and opened the folder.

It was certainly not as I had left it. The outside file was a universal folder with details of more than one company, but someone had since gone through the file and changed the paperwork within. Now it only contained papers from one company. These were copies of receipts, payments and shipping orders for a company called Fairlight Healthcare.

Chapter 4

I immediately started going back in my memory to recall what work my company had done for them. According to this paperwork, the printing Fireflight Healthcare had ordered had been completed months ago, but they were paying in instalments over several weeks. I had authorised the receipts myself and agreed the shipping orders. Once I had done that, the work was cleared for dispatch, but it seemed the printing had never left us.

I was confused. I'd been in the stores only last week and there were no outstanding orders, everything that should have been dispatched had been. Why were they still paying for work that had already been done?

There was only one possible answer I could think of; more work had been added to the original request over and above what I had originally billed for. I realised with dismay, there were only two people who could authorise that change above me; Andrew, my boss and Tony Brownlow, Andrew's uncle and owner of Brownlow Print.

Whatever work they had authorised, they had chosen not to go through me and, as far as I knew, Andrew had never kept me in the dark like this before. He'd always trusted me completely, and I'd never betrayed that trust.

Stapled to the back of each authorised shipping order was a print-out of the payment details which I logged into the computer at the close of each job. I immediately noticed the account numbers had been changed. I had logged the payment as going into our general payment account, but the money had been transferred to another account, not Brownlow Print. This was not our normal sequence of events. Why would our payment be sent outside the company?

It was while I was reading the account change details that I discovered an attempt had been made to withdraw a significant sum from the account, but the withdrawal had been refused by the bank. This was because I'd used my own access code when I had logged the payment and closed the invoice. Our system didn't allow any employee access to the company accounts without a passcode and although both Andrew's and Tony's codes trumped mine, they couldn't change what I had done. This was an added security measure that Andrew had approved himself. He would have to re-enter my access code and reopen the invoice to get at that money.

Andrew would have known that asking me for my codes, or tricking me into revealing them was unlikely to work. Previously I would have balked at the idea of betraying the company, but now I was changing my mind. I didn't really care about the money, and I certainly didn't care about my kidnappers. All I wanted to do was get out alive. I'd give them what they wanted and get the hell out of Dodge.

I wasn't going to be given a computer in this room; I wasn't going to get that lucky, but if they needed my access codes that badly, they'd have a computer here somewhere, possibly set up in one of the other rooms.

I had to find it. Maybe they had email. I guessed there was a bigger chance of finding the computer and getting a message to someone than escaping from the cottage by myself.

I tried to think logically about what I could do. They weren't going to leave the door open for me so I could go looking for the computer and they weren't going to let me input the access codes on my own. Most likely the folder would be taken from me. I would have to break out of the room and find out where they were taking it.

In the bottom of the folder was a cheap ballpoint, and after a few scribbles on the outside of the folder, I got it to work. I went back over the payment printouts and wrote in my access codes and the date I'd applied them. I've never had any trouble remembering figures like that. Dates, times, amounts; it doesn't really matter what the figures are or what form they take, if they have a sequence I can usually recall it.

When I'd finished, I closed the folder and left it by my chair. I wondered how long it would be before Peters came to collect it. It felt like an unclean presence in the room.

I went over to the window and tried to look out. I was keeping my back to the folder as much as possible and trying not to think about it. I felt like a traitor. I'd revealed details about my company's payment methods, and I wasn't sure it would do me any good. In fact, I was pretty sure it wouldn't. I might escape from here but who would give me a job after this?

I imagined newspaper headlines. 'Search for Missing Woman Continues.' Were they looking for me? Was my husband asking friends and neighbours about me? Had he called my office? What lies had they told him? I was sure Nick would be looking for me.

Sharp tears stung my eyes. I commanded myself to stop. I had to keep a clear head if I was to get out of here and blubbering like a baby wasn't going to help.

It was no good. As soon as I started thinking about my family, the crying started and once the flow began, the trickle became a flood.

I wasn't just upset; I was angry and indignant. I could not believe that anyone could kidnap me in daylight, hold me prisoner and coerce information from me. How dare they?!

I pushed my hands against the window frame, giving it a useless shove. How dare they? I banged my fists against the sides of the frame.

'How dare you!' I exclaimed to no-one in particular. I banged my fists against the frame again, almost relieved to feel the pain in my hands and wrists. 'How dare you!' I screamed. I knew there was nobody to hear who could help me in my predicament. It seemed more realistic to vent my anger at those who inspired it. I smacked my hands against the glass and didn't care if I pushed my arms through it. 'How dare you do this to me!' I yelled furiously. 'How could you do this? How could you just take me away like that!' I ran out of breath and stood there sobbing with my forehead against the cruel glass, separating me from the freedom of the outside world.

I whispered between sobs, 'How could you?'

My blurry vision created a dim watercolour impression of the restricted view I'd been given. It was a grey day outside. The wind was blowing roughly and I could see leaves being torn around. There was no sunlight trying to fight its way in through the shutters today.

I heard the sharp high-pitched whining of a reversing car and the crunch of tyres over gravel, the persistent noise forcing my attention towards the sound. I lifted my head and tried to look. The back end of a vehicle came up the drive and, although I couldn't be sure, my heart beat faster as I wondered if it was the same car I'd seen before and if it was the one that brought me here.

I don't think I was meant to find out. Footsteps on the stairs told me someone was coming, and they wouldn't be too pleased to find me trying to attract attention by standing by the window.

I swiftly stepped back to the middle of the room just as the lock clicked open and Peters walked into the room.

The door was too far away for me to make a run for it, not that I thought such a move was wise. Peters didn't speak as he closed the door and stood watching me for a moment. I held my breath. What did he want with me?

Peters stayed silent as he picked up the folder and slowly

made his way back to the door. His eyes were diverted for a second as he reached down for the handle.

I didn't allow myself time to think. I really didn't care how sensible or foolish this was; I considered it my duty as an unwilling hostage to attempt an escape.

I ran towards him as fast as I could and made a frantic and determined grab for the door handle. My technique at ambush wasn't as polished as his had been, but mine was unrehearsed. For a few stupid seconds, we were like two children fighting over the possession of a toy; smacking hands away, pulling at clothes, tugging and scratching.

Peters easily pushed me off and I guessed what he was about to do next. When his hand came up towards me, I caught it with my right hand. I hadn't forgotten he was left-handed.

A flash of surprise lit his face for a second before he shoved me hard and I fell down on my butt once more.

By the time I was up on my feet again he had the door open and was already on the other side of it. I wasn't about to give up quietly. I banged on the door with the flat of my palms and kicked it too. That was a mistake. Without protection on my feet, I was only doing myself damage.

I continued to yell and scream, making as much noise as I could manage.

'You bastard! How dare you do this to me! I demand to be released. How much longer do I have to be here?'

None of my comments or insults were answered. Once I had stopped shouting I realised I was hungry. 'When am I

can make a lot of difference to a small volume, but not to the huge amounts this company was ordering. It was big enough to make a difference to somebody, but small enough to be missed by someone not in the know.

What the hell was going on?

Chapter 5

I scrambled through the folder and again found the usual ball point pen.

As I reviewed the changes they'd tried to make, I realised that this time they wanted individual account numbers for the client and the dates the payments were to be made available. It seemed that the codes I had given them had allowed them through one door, but now they needed more information to get them through the next.

How much was this worth, not just in monetary terms but generally? As far as the costs were concerned, I reckoned that Fireflight Healthcare's work was probably about 25k. In our business, that made them a very good client but was money the only consideration? How much was £25,000 worth to Peters and Gloves, and surely there had to be easier ways to get it than to go to all the trouble of kidnapping someone.

I made a very rash decision to find out just how important £25,000 was to them.

The account details were listed in the usual fashion and I assumed that I had to do the same as before and write in my remembered information next to the relevant details.

All the account numbers I wrote myself were correct but I put them beside the incorrect account details. I then changed the written order of two of the payment dates, putting the month before the day the way the Americans do.

It was a running joke in the office that I never made mistakes like that. Apple pie Anderson, that's what they called me, but having a head like a calculator isn't always a blessing. Frequently when a female colleague had a '37th' birthday celebration, I'd missed the cue for subtlety and bought her a card that said 'Happy 40th'.

I knew I was being foolish, but I had to find out what they were up to. The only way I could think of, was to provoke a reaction.

I was now pretty sure there was a computer here. Peters' reaction to the previous folder had been a bit of a giveaway and if my suspicions were correct, then so would be his reaction to this one.

I deepened my resolve to find the computer. But first I had to devise a plan to get out of this room.

I put the folder back together, trying to make it as I had found it, and left it beside my chair.

Outside, it was starting to get dark and I was feeling a sharp chill. It was going to be cold tonight.

A few hours passed before I heard the familiar creak on the stairs.

Peters brought me soup and crackers for my tea. Although it was obvious that I was being used for some private purpose, I had to admit, I was being well looked after.

'My feet really hurt,' I complained.

I had gone the whole day without any protection on my

feet and now, at the end of the day I was beginning to feel the effects of this neglect.

I rubbed my toes as I sat on the mattress. I could feel the sharp pin-pricks of tiny splinters.

'Do you think you could find me some socks or slippers from somewhere?' I asked, 'Or doesn't the kidnap budget run to that?'

Peters walked over to the chair and picked up the folder. I was surprised, I hadn't expected Peters or Gloves to come back for it until morning but I had thought it wise to have it ready in case.

Peters didn't even acknowledge me and left the room without commenting. He had either received some sort of briefing from Gloves about how to handle me or had suddenly learned how to manage me on his own. I knew which I thought was more likely.

Some time had passed after I'd finished my soup when Peters reappeared. He quickly unlocked the door and came storming in. He was not in a good mood.

'What the bloody hell do you think you're doing?' he yelled, and then more quietly and menacingly, 'If you have no regard for your own safety, then just carry on and I'll be happy to administer your punishment.' He was standing right over me and gripped my tee shirt firmly, holding me steady in preparation for a beating. He already had his other hand raised and looked as if he was about to give me the thrashing of a lifetime. He also looked like he was going to enjoy it.

A stern cough from the stairway made us both jump and I realised, with a huge surge of relief, Gloves must have followed Peters up the stairs.

Peters leaned close to my ear.

'Later, sweetheart,' he whispered.

I was so scared I thought I was going to be sick, but Peters didn't leave straight away. He reached inside his belt and pulled out another plastic tie.

'Oh God, no, please don't,' I begged. 'Not again. I won't fight, I promise.'

Hot tears stung my eyes but I tried to harden myself. I wasn't above a bit of begging but I'd be damned if I'd let Peters think he'd succeeded in making me cry.

He ignored me and very quickly the hood, discarded in the corner of the room, was retrieved and I was deprived of light and vision yet again.

The plastic tie held the hood in place and once Peters was sure it was secure, he left and I heard the door close. Yet I wasn't alone. I heard the sounds of different items, and also something bulky, being put down and then the scraping of the chair being dragged into the centre of the room.

The firm grip on my arm needed no introduction, and I was soon sitting in the chair.

'So, I guess you've tried the account codes, then,' I said. 'Didn't you get what you wanted?'

Gloved hands gently pulled the cuffed edges of the jogging bottoms up the calf of one leg and then the other.

'Maybe I've made a mistake,' I continued as the bulky

object was dragged nearer.

'Maybe you should let me take another look at the file and I'll go through it again for you.'

My knees were bent and my legs lifted before being slowly lowered again. The gentle warmth of the water comforted my feet like a soft blanket and I couldn't help letting out a small sigh of relief.

The astringent smell of something medicinal rose out of the bucket as cupped hands behind my knees alternately lifted and lowered my feet in the bucket. My feet were only submerged in two or three inches, but this was enough to help ease away the aches and pains that had troubled me for most of the day.

The assistance stopped momentarily and when I realised I was moving my feet on their own I wondered if he had left.

'Are you still there?' I asked. I can't explain why but I was suddenly worried. Not mistrustful of being hurt, but concerned that he might leave me alone and I hadn't heard him go.

In answer I heard a shuffling and then a familiar click. Within seconds the hood was loose.

This guy was behaving very strangely. He wouldn't hurt me, but wouldn't let me see his face. He wouldn't let me leave, but he wouldn't let me be mistreated and he trusted me enough to let my hands be free.

I instinctively rubbed my sore and aching neck.

Immediately he reached forward and gripped my forearm and I froze.

'It's OK,' I said, trying to reassure him. 'I won't lift the hood. I promise.' Cautiously, he released his grip.

I heard him move and walk around to the back of my chair. I cannot describe what it felt like when he started to rub my shoulders for me. My muscles resisted at first but soon I felt much better and as he moved on to the back of my neck, I dropped my head co-operatively. Strong thumbs pressed deep circles into the groves at the top of my spine and I couldn't help but take a deep breath.

His thumbs dropped lower below the collar of my tee shirt and a gasp left me as he applied gentle, but persistent pressure.

'Who are you? Why am I here?' I flexed my toes as I squirmed uncomfortably in my chair and heard the sound of cascading droplets splash on the harsh wooden floor. I felt the weight of his head and the warmth of his breath against the back of the hood as the rough sacking was dragged up, up and away. I felt it rise up against my cheeks, over the top of my nose, and suddenly I could see again. My hair fell against my face and obscured the dim view of the bucket and towel I saw on the floor, casting strange shadows across the room.

His hands had never left me, so he'd pulled the hood off with his teeth and let it fall to the floor by his feet.

His breath brushed my skin as gently as a summer wind as his lips began a journey where his thumbs had paused. He pressed his nose against my neck and took a deep breath of his own.

'Why are you doing this? Who are you?'

I should have been scared; terrified, even. But I didn't feel like I was being attacked. Strangely, I felt as though I should know this man, as if I was being seduced. His fingers pressed against my neck, my ears and up into my hair. His nose continued to breathe me in as his mouth meandered through my hair to the top of my head, where his cheek came to rest at the crown.

My husband always hugged me this way. Nick always held me from behind and rested his cheek against my head. He said I had a funny shaped head that was made to fit his funny shaped cheek.

Gloves moved his head to kiss the spot where his cheek had been and it was then that I realised I had to stop him. I reached up and held his head between my hands and uttered the killer word.

'Don't.'

Thoughts of my husband and home swirled in my mind and a wave of guilt rushed over me as I thought about how close I had come to giving in to temptation.

Gloves didn't move at first, everything just stopped.

'I'm sorry,' I muttered, feeling foolish. 'I just can't. I'm sorry.'

I didn't know why I was apologising, I couldn't explain.

Slowly he backed away and I felt the rough hood being lowered over my face again. I heard him pick up the bucket and heard the water pour from it. No words were exchanged and soon I heard the door close and the key locking me in my prison.

I pulled off the hood and simply sat there for several moments. Maybe, if I was strong enough, I could have used a romantic moment to take advantage of the situation and bribed my way out of here. Could I do that? I didn't think I was brave enough even if the thought had occurred to me.

When I looked around me, I saw the towel on the floor and picked it up. It was warm and soft. Not the kind of rag one would throw before a worthless victim.

Beneath it was the folder that Peters had collected earlier.

So, he had brought it in with him.

I glanced over to where my original bucket had been. The one in which my feet had been bathed, was in its place. I looked inside and it was empty. I let out an incredulous laugh.

The perpetrator of this crime, the brains behind the kidnapping and reason for it, had protected me from his violent partner, had bathed my feet, revealed a romantic interest and now had changed my chamber pot.

I remembered something. I hurried over to the mattress and checked around the edges, picked up the blanket and gave it a shake. It was gone. I couldn't find the handkerchief anywhere. He had taken it.

This confirmed something to me, without a doubt. I knew it when I touched his face, when I was close enough to smell his skin. Gloves was not whom I'd thought he was. AB was not Andrew Brownlow.

Chapter 6

I noticed that Gloves had not taken my empty soup bowl away. This gave me an idea. I cleaned off the spoon as best I could and hid it beneath a corner of my blanket.

Once that was done I got on with the job in hand and did the work I was supposed to do.

I went through the folder again and gave correct details in correct places, this time noting which numbers went against which details. Once out of here, it was likely that I would have to report to the police. With a memory like mine, they would expect me to be able recall exactly what information my kidnappers had wanted from me.

This reminded me of a disturbing realisation. I couldn't recall the registration of the car that brought me here. That sort of thing was supposed to be easy for someone like me. A registration had both letters and numbers. These were details I handled every day and which made up the bulk of my working life. Why on earth would the image not come to me? I remembered seeing the vehicle; I could describe its shape and style. I wasn't surprised at not immediately remembering the colour, that sort of thing I probably would forget, the registration number I certainly should remember.

Again, once I had finished I put the folder back as I had

found it.

The information I was about to give them would free up access to the £25,000 I knew they were after. There was one more stage in the process. There would be one more folder for me to look at: the pink one that authorised despatch. This was the last payment in our work process to be received. Had they changed the values of those payments, too? Once they had the access codes to the despatch accounts, it was all systems go. They'd get what they wanted, but where did that leave me?

It was now late evening and soon my kidnappers would be preparing for the night. I should have tried to get a few hours' sleep but I was restless. At home I slept like a log, but here in strange surroundings, I didn't want to be unaware of things. I guessed it was pretty quiet here at night, but that was soon to change.

I had no idea how long I'd waited, or what time it was, but I didn't want to leave it much longer because if I was tired, my responses would be slow.

I crept over to the door and gently tried to open it. Unsurprisingly it was locked. Then again, stranger things had happened. I knelt down and peered through the lock. The key had not been left in and I thought I could just make out the door opposite.

I examined the door hinges. I'd seen similar ones before but this was the first time I'd truly taken a good look. When I helped my Dad redecorate last summer, he had painted similar hinges the same colour as the door frame.

The hinges looked like long narrow tubes sitting on top of one another, each pair as long as the width of my palm. Looking at the top of the lower hinge I saw what I presumed to be a long pin running down the middle of the hinge, through both halves. I couldn't lift it with my fingers.

I retrieved the spoon I'd hidden earlier and tried first the handle and then the bowl end to lever the pin out. It seemed completely stuck and I had to work the spoon round the top of the pin several times to free trapped dirt and several layers of chipped and peeling paint before I could try again.

This time, when I used the bowl end of the spoon, I was successful in getting the edge under the head of the pin and after much levering I thought I felt it nudge upwards. I tried again, and it nudged a little more. This was painfully slow, but it was working.

Nudge after tedious nudge, I eventually brought up half a centimetre's worth for me to grip with my fingers and coax loose. With a lot of persuasion, it finally gave in and I lifted the pin out.

I balanced my hand against the door and released it very slowly, just in case the door gave way and fell in. I need not have worried. The hinges had been left for so long, the door didn't move.

I had to stand on the chair to reach the top one and after many minutes of brute force and silent swearing, that pin also started to free up.

Once I had both pins out, I pocketed them in my jogging bottoms with one hand and kept the other on the door.

Then I walked my hands down the door, until I could step off the chair and push it out of the way with my foot.

Here came the really difficult part. I braced my hands and the weight of my arms against the edge of the door and with more strength of will than strength of body, I pushed in and up as hard as I could.

The door only shuddered slightly. I prised my fingernails into the tiny gap between the door and the frame and gave another shove.

The door gave way and dropped about two inches. It made no noise, as the inside edge landed squarely on the tip of the middle finger of my left hand. Indescribable pain surged through my finger, into my hand and I immediately put my finger into my mouth and sucked hard, not just to ease the pain but suppress the sound of an impending scream, threatening to give me away.

I forced myself to get a grip and focus on what I was doing. I tried to lower the door on to the floorboards but it was too high up to be lowered that far. This room had obviously once been a bedroom and as such probably had a soft carpet which may have been high enough to cushion the drop. I would have to find something else.

I held the weight of the door against my left hand and gently wedged my left foot underneath. Balancing the door between hand and foot, I had my right hand free.

All I could think of was using my tee shirt. With my right hand only, I pulled the shirt up to my chest and holding the edge under my chin, wriggled my arm out and then pulled it over my head. I reached across the door with my right hand to hold it steady and with my left shook the shirt off and wedged that under the door.

Hoping and praying that this would work, I slowly pulled away my foot and let the door drop on to the cloth. It held.

I had no other clothes, and shivered with apprehension as well as cold when I realised I'd have to brave the house in just a vest.

I knew that with a few hefty pulls, the door frame holding the lock would give way and I'd be in the hall easily. I also knew that if I did that, either Gloves or Peters would hear me and the consequences of discovery didn't bear thinking about.

The gap still wasn't big enough for me to squeeze through. With both hands, one either side of the door I half lifted and half pulled to make the gap bigger. The dry and aged frame protested and squeaked noisily as it started to splinter.

I stopped and held my breath. If anyone had heard that, I was done for. If no-one had heard the noise, I'd been very lucky and wouldn't get away with it twice. I didn't move, didn't even dare to breathe, but nothing happened and no-one came.

I inched the door a little further and then pulled again, tiny fraction by tiny fraction. Every time there was a creaking sound, I stopped and prayed that I was still going to succeed in my plan. Failure was deadly.

At last, I had a reasonable space. I squeezed first my left leg through and then my left hip. I wriggled to get my butt through the gap and breathed in as hard as I could. I almost yelled again as half the hinge from the frame scrapped against my right ankle. I bit my lip as I pulled my right leg through.

I could scarcely believe this. Now, I was standing in the upstairs hallway looking at my broken door. I was finally outside of my cage and unbelievably, I felt a little lost.

I wrapped my arms around my chest and wished I had my tee shirt. It was time to get moving.

I tiptoed to the top of the stairs and paused. There was no sound, so I edged to the first stair and tried to look down through the darkness. Most of the stairs were obscured but I had to risk it. I'd come this far and passed the point of no return.

There were no banisters. The stairs were walled on both sides, adding to the darkness and the gloom.

I kept my back to the wall on my left and stepped one foot over the other, avoiding the middle and slowly making my way through the darkness.

Every creak made my heart jump and I didn't really notice until I reached the bottom, that I'd been holding my breath. I exhaled slowly and tried to calm my rapid heart, which by now felt like it was doing the Can-Can.

I was now in a downstairs hallway, which actually looked a little smaller than the one upstairs. Facing the stairs was a door, beyond which was the black, menacing night. I tiptoed over to it and put my hands against the cold wood. It wasn't as fancy as I expected a front door to be, so I assumed this was the back door and the one through which I was bundled when I was first brought here. Tentatively, I tried the handle.

It was locked, of course.

Over my left shoulder was a passageway that seemed to run the length of the house. I turned a hundred and eighty degrees and faced the passage. There was a door left ajar to my right. Nervous and shivering, I edged towards it and peeped through. It was the kitchen.

Pale stone tiles covered the floor and appeared in need of a thorough scrubbing. The cabinets, which looked like they dated back to the 1950s, were equally dirty and had paint peeling away from the edges. There was a rough and worn wooden table dominating most of the floor space but no chairs. Dirty plates had been left on the table and more cluttered the sink. A teaspoon had been abandoned on the floor where it fell, beside the overflowing bin.

I silently pulled my head back and continued further down the passageway.

The stairway wall showed dark square shadows, where pictures once hung.

There was another door on the right. This door was wide open, and revealed what looked like the main front room. The fireplace, in its heyday, alive with flame, was now a cold and empty space.

Two worn and overstuffed chairs were the only furniture in the room. Against two of the walls were cardboard archive boxes stacked on top of one another. I recognised them straight away. They were the boxes in which we sent completed work back to the customer.

I tiptoed into the room and glanced around. My kidnappers were nowhere to be seen.

At the far end of the room was another open door. In front of the fireplace, two boxes were being used as a coffee table and on top of them was what I had wished to see since I was first brought here: a laptop.

It was open but the screen was blank. I rushed over and gently ran a finger over the touch pad. It lit up immediately.

It was already open at an email and although I was desperate to send a mayday one of my own, I was drawn to reading this one because it was worded so strangely. It was from someone called Hermes at Fireflight and sent to Ares at Fireflight. It said: Demeter will travel to Hades' land March 1st with Hermes. Ares will not trouble his sister unless he expects Hades to return. Hermes expects to find Irene waiting for him with the bird of Hephaestus.

I scanned my memory for my secondary school Greek mythology. I thought I could remember who most of the characters were but why they were being referred to here would need guesswork more than knowledge.

I looked at the boxes. They were obviously cargo of some kind. I went over to the ones by the wall and lifted the lid. I was amazed by what I saw. It was full of small square boxes with a medical logo on them. They were neatly stacked to fill the box carrying them. I opened one of the small boxes and found it full of syringes. They were wrapped in sterile packaging and were clearly meant for a hospital or clinic.

What were they doing with such things? Was I now caught

up in a drugs war of some kind?

A voice came from the front of the house. It was Peters.

'The next lot is ready to go. Don't worry. I'll have the information input tonight.' He was talking on a mobile phone.

'No,' he continued, 'haven't heard a peep from her all evening.'

I almost laughed.

His voice was getting closer. I felt a rush of cold air and the acrid smell of cigarette smoke came in through the open door.

I replaced the stuff I was holding and put the lid back on the box. I backed up towards the door and had just stepped backwards into the hallway when I heard his footsteps suddenly stop.

I couldn't see where he was standing, but I could guess. When I entered the room the laptop screen was blank. Now it wasn't.

I clasped both of my hands over my mouth and willed myself to stay calm.

Peters' voice remained perfectly level and betrayed no emotion. This frightened me more than anything else.

'Look, can I call you back tomorrow?' he said. 'I've just remembered something else I have to take care of.'

Chapter 7

I heard the mobile phone bleep off, but by that time I was already half way back up the stairs and I didn't care how much noise I made.

I was literally running for my life.

Peters was hot on my heels and was no more than five paces behind me when I reached the top of the stairs. I couldn't turn right into my room. That was a cage with the door burst open.

I turned left and pushed open the door opposite mine. As I shut it behind me, Peters was banging his shoulder against it and screaming curses at me as he did so. I fumbled with my right hand and, feeling the key in the lock, turned it and removed it in a single swift movement.

Peters slammed against the door and it shook inside the frame. I backed away slowly, wrapping my arms around my body and realised that my left hand was throbbing with a burning heat.

With a final stream of obscenities, Peters kicked the door and issued a threat.

'I may not be able to get to you at the moment, but there's no toilet in there and nothing to eat. Enjoy your stay, Kim; it won't be for very long.'

I heard his footsteps pause in the hallway, before going downstairs. He was probably surveying the damage I had caused to get out.

Perhaps I had shot myself in the foot a bit. I couldn't go back to the safety of the familiar as I'd damaged the door too far to be safe inside.

I felt like I already had been shot in my hand. When I took a look, my middle finger was a purplish blue. The rest of my hand was starting to change colour to match it and the nail, swollen with blood, was causing me the most pain.

I transferred the key from my right hand into my left and was immediately grateful for the coolness of the metal.

I looked around me. This was presumably Gloves' room. The décor wasn't much better than the room that I'd been in, but he'd done what he could to make the place as comfortable as possible.

There was a proper bed in this one and the covers were clean and neat.

A shabby chest of drawers sat opposite the bed, on top of which were a hair brush, an empty glass, a shaving mirror and pair of cufflinks.

I opened the first drawer and saw a mishmash of clothes within. Nothing had been sorted or separated. Socks tangled with each other and a sweater wrapped its arms around a tee shirt in an untidy embrace.

I pulled out the clothes and without realising what I was doing, started to tidy with my working right hand. After I'd paired socks and folded the sweater, I saw that although there were about three pairs of socks, there was only one of each other item. This suggested to me that Gloves wasn't staying here full time. He hadn't left his home to live here. For all I knew, he could have a wife and children blissfully unaware in suburbia.

I claimed the tee shirt and sweater and immediately felt a little more protected. I also took a pair of socks and it was then that I noticed dried blood dribbled over my right foot.

I'd hurt my ankle when I climbed through my broken door, but fuelled by adrenalin, I had barely noticed. The socks were warm and I appreciated the comfort.

I lay down on the bed on top of the covers, and fell asleep before my head hit the pillow.

The room had an unbarred window and, in the morning, the sun pouring in through it woke me rudely as sharp fingers of daylight poked me in the eye.

I went over and took a look outside. I was pleasantly surprised. And especially surprised to be pleased by what I saw.

Sunlight was dancing off the crops in the fields and dispersing bright slivers across the horizon. The farmland looked beautiful in the morning.

Below me an unkempt patch of garden was slowly being invaded by intrusive beauty. Bluebells and honeysuckle were fighting for dominance, with wisteria beating them both.

Just beyond this, the driveway I had only glimpsed before was laid out clearly. The gravel was rough and churned over, suggesting a lot of traffic. There were persistent weeds pushing their way through the stones.

There was no vehicle in the driveway this morning. I tried to open the window and managed to lift it about six inches.

It didn't look as if I was going to be able to climb out of it. The nearest drainpipe was a couple of feet out of my reach and the ground looked a long way down.

I retrieved the key I'd kept and tried unlocking the door. The key wouldn't go all the way in and I couldn't get it to turn. Peering into the keyhole, I saw it was clogged with something.

Peters! He had been busy last night. I could smell something vaguely familiar. I realised it was superglue.

His actions were simple but effective and also, I thought, quite bullying, in a schoolboy kind of way. He'd stuffed the lock with toilet tissue doused in glue. The only thing the bastard hadn't done was set the stuff on fire. I was grateful for small mercies.

Peters couldn't keep me in one prison, so he'd do everything he could to keep me in another.

I had to get out quick. This wasn't just another desperate desire to escape; my hand was really killing me and I desperately needed to pee.

Well, I thought. First things first.

I went back to the chest of drawers and picked up the glass. The inside was damp and odourless. Likely it was Gloves' water glass. It was about to get a lot wetter.

Feeling a bit better, I left the glass on the floor by the

window and turned my attention to the cufflinks.

I swung out the central pin on both and tried to use them as a primitive pair of tweezers, to pull out the tissue from the door lock.

The cufflinks were a little too fat to be fully effective and only seemed to succeed in tearing the tissue into tiny shreds.

Then I remembered I still had the pins from the door hinges in my pockets. I pulled them out and tried to dislodge the tissue again.

Something was needed to moisten the tissue and break down the super glue.

I had just the stuff to hand.

For now, all I had was time and I was spending it tediously pulling tissue out of a lock with pins dipped in pee. This worked quite well. I'd remembered from chemistry at school that superglue is predominantly alkaline and urine is acidic.

Other things were coming back to me as well. It's amazing what a good night's sleep can do for you, and now the email I'd read the night before was becoming clearer. I considered the possibilities carefully while I worked on the lock.

I doubted that I'd get a second chance to get my hands on that laptop, so I tried repeating to myself as much of the email as I could remember. I'd only read it once and school was a long time ago, but I thought I could decipher most of it.

Three main characters were mentioned in the email: Ares, Demeter and Hermes.

Ares was the god of war and destruction. Now who did

that remind me of?

Demeter was the goddess of fertility and the harvest.

Hermes was the messenger of the gods. I was puzzled by this. If this was Gloves's describing himself, then why not Zeus? I thought it was quite strange that someone of his importance would give himself that job.

I thought of something else, too. Athena wasn't actually mentioned by name, but described as Ares' sister. She was the goddess of knowledge and wisdom. Not usually one to blow my own trumpet, I assumed that meant me.

The email had said that Ares would not hurt his sister unless he expects Hades to return. I smiled when I thought of this. It seemed like a warning to Peters to leave me unharmed or else face the god of the underworld when Gloves got back. That sounded more like the voice of a man in charge.

Clearly I was still important to him. Even though I had halted the romantic moments of the night before, I was still needed in their operation and reasonably well treated, if only by Gloves himself. I wondered where he was.

The email had said he was travelling to Hades' land with Demeter.

Well, Hades was the god of the underworld, so his land would be hell. I could think of any number of places that would fit that description, but this would have to be somewhere specific.

But who was Demeter? Was this another person I'd yet to meet? This seemed unlikely. Of course, I couldn't be sure, but the more people involved in a situation, the greater the risks.

I remembered that what I'd seen in the archive boxes downstairs weren't printed documents but boxes of syringes ready for a hospital or clinic. Could Demeter be a drug?

I started to feel a bit sick, and not just because of hunger.

Were they using me to get access to money for drug running?

There was more of the email I hadn't considered. The last line said that Hermes expects to find Irene waiting for him with the bird of Hephaestus.

Irene was the goddess of peace and tranquillity and Hephaestus was god of the fire and the forge. Did Gloves want a peaceful home with Fireflight? That was unlikely to happen here. Maybe he didn't mean the house. Maybe he meant a deal.

There was another question to answer. Why write the email at all? Why didn't Gloves just tell Peters what he wanted? Gloves evidently had some sort of hold over Peters that kept him in line. Peters clearly had a changeable personality, like dangerous and stormy weather. Now that Gloves had gone somewhere, that hold keeping Peters in check would be weakened.

Everything I was thinking was pure guesswork, but maybe Peters and Gloves didn't stay here together all the time. Gloves didn't. I knew men didn't always place much importance on packing the right kind of wardrobe, but the number of clothes here clearly wasn't enough for many days.

Maybe he hadn't expected to be here for very long.

I then remembered that at the start of my imprisonment here, I had half glimpsed a man through the shutters of my window, whom I knew was not Peters. He had been loading boxes into the back of an SUV.

Was that Gloves? I still didn't know who he really was.

Chapter 8

I conjured more guesswork and tried to marry it with what I thought I knew.

Yesterday, on the night of our romantic moment, Gloves must have quit the house very soon after he left my room. Peters could not have been around at the time Gloves left, or why else write the email?

Later that same night I had escaped my room and discovered their cargo and the message. I had imprisoned myself in Gloves' room in what must have been the early hours of this morning, and was once again trying to escape.

Peters and Gloves had other jobs to do, they didn't have huge amounts of spare time to babysit me. I started to wonder, when would be the next time I was in the house by myself?

With just a little more teasing and a few more swear words, I cleared the lock of all the remaining tissue.
I tried the lock and turned the key very slowly.

Opening the door only by fractions, I peeped out into the hallway. I could see nothing. Leaving the door ajar, I hurried over to the chest of drawers and took the shaving mirror. It was one of those funny little travelling ones that have a spring which acts as a stand so it could stand up in its own case.

I stood with my back to the wall on the opposite side of the open door and held the mirror in my right hand. Very cautiously I extended my right hand through the gap and tilted the mirror so I could see down the stairs.

I was impressed to note that I saw the stairway very well up to the first bend, but the rest was tantalisingly out of view of the mirror.

On a clear morning such as this, the stairway looked much less threatening than it had last night, but I knew the danger would be the same.

I braved sticking my head out of the door and listened carefully. I could hear no sign of Peters so decided to explore the downstairs rooms again.

Another need, apart from curiosity, was becoming apparent. I needed to get a dressing on my hand soon. My finger felt like a balloon about to burst and the nail was a disgusting colour. If I didn't do something about that quickly, I wasn't going to have a finger left to worry about.

I tiptoed out on to the landing and paused as I listened again. No sound was coming up the stairs.

It was while I was standing between the two rooms that I noticed something I'd been unaware of before. There had to be hidden rooms in the house.

The stairs ran up one side of the downstairs hallway and at the top there were two rooms; the one I'd been imprisoned in and the one Gloves used.

In the hallway downstairs the ceilings were of normal height. There had to be another two rooms on the first floor, but from where I was standing I could see they weren't accessible from up here.

I remembered my earlier suspicion about the house. It was larger than it first appeared and must have another staircase. I believed that I'd been bundled through the back door and up the back stairs. Clearly there was a front door and main stairs somewhere else in the building.

I left the door of Gloves' room open. If Peters found me, I'd need somewhere to run back to.

Gingerly, and nervous of squeaking floorboards, I made my way back down the stairs, one step at a time. At the bottom, I crept over to the back door and tried the handle in vain hope once more.

I stopped in the downstairs hallway and listened carefully. Still no sign of Peters.

I remembered the first room was the kitchen and that was where I had to go. It was as dirty and disgusting this morning as it had been last night, only this time the sink was even more packed and a box of cornflakes had been abandoned on the kitchen table.

My left hand felt like it was going to explode any minute and the finger worst affected was the same colour as the nail. My first priority had to be to relieve the pain and that meant relieving the swelling. I'd only seen this done once, and that was on a TV show, not even a real event, but if I didn't risk losing my fingernail I'd definitely risk losing my finger.

I eyed the sink warily and shuddered inwardly.

In a drawer under the sink I found a metal kebab skewer

covered in dust, and sticking to the inside of the drawer. I almost heaved as I peeled it away and lifted it up. Glancing around the work surfaces, I spotted an electric kettle plugged into a dangerous looking socket against the far wall.

Tucking the skewer under my arm, I unplugged the kettle and carried it over to the sink. I really needed two hands for this but I was just going to have to manage as best I could.

Beside the sink was a sticky bottle of washing up liquid. I laid the skewer on the least dirty work area I could see and coated it with the washing up liquid. I rubbed and massaged against the grime as much as possible with my right hand, then balanced the skewer against the top of a saucepan that had something burnt and congealed stuck to the bottom.

I poured the contents of the kettle over the top to wash off the detergent, and although still unsatisfied with its cleanliness, decided that it would have to do.

There was no paper kitchen towel to be seen, only a grubby tea towel on the kitchen table. My heart sank a little more.

I wrapped the tea towel a couple of times around my hand and pulled it tight with my teeth. It stank badly.

I laid my hand down on the kitchen table and spread my fingers to keep it as flat as I could. Peeling the tea towel back a little to expose the damaged nail, I took a deep breath.

With gritted teeth and my heart pounding, I lifted the skewer a couple of inches above my hand and stabbed myself.

Intense pain was swiftly followed by a flood of relief as a small pocket of blood and pus vomited over the top of my finger.

Hobbling over to the sink again I tried the taps, to find that only the cold one worked. I let it run until the water looked nearly clean and discarding the grubby tea towel, rinsed off my hand.

I was quite proud that I'd not made a lot of noise, only a sharp intake of breath, but I couldn't stay in one place for too long and give Peters the opportunity to find that I'd escaped again.

I crept back out into the passageway between the rooms and, believing that this was a bad idea anyway, decided to check the main living room.

Whatever I was hoping to see wasn't there. The whole room had been stripped. There were no boxes and, perhaps unsurprisingly, no laptop.

The door leading from that room, which had been open before, was now shut tight. I remembered I had smelt Peters' cigarette from that door. Could this finally be my means of escape?

I had no way of knowing what lay beyond that door, but all I could think of was freedom.

The door was unlocked but protested at being disturbed as soon as I touched the handle. If Peters or anyone else was on the other side of that door, they already knew I was here. There seemed no point in being cautious anymore.

I pulled the door open and it shrieked as it swung inwards.

The door led out into what was once a very grand hallway.

Just to the left of the hallway was another door and I presumed that led back into the main passageway between the downstairs rooms and the back stairs. That seemed a safe assumption, because beyond it was a much more imposing staircase going up to the first floor.

Opposite the staircase was an archway with crumbling plaster flowers surrounding two large mahogany doors, now coated in a grimy mixture of dirt and cobwebs. The hallway itself looked as if it ran across the whole of the front of the house and was about the depth of a large room.

I went over to the main front doors and tried the handles. The large round brass roses rattled in my hands and the doors shook within their frames but would not open. Beneath the handles was an ornate keyhole and when I peeped through it, an overgrown bush obscured everything.

Sheer frustration threatened to overtake me completely. I had fought against my imprisonment from the start, escaped from two rooms and was now starting to uncover the secrets of the house, but however close I got to the outside, there was always one more barrier for me to break through.

I screamed with pent up anger and slammed my fists against the doors. I kicked and screamed some more, but I wasn't going to get out of that door today.

My hand was throbbing again and without a dressing, my finger was dripping blood over my hand and wrist. When I turned around to look at the door I'd come through, my blood had smeared the frame and there were a couple of drops on the hallway floor. If I was going to be shut up in here a little longer, I would have to clean up the trail, or Peters and Gloves would know where I'd been.

I wanted to keep my exploits secret as long as I could, because the more I could learn about the house, the more I might learn about my captors and gain an advantage.

The sound of an approaching car told me that would have to wait. Someone was coming to the back door and the internal doors that I'd left open were going to give me away.

By the time I got to the living room door a key was being turned in the back door. I just had time to shut the living room door in front of me before the back door opened.

Someone walked through the passageway and into the living room while I was rooted to the spot, listening to him make his way through the house. He stopped in the living room and seemed to settle there, not knowing that only a single door separated him from me.

I tiptoed backwards into the hallway and noticed again the blood smears on the door frame.

Pulling my tee shirt up from under my sweater, I licked a corner, then rubbed it over the smears, cleaning up as best I could.

I knelt down and tried to do the same to the floorboards, hoping that no one would notice what I couldn't remove. I was rushing and trying not to make any noise. A single door between one of my captors and me really didn't feel like enough.

After my meagre housekeeping efforts, I realised I had two choices. I could either brave my way back down the hallway past the living room or carry on the adventure and explore upstairs. I decided to go exploring.

With pigeon steps across the hall, I tiptoed my way up the once beautiful staircase and wondered how anyone could allow such a lovely house to decay like this.

The stairs made surprisingly little noise and soon I found myself on the upstairs landing with two rooms: one to my left and one to my right. The stairs had spiralled in their journey upwards and I quickly saw that this layout was a mirror image of the other side of the house. The two upstairs rooms must, therefore, sit above the hallway.

There was nothing decorative up here and heavy cobwebs drooped from the corners of the coving.

I moved to my right and tried the handle of that door. It was unlocked and cautiously I peeped in. My guess was this was Peters' room. There was a makeshift camp bed against the left wall and a small three-drawer chest on the right. But it was the window opposite that grabbed my attention and I ran straight to it. I pushed against the wooden frame, which rattled, but did not move. No lock was visible, but the window stubbornly refused to open.

There were no shutters on the window, no curtains and nothing to restrict the view. Now that I knew I was at the front of the house, getting someone's attention should be a lot easier.

There was a long driveway in front of the house, almost as long as my small garden at home, and a road just beyond the broken, white-painted gates.

A car drove up the road. My mouth went dry as I practically danced with excitement. I waved my arms frantically, like a child on a fairground ride and the car drove on, oblivious.

No-one was going to give this house a second glance. It had probably been empty for years and still looked deserted. The front of the house was too far back from the road for anyone to see a vehicle parked here and even if they did see one, so what? Who would care?

Had my husband driven up and down this road looking for me? Had the police? I dejectedly turned away from the window.

Peters' room was much sparser than Gloves' had been. There was nothing on top of the drawers and the bed looked temporary.

I opened the top drawer out of curiosity and instead of clothes saw a couple of items I recognised. There was a pack of cigarettes and a box of the clinical syringes I saw ready for dispatch downstairs.

I swallowed down a lump in my throat. Was Peters a distributor? I thought he was just a hired heavy working for Gloves.

I took the cigarettes and one of the syringes. Already a plan was forming in my mind. I wasn't sure how I was going to pull this off, but I knew I had to try.

Chapter 9

I needed a safe and quiet place to carry out my plan. I was going to have to get back to Gloves' room. Peters was a dangerous guy and if he decided to come upstairs for a nap, I don't think he would be too pleased to find me snooping in his room.

I hurried out of Peters' room and back downstairs. Staying close to the walls, I made my way to the door I'd seen in the hallway. Hoping that my presumptions were correct, I had to believe that the door led back into the passageway by the living room.

So far almost all the doors I'd tried had creaked. I nervously opened this one very slowly. It made a little noise but, fortunately, not a lot.

I held my breath as I squeezed through the door and into darkness. No light was on and the daylight coming into the house couldn't reach into the passageway. No sound was coming from the living room, but my heart felt like it was going to beat its way out of my chest. As I made my way back, I could see that the door to the living room was open. My captor had come back into the house and entered the living room, leaving the door open behind him. How the hell was I going to get past undetected?

I crept forward as carefully as I could. I reasoned that if I turned around and tried to make my way back, I stood as much chance of getting caught as I would if I carried on.

With nervous steps, I approached the door. Peeking first through the gaps and then round the door, I saw Peters slumped in an armchair. He had his head back and his mouth open, with his arms flopping over the top of the overstuffed armrests of the chair. His hips were forward and his feet apart. Normally well dressed, he looked as if he had slept in yesterday's clothes, with his tie askew and collar open. At first I thought he was dead. I tiptoed forward to take a closer look. No such luck. I could see his chest rising and falling with heavy breaths.

Suddenly without warning, he lifted his head slightly and let out an almost hysterical laugh. It was very loud, but very brief and he slumped back into the same position as when I found him. A discarded bottle of Jack Daniels lay on its side by his chair. The square shape of the bottle had saved most of what was left, but the bottle cap was nowhere to be seen.

By his feet was an empty vial and I could only guess at what had been in it, but my imagination was running wild and I could feel my blood pulse with rage. Was this why they had brought me here? Was this a sordid drug operation? Images of packs of Heroin swam in my head and my heart beat fast at the thought that Brownlow Print was laundering drugs money. If this was what they were using the information for, then all that I had suspected was true and I'd been used badly. They were going to pay.

I couldn't believe that when we'd first met, I thought Peters was good looking. He had dark tousled hair and blue-grey eyes, the kind of guy I'd expect to be a salesman. Perhaps he was.

I pulled out my tee shirt to cover my hand as I picked up the vial and backed out of the room.

Hardly breathing, I hurried upstairs to Gloves' room, locking the door behind me. I sat on the bed and finally allowed myself to exhale. Oh, God. Could I really do this? Could I really get away with finding out what they were up to? Or, was I now 'surplus to requirements' and soon to be disposed of? I had to carry on. Even if it meant my own downfall, I had to make sure they faced downfall too.

I laid out my gathered supplies on the bed. Most were covered with blood, but I decided to view that as a good thing. If I did manage to get the package outside of the house, someone might be able to identify the bloodstains.

The packet of cigarettes was almost full. I tipped out more than half, but left the rest in there. They would act as cushioning. I dropped in the vial and the syringe and closed up the packet.

I thought about wrapping it in something, but that might not be effective. I'd need something heavy to wrap with it, but even if that worked, who would know to unwrap the bundle and look inside?

No, small was beautiful and a pack of cigarettes falling into the hands of a grateful smoker was more likely to be opened than a tied-up bundle.

It was still morning but already too late for me to initiate my plan. I'd have to wait another day. I didn't want to stay here one more night, but if my only way of escape was to send a message, then I had to be patient and bide my time. I hid the packet of cigarettes under my pillow and dropped the loose ones into the top drawer of the dresser.

By now, my hand was smeared with dried up blood and my finger felt a lot better, but was still quite painful. With no dressing to put on it, I had to find some protection from somewhere.

I undressed my top half and gripped the tee shirt between my teeth. I tore at the hem and hurt my tooth. This was not easy. There were no scissors up here and I didn't want to risk another journey downstairs.

I remembered Gloves' cufflinks and used one of them against the stitching. It seemed to work and after a little while I had a small strip that I was able to tie around my finger and fasten roughly with my teeth.

I didn't want to put the clothes back on: they didn't smell very fresh, but then, neither did I. I was also very hungry. I was starting to lose track of time. I couldn't remember the last time I ate something or even exactly how long I'd been here. Was today the second or third day? So much had happened and yet I still couldn't figure out what was really going on.

Movement in the rooms below told me that something was happening. I heard doors opening and closing and suddenly raised voices. The angriest one wasn't Peters and seemed vaguely familiar.

Daddy was back and had found his naughty kid high in the living room.

A quiet minute or two followed. Peters must have been trying to explain himself. That meant that Gloves was going to find out what I had been up to.

Sure enough, I soon heard a creak on the stairs and footsteps pausing in the middle of the upstairs hallway. The footsteps came up to the door and stopped. I walked to the door and pressed my ear against it. I heard nothing but I knew Gloves was still there.

'Yes,' I confirmed to the door. 'I read the email, and I understood it.' This was still only partly true. I only understood some of it. 'So where is Hell, then? The streets where you'll sell your poison?' I still didn't know exactly what Demeter was. But I was determined to find out.

I'd guessed that while Gloves was away last night, Peters was expected to deliver the boxes to one location, while Gloves delivered the drug to another. Clearly it was too risky to deliver both the syringes and the drug in one haul.

Peters' delivery must have been late. My escape and discovery of the email had thrown an enormous spanner in the works and he'd had to find a way of keeping me in Gloves' room while he was out of the house. But there was one thing he couldn't explain away. He'd sampled the merchandise.

Were they now looking for the missing vial? I hoped I'd left no clue that I'd seen Peters in the living room, but there was no way to be sure.

'Well?' I yelled. 'Don't you have anything to say?'

Of course, Gloves didn't answer, but I heard heavy objects put down on the floor and his footsteps disappearing down the stairs.

I waited a few minutes before feeling brave enough to open the door. There was a small plate with a couple of slices of buttered toast pushed to one side. Next to the toast was a cotton face cloth wrapped around something. When I opened it up, I found a bar of soap. Standing next to the plate was a bucket of hot water.

'Nice,' I thought. 'Room service has delivered breakfast and a bath.'

I dared to tiptoe across the landing and peep through the broken door of my former prison.

I pushed against the broken frame and the lock, the only thing holding the door upright, gave way with a protesting screech. The bucket beneath the chair was still there and the fluffy towel that Gloves had given me when he washed my feet remained discarded on the floor.

With just a quick glance over my shoulder, I ran through, retrieved the towel and ran back to Gloves' room. I quickly pulled the bucket and the plate into the room and locked the door behind me.

After breakfast, I washed as best I could and tried searching for clean clothes. I remembered there wasn't much to choose from. There was no tee shirt and I was wearing the only jumper. At least I could change into a clean pair of socks.

I could have done with a cup of tea to accompany my toast, but I didn't think I was in a position to ask for one. Besides, movement downstairs told me that I'd have to wait. Peters and Gloves were busy.

I went over to the window and saw the SUV in the driveway again. It was Peters who had drawn up in the car, while I had been in the hallway. I hadn't heard Gloves arrive until the argument earlier. Peters must have reversed the car into position. I didn't remember him bringing anything noticeable into the house, so he must have been getting high while I was in his room and a small vial would have been easy for him to pocket.

From the position I had at the window I could clearly see the front of the car but something seemed to be missing. I wasn't terribly familiar with SUVs but I couldn't see a number plate on the front of the car.

Peters walked into view, lurching like a puppet on broken strings. He went over to the car and tried several times to press the button on the key. He swore like a sailor and demanded that the key do as it was told. The cussing must have worked, as he finally managed to open the door.

Instead of driving off, as I expected him to, he reached in and retrieved a jacket before relocking the door and re-entering the house. Peters really wasn't in fit shape to retrieve anything from anywhere, and I was surprised he could remember where he left it.

Why hadn't Gloves retrieved the jacket himself? He must

have known that from this room, I could see the car. He was still being enigmatic and mysterious. Peters must have left something personal in his jacket that wasn't safe to leave in the car; maybe other keys, or even a mobile phone. If I could get my hands on a phone, I'd be laughing.

Obviously Gloves had thought of that too and was securing any opportunity I might take advantage of. Well, the day was still young. We'd just have to see what it would bring.

Chapter 10

It was a couple of hours before anything happened. I was stuck in the room and unless I wanted an unpleasant confrontation, I had to stay there until Gloves or Peters left. I had already pushed my luck trying to sneak past one of them. I wasn't dumb enough to try to fool both. Besides, Gloves was smart and it would be a mistake to underestimate him.

Stumbling footsteps on the stairs again drew my attention to the door.

'Hello, Kim,' said Peters.

'What the hell do you want?' I demanded.

The drunkenness had all but disappeared from his voice. A lower tone was all that gave him away. I hoped he had run out of paracetamol. He was going to get one hell of a headache later.

'I've come to collect your plate and bucket.'

I was immediately suspicious. Peters would not provide room service out of the kindness of his heart.

'Oh, there's really no need,' I protested. 'I'll drop them off myself later.'

'Look, we need the bucket. Just open the door and hand it over or I'll break down the bloody door and get it myself.'

I knew he would, too.

'All right then,' I agreed. 'I'll get it.'

I had just turned towards the bucket when an engine sparked into life and heavy wheels crushed gravel as the car moved away.

I ran to the window and watched as the SUV disappeared out of view. I'd been conned by a classic diversion tactic. Peters had kept me busy at the door while Gloves had made a run for it.

I was furious. A good chance at finding out who Gloves was, had slipped through my fingers.

'Ok,' I said to the door. 'I've got the bucket. Get ready.'

I'd left the key in the lock and turned it with one hand while I held the bucket in the other.

The key moved slowly, but I opened the door swiftly and before Peters could say anything, I swung the bucket up and forward drenching his head and shoulders with the dirty water.

Peters staggered back and gasped for air, his mouth opening and closing like a caught fish as he took the full force of the water in the face. I slammed the door, dropping the bucket as I did so. It fell on my side of the door. As I turned the key, Peters was trying to break his way in.

Every obscene name I'd ever heard before was flying at me from the other side of the door.

'Open the door,' he demanded. 'Open this bloody door.' He banged his fists against it and I'm sure that if I did as I was told, he'd be banging his fists against me too.

'No chance,' I yelled back. 'You'll just have to find something else to contain your next batch.'

Loud and angry steps stamped back down the stairs, accompanied by more swearing.

I sat on the edge of the bed and tried to think. Strange as it all was, a few pieces of a complicated jigsaw were falling into place.

Knowing one thing made me feel a lot better. At least now I wasn't losing my mind. The reason I couldn't remember the registration number on the SUV was because it didn't have one. I didn't see one on the front of the vehicle and there was nothing on the back when Gloves drove it away. This gave me another clue. Gloves wasn't dumb enough to drive around anywhere without number plates on the car; he'd be drawing attention to himself if he did. There would have to be somewhere he could go to fix them on. As people were, generally, creatures of habit, it would probably be the same place each time and could be the abandoned barns where I was first kidnapped.

If Gloves had come back to the house for something, what was it and where was he going now?

When I last saw the living room, all boxes had been removed and presumably the delivery had been made. Was Gloves was oη his way somewhere, to pick up another supply? But where from?

I already had big ambitions of wanting to destroy their drugs ring, but until I had more answers, there was nothing I could do. Even if I tried, I could be biting off more than I could chew.

I tried to be as patient as possible until hunger got the better of me and I decided to venture downstairs again. It had been pretty quiet in the last hour or so, but without a watch I wasn't sure if my concept of time was right, or if I was wishing my time away.

I pressed my ear to the door and listened carefully. All was quiet and I could only hope that Peters had gone out and left me alone again, or was slowly killing himself in the living room. I opened the door slowly and left the key in the lock on my side of the door. I paused and listened for any sign of life.

I crept down the stairs as carefully as I could, thinking I was getting pretty good at this. By the time I reached the bottom of the stairs, I was fairly sure that Peters wasn't in the house. My shoulders relaxed a bit.

I walked past the kitchen and peeked in the living room. It was empty and looked completely bare.

I went back to the kitchen and saw what Gloves had brought back earlier. He'd left a carrier bag on the kitchen table which Peters didn't seem to have touched.

In it was a sliced loaf with a few slices missing, a tub of supermarket margarine, and a two pint bottle of milk. An almost clean knife was on the kitchen table and I used it to do myself a makeshift sandwich. If Gloves were here, I might get something to eat, but in Peters' tender care I'd get a beating before I got lunch.

I pocketed the knife. It wasn't sharp, just a regular

spreading knife, but you never knew what might come in handy. I ate my sandwich standing up there at the table and swigged milk straight from the bottle.

When I was finished I decided to take another look at Peters' room. This time I wasn't as worried about being as quiet as I was before. Peters and Gloves wouldn't worry about me wandering in the house as long as they could be sure that I couldn't leave it. I had the key to my room. That meant they had to be prepared to negotiate a bit, however reluctantly.

I remembered that Peters' room looked a lot more temporary than Gloves' room. The bed was a camp bed and there hadn't been any clothes, but what I was really looking for was something else I could put in the cigarette box. I didn't know what that would be until I saw it, but it had to be something that would identify one of them; Peters' cigarette lighter, perhaps.

When I reached his room again, nothing appeared different. That was not what I expected. I had expected to see clothes lying about, loose change on the chest of drawers or another cigarette packet. There was nothing.

Apart from his name, I knew nothing about Peters; even less about Gloves. If there was something to identify them, it would be here, unless they were smarter than I gave them credit for.

I opened the drawers again and found nothing more than I had seen the last time. Peters had not replaced the cigarettes I'd taken and there were no clothes in any of the drawers. It was if no-one occupied this room at all. Gloves used Peters to keep me in line. I'd guessed Peters was obviously unreliable, but he'd still need certain things to be here. There was not even a change of underpants.

I ran my hands over and around the bed, checking the covers and under the pillows. Nothing: no lighter, no wallet, no keys. Then, I realised I must be in the wrong room.

If this part of the house was a mirror image to the side where I was kept, then I needed to see the other room across the hallway from this one. I checked for sound before I left the room and hurried across the hall. I tried the handle and crept in.

This room was in complete darkness. Instead of curtains or blinds, chipboard sheets had been cut to size and fixed to the inside of the windows. Neat and tight screws secured them in place.

The nails fixed to the windows of the room I'd escaped from had been hurriedly banged in, but whoever had done this job had been a lot more careful and, perhaps, purposeful.

There was no bulb in the light fitting and no lampshade. The wire was hanging down and had been taped over. There was a mattress on the floor and a bucket in the corner. For one moment, I thought this must be where I was going to be moved to. The only difference here was that this room looked slightly smaller than mine. I couldn't understand why that would be.

I went over to the nearest wall and knocked it a couple of

times. It sounded solid enough. I walked to the wall by the side of the door, then realised what I'd seen without my knowing it. The wall into which the doorway was fitted, was considerably thicker than in any of the other rooms. This alteration made no difference to the width of the hallway, but reduced the size of the room slightly.

I ran my hands over the wall. I wasn't sure what I was expecting to find until I found it. There was an indentation about two thirds of the way down the wall, which reached to the floor and was about a foot wide. It had been made to look invisible and wallpapered over. The wallpaper itself was grey and faded, the green leaves that once adorned it, now shadows of their former selves.

This could not be a recent alteration made by Gloves or Peters. But then, Peters would not have created a room like this if he was to stay here himself. I couldn't peel back the wallpaper and take a look without it being obvious I'd been here. The wallpaper was too old and brittle to be repairable and any tear would be noticeable.

I looked back at the bucket again. Maybe it needed replacing. Perhaps that's what Peters wanted it for.

I knelt by the mattress. There were warm looking blankets and a soft pillow on top, better quality than those I had been given. Could this room be meant for Peters? If he was an addict or an alcoholic, Gloves could be keeping him prisoner in here when he got out of hand. If so, Gloves might be blackmailing him too.

I lifted up the pillow and felt how soft it was, but glancing down, I noticed what had been hiding beneath it. My breath caught in my throat and I almost laughed with shock.

When Peters brought his mobile phone back into the house he must have hidden it up here. But why not take it with him? That, although a puzzling question, was not something I was going to dwell on; I wasn't going to look a gift horse in the mouth and besides, I was too excited to care. I could hardly believe it! At long last, I finally had the key to my escape, right here in my hands.

Then it rang.

Chapter 11

I just stared at the phone as it played a movie theme tune and vibrated in my palm. The identifying display on the front of the mobile said the call was from Hephaestus. I swiped it open and said nothing. I didn't need to speak.

'Ares,' said a man's voice, clearly assuming that I was Peters, 'you're late. You should have been here an hour ago. Listen, there's been a development. Persephone isn't working. You'll have to tell Hermes before the next delivery. If we can't fix this, the only outcome is Thanatos. Ares? Ares, are you there?'

I ended the call.

What the bloody hell was Persephone? Or Thanatos? They sounded like more Greek gods and my knowledge wasn't good enough to identify them. Whoever had made that call was at the place where the boxes had been delivered and I was sure they must be manufacturing drugs.

I hurried out of the room and back through the house. I ran down the main stairs, lost my footing and fell over the last two steps. Crashing to the floor, I skidded along the parquet towards the main front door and banged my shoulder against the frame. The phone flew from my hand and bounced along the floor. The screen fractured as a crack stretched like a scar across its face.

Crawling on my hands and knees, I retrieved the mobile, terrified someone would come back and find me there. I didn't want to even imagine what Peters or Gloves would do if they found me with a phone.

I tried with shaking hands and an aching arm to check that it was still working. What if I had broken it? Had I just lost my only chance?

I pressed the side button and it lit up. I heaved a sigh of relief and closed my eyes in a vain attempt to quell the tide of frantic desperation. I limped through the hall and passageway and took the stairs to Gloves' room one single stair at a time.

With fumbling hands I scrambled through the bedroom door and turned the lock. I sat on the edge of the bed and looked at the phone again.

An emergency call would override the need for a passcode, but there was only one per cent of battery power left on the phone. Would this work? There was only one way to find out. I pressed 999. The time was 16.24.

'Hello, Emergency, what service please?'

I let out a long breath as if I had been holding it all my life.

'Police, please. I'm being held against my will.'

Suddenly the phone bleeped. The battery was dying.

'Are you in immediate danger?' asked the dispatcher.

'No, I think they've left me alone for a moment, but I don't know when they'll be back.'

'What's your name?'

'Kim Anderson. How soon can you get here?'

She gave me the routine customer service response.

'As soon as we possibly can, Kim. Please try to stay calm. Where are you now?'

'I'm locked in a rear bedroom, overlooking a narrow road no more than thirty minutes' drive from the local train station.'

'Do you know the address?'

I was immediately annoyed. 'No, they didn't tell me that when they brought me here.'

I knew I was sounding snappy, but I felt justified. I didn't know how long I had left.

'Please remain calm. We'll trace you by the telephone number. What is it, please?'

'I don't know; it's a mobile.'

The dispatcher couldn't hide her surprise. 'They let you keep your mobile?'

'No, it's not mine; I stole it from one of their bedrooms.'

'So, the people who are holding you against your will and locked you in a bedroom left a mobile lying around.'

Clearly the dispatcher was starting to think that this was a hoax call.

'No, I locked myself in the bedroom for protection. Finding the mobile was just lucky.'

'I see.'

It wasn't going to be so lucky if I ran out of battery. The phone bleeped again, just to annoy me.

'Look,' I said, trying to be patient. 'Can't you just identify the mobile number and trace from that?'

'One moment, Please.' I could hear the tapping of a computer keyboard. 'Is this some sort of a joke?' she asked.

'No, it's not a joke,' I responded, desperation creeping into my voice. 'Please, can you locate the phone?'

'It is actually an offence to make a crank call, Mrs Anderson,' she responded, irritably. 'Why would you use your own mobile phone to call for help with such an absurd story?'

'But it's not my mobile,' I cried, panicking.

'It's registered to you at your home address,' she said coldly. '12, Alexander Road; that is where you live, isn't it?'

'Yes,' I whispered, shocked. As my thoughts came together I guessed what had happened.

'Please,' I begged. 'Please, send someone. Anyone....'

The phone bleeped a final three pips and the screen went blank.

I started to cry. So many times I'd willed myself not to give in to tears. Crying may relieve stress but it clouds my thinking and raises my temperature. I genuinely get hot and bothered.

I dropped the phone into my lap and sobbed my heart out. I thought I would never get out of this wretched place.

When Hephaestus realised he wasn't talking to Ares, he must have called Gloves. A quick call to the network provider, with a few easy lies and my personal details, changed the ownership of the phone. A desperate person who will say anything would be easy to discredit. They couldn't stop me from making an emergency call, but they could make me appear crazy.

I picked up the phone again and looked at the dead screen. I would have given anything at this time to call my home, not just to beg for rescue, but to speak to my husband. Even if it was just a moment, just to say 'Hi'. I would have sold everything I own to hear his voice, even on the answering machine.

I held the phone up to my ear.

'I love you,' I said to no-one. 'I miss you. I want to be back with you and I'll do everything I can to get back home.'

I put the mobile in one of the drawers. It was no good to me now, but there might be a way of using it again. I'd need time to think about how I could use it to my best advantage. This was assuming, of course, that Peters, or Gloves himself, didn't take it from me before the opportunity arose. I'd be surprised if they didn't try.

In the meantime, I'd have to fall back on plan B.

I retrieved the cigarette packet from under the pillow and took another look at the contents. Eight cigarettes, an unused syringe and a small vial of suspicious origins; it wasn't a lot of evidence to offer and it would only be considered evidence if whoever found it was wise enough to take it to the police. If they were frightened off by these contents, they might think it safer to bin the packet and forget they ever saw it.

Trying to look on the bright side, I concluded that even

if that did happen, I'd be no worse off than I was at present. What I could really do with was a pen. Just to be able to write a quick SOS to someone would, at least, make me feel that I was doing something positive.

I went back over to the window It only opened about six inches, but I knew that if I crouched down, there was just enough space for me to stretch my arm through.

Holding the cigarette packet in my right hand, I pushed my right elbow through the gap and prayed for a miracle. I took a deep breath and with a curling arch, flung the cigarette packet through the air. I heard a faint plop as it landed on the driveway, out of view of my window. At least it hadn't landed in overgrown grass. There had to be an exit gate that Gloves used when he drove the SUV. With fingers crossed, I hoped and prayed that the packet had landed nearby.

This wasn't the best time of day to be doing this. No postman would be visiting this house anytime soon. If Gloves or Peters found the packet outside, I'd get a beating or risk even worse. If they hadn't seen it, there was still a chance that one of them would crush it under the car. Even so, I thought the risk was worth it. Now, my fate was in the lap of the gods: Greek ones.

I looked up at the sky and noticed it was already grey. In another couple of hours it would be dusk.

If I were free, I'd be looking at the office clock and wishing it was home time. At five o'clock I'd leave work and hurry home to shower and change before Nick arrived back from work himself. He'd hug me from behind and tickle me with the stubble on his chin while asking me what was for dinner. We'd eat about 7pm, moan about our days and watch telly together.

I used to think we had a boring life and I thought the fact that we'd inherited a kitchen I didn't like and a painted bedroom I liked even less, meant that our life wasn't perfect. Kneeling by the window now in an unfamiliar and unfriendly environment, I thought heaven couldn't be more perfect than my own home.

I was hungry and my throat was dry. I desperately needed a glass of water. I wondered what Nick was eating. Was he eating? Was he coping without me there or was he dying without me?

I heard the familiar crunch of tyres on the gravel as the SUV slowly rolled into view. Usually the car was reversed up the gravel driveway, presumably to make deliveries easier. Today they drove in forwards which put the driver's side closest to the door.

I pulled down the window and stayed still to watch. I could see two figures in the car and recognised the outline of one as Peters. Was Gloves going to reveal himself at last?

If I stood up and leaned forward I would have a clear view of the whole of the car and see Gloves. But then, he would have a clear view of me too. If he still had a reason for keeping his identity secret and I blew it, I could put myself in unnecessary danger. By staying where I was, I was out of sight but could only see half of the car. Peters got out the passenger side and entered the house. I heard Gloves get out of the car and pause for a moment before his steps came into the house.

Running steps thudded through the house and started up the stairs before stopping and slowly returning. I could hear Peters shouting and calling me names. I involuntarily glanced at the drawer where I'd hidden the phone and swallowed hard.

Another voice, lower pitched, seemed to be trying to bring reason to Peters' hysteria. There was a dull thump and the yelling just stopped. Movement continued downstairs for a few more minutes.

It was already dark when I heard footsteps on the stairs again. Things had been left outside my room and the only person who brought me anything was Gloves. I wondered what he had done with Peters. Was he now also under lock and key, imprisoned in that little room with the board up at the windows?

Chapter 12

I waited several minutes before opening the door and found a mug of soup, a couple of slices of bread, balanced on top, and a mug of hot chocolate. I hadn't been given hot chocolate before; presumably they'd run out of tea. I gulped down the soup quickly. I seemed constantly hungry lately. This wasn't too surprising as the only food I was getting here was soup or sandwiches.

'I could really go for fish and chips, one night,' I yelled uselessly to the room. 'If you want to give me my handbag back, I'll go get it myself.' I couldn't help smiling at the thought. Well, it was worth a try.

I slumped on to the bed when I'd finished my hot chocolate. I didn't have the energy to worry about getting indigestion, I just felt so tired. My legs were heavy. I hadn't felt overcome like this before. What the hell was happening to me?

I grabbed at the mug that had contained the hot chocolate and did that twice, missing the mug the first time. I barely had enough time to see the gritty remains in the bottom of the mug, before I collapsed back on the bed. The mug dropped to the floor where it landed with a muted thud and bounced, soundlessly.

'Bastard,' I mumbled into the bedclothes, as my eyes closed and my mind gave way to unconsciousness. 'You bastard.'

It was already morning and cold, damp daylight was making a weak effort to start the day. God, what day was it? I couldn't remember. Maybe Wednesday, maybe Thursday? I had a sore and aching shoulder and a rough, bitter taste in my mouth.

I looked around the room and saw that any remnants of the night before had disappeared. I checked the floor to see if I could find the mug that had contained the drugged hot chocolate. Nothing remained but a dark brown stain in the unprotected floorboards, dry and lemon scented.

I looked at the door. The lock, the handle and finger plate had all been removed. That was how he had got into the room. Rather than breaking down the door, he'd removed everything that held it shut. Now, where the lock had once been, there was a rectangular field of unprotected wood with a two inch hole bored through the door, like some kind of gratuitous peephole. The door was now standing ajar and any attempt to push it shut was futile.

I went over to the chest of drawers and immediately started searching for the mobile phone.

'Shit, shit, shit! Bastards!'

I knew they'd try to take it; I knew they had drugs here. Why hadn't I taken better care to hide it? Cursing myself again for being such a fool, I realised that I'd assumed that if Gloves liked me, he wouldn't want to risk hurting me. He didn't really know how I'd react to the sleeping pills, after all, assuming that's what they were. But, of course, I understood now, that whoever he liked and whatever he cared about, there would always be something more important to him.

There hadn't been any usable clothes left in the drawers the last time I'd checked, but today a pair of boxer shorts was lying alongside a clean tee shirt, jogging bottoms and another sweatshirt. These were men's clothes and not new but I was pleased to see them, just the same.

I hurriedly undressed and grimaced as I pulled my hand out of a pocket. I had forgotten that I'd taken a knife from the kitchen yesterday and now my hand was slimy with cheap margarine.

This told me something. If Gloves had come into my room to look for the mobile phone, he must have searched the room, but he hadn't searched me, or else he would have taken the knife. I already had an idea about what I could use that for.

I wiped the knife on the dirty tee shirt and quickly put on the clean clothes.

I listened outside the door and could hear nothing. Cautiously, I tiptoed down stairs and was confident that I was alone by the time I reached the bottom. On the very obscure off chance, I tried the handle to the back door. It was locked, of course.

In the kitchen, there was a clean cup, plate, a pint of milk and half a loaf of bread waiting on the kitchen table. I went over to the kettle and pressed my hand to the side. It was still warm. Gloves must have made himself some breakfast before he left.

I tipped their toaster upside down over the remains of yesterday's washing up in the sink and the other half of the loaf came tumbling out in several handfuls of crumbs, coating the grubby plates in burnt offerings. I made toast as best I could and drank a cup of discount coffee that tasted a lot like mud.

I then wandered through to the living room and was surprised to see a new delivery. Gloves had been busy last night. There were new boxes stacked up against the walls: our company archive boxes with the Brownlow company logo on the front.

The suspicions that had only recently been planted, were starting to grow. I didn't want to believe that the company I worked for was crooked. Were they being taken for a ride or in on the deal? I'd been the Finance Officer there for just under three years and never before had there been any hint of dodgy dealings; at least, none that I was aware of.

Brownlow Print was a small printing company producing brochures, magazines and pamphlets for local businesses. They had a healthy turnover, but nothing I had seen suggested their money came from illegal operations.

I lifted the lid off one box and then another. They were stuffed full of pamphlets, in neatly banded bundles, arranged to fill the whole of the box and there were six of these boxes in the room. I was used to handling documents of all shapes and sizes, so I picked up a bundle and counted the pamphlets. There were a hundred. The archive boxes were a fairly standard size and it was possible to pack quite deeply.

Roughly estimating five thousand pamphlets to a box, it made thirty thousand pamphlets in total. That was the kind of volume used for a marketing campaign, and I would have remembered authorising a volume like that. Either someone more senior than me had given the authorisation or, more likely, they had been printed within the last few days. Even so, someone would still have had to give the go ahead.

Not caring if someone came back to see me, I un-banded one of the bundles and sat down to read the pamphlet. It was a fancy design and not one that I'd seen on our printed documents before. Many printing companies have templates for standard documents and I'd seen hundreds of different pamphlets for hundreds of different companies. They had all followed a similar pattern. This was not one of our own company designs.

It showed a classical depiction of a mother cradling a baby, flanked by carved pillars and with gifts of baskets of fruit and grain at her feet. She was standing on a step bearing her name as Demeter. The whole picture seemed to owe more to Hollywood than to history.

I opened the pamphlet and read the contents with growing unease. It was promising the earth.

'Thousands of women all over the world carry the pain of empty arms. With so much love in their hearts, they cannot bear to be without children. We at Fireflight Healthcare believe that they suffer needlessly. Using unique and revolutionary techniques, we have formulated a new treatment which practically guarantees pregnancy within six months.'

There was no treatment I had ever heard of that could guarantee anything, except to improve a woman's chances of conceiving. What the hell was this treatment and how could they claim such success?

'Demeter, named after the goddess of fertility and the harvest, is a completely different type of treatment. We have created an innovative method of enhancement that we've called Persephone, named after Demeter's daughter.'

I recalled the one-sided telephone call when I'd found Peters' mobile. Hephaestus had said that the Persephone wasn't working. Was that some kind of accelerant?

'Together they promise to bring you the joy of motherhood and the love you have always dreamed of.'

'Yuk!' I thought. 'Talk about giving it the hard sell!' But another thought sat less comfortably. If Hephaestus had already reported that the drug wasn't working, surely they would have stopped production. My father had once been a research scientist. I was sure that if a drug wasn't working as expected, even if it was only ineffective, then it could be thought of as potentially dangerous. They would have to stop production. Or wouldn't they care?

The other box I'd opened contained the same pamphlets, banded in the same way, but this time in a foreign language I didn't recognise.

Where were they going to? Who were they trying to target? If Gloves was manufacturing a fertility drug, exactly whom was he selling it to? I pulled the lids off other boxes and lifted the bundles from those.

Each box had pamphlets in a different language. The scale of it took my breath away. There were thirty thousand pamphlets, five thousand pamphlets in six different languages.

If Gloves was thinking internationally, then this would still only be the tip of the iceberg.

As I stood here in this room, there would be more pamphlets being printed, more women being promised the impossible and more of an unreliable drug being produced. I started to pace, as angry as hell. I wished I had a box of matches and then I could show Gloves what I thought of his plan to 'help' the childless.

'Well?! Where the bloody hell are you then!?' I yelled into the empty space. 'Come on out and then you can tell me to my face what all this bullshit is about!' I waved a handful of pamphlets angrily in the air.

Dumping the pamphlets on the floor, I ran to the back door and yanked at the handle again, wishing I was strong enough to pull it from its lock, this time not just so that I could escape, but to go in a possibly fruitless search for a man whose identity I didn't even know.

Kicking and cursing at the door, I turned and ran up the passageway towards the front door and grabbed at the ornate doorknobs once again. The loose and damaged knobs shook within my hands, rattling in the lock.

I charged up the grand stairway and in through the first open door. Nothing had changed in this room and it looked as temporary as it always had. I didn't stop to admire the décor; I was still angry and looking for Gloves.

I tried the handle of Peters' room. I'd found the mobile phone in this room; perhaps lightning could strike twice. The door was locked. The key was in the lock and I was about to turn it when a massive thud hit the door. The only time I'd seen a door shake in the frame like that, was when Peters had been on the other side of it. He tried to break out twice more and then was suddenly quiet. Maybe he had hurt himself. I hoped so.

I was about to speak when he broke the silence.

'Hermes,' he called, 'Hermes, look, can't we just shake hands and agree I overstepped the mark?' He sounded genuinely sorry. 'Hermes, you were right,' he conceded. 'I was careless, but it was a genuine mistake. Haven't you ever forgotten anything? There must have been times you've left your house without your mobile.'

Peters was trying to make his excuses sound reasonable, but clearly, he had angered Gloves. If Peters was an addict and an alcoholic, as I suspected, there were bound to be times when he would become careless and therefore unreliable.

'C'mon,' persisted Peters, 'I'll do the re-boxing for you.'

The re-boxing!? The pamphlets were not going out in Brownlow Print boxes, then?

'Plain white archive, right?' he continued. 'Call it penance. All I'll need is half a glass and two drops, just enough to take the edge off.'

That would be half a glass and two drops of what? Maybe it was half a glass of Jack Daniels and two drops of Demeter. Someone with a drink problem would need more than half a glass to 'take the edge off'; even if they could convince themselves it was all they'd need.

Peters bounced against the door again.

'C'mon,' he yelled, more demanding this time.

Half of me wanted to tell him the truth, that I wasn't Gloves. The other half of me wanted him to suffer and to feel as frightened and imprisoned as I had felt.

I slowly backed away from the door and crossed the hallway into the neighbouring room. I walked over to the window and could see the distant road beyond the grounds of the house. For whoever had lived here before, it might have been no more than a thirty second walk to reach the road. For me, it may as well have been a hundred miles away.

The last time I had stood before this window, I had been excited by the sight of a passing car but, while I had been practising semaphore impressions, it had driven by unseeing. In the grey, dreary daylight of this damp morning, I could see another car approaching in the distance. I didn't jump up and down as I had before, what was the point? But, as it came ever nearer and more into focus I could feel my heart beat a little faster. I recognised the markings of a police car and held my breath as it approached. My heart was pounding now, as I begged the driver to look up and see me.

I smacked my palms hard against the glass and held them there, but all I could do was watch the car as it continued by. Again, I frantically tried to open the window, but it wouldn't budge. I hit my fists hard against the frame, but only succeeded in hurting my fingers. I turned and stared despondently at the room.

'Always the same,' I thought. 'Like a bad relationship; the promise of freedom without release.'

It was then that I realised that Peters and I were not alone in the house.

After coming here, I'd been given work to do: I'd been made to reveal the account codes for work detailed in two coloured folders. The pink folder would be the last in the chain of work.

Now I noticed that the pink folder I had kept with the others in my desk drawer at the office sat on the dressing table.

Gloves was back.

Chapter 13

I ran towards the door and ignoring the folder, raced out of the room and down the stairs. I spun round in a circle when I reached the downstairs hallway, unsure of where to go next.

'Where are you?' I yelled into the emptiness. 'What are you up to? You'll never get away with any of this!'

Nothing I said was provoking any kind of response. I pushed through the door into the living room and saw the boxes still neatly stacked against the wall. The only difference from when I left them was that the box lids and pamphlets I'd discarded on the floor were back with the boxes they belonged to.

I hurried out of the room and into the passageway. Checking left and right, I then ran into the kitchen. It looked unusually clean and tidy. The table was clear of debris and the only thing on it was a hot mug of coffee, still steaming.

I rushed to the back door and tried the door handle. It was locked fast. I swore and kicked at the door. I must have missed Gloves by seconds.

A loud thumping made me jump. It was coming from behind me. Someone was at the front door, banging against the frames and shaking the handles. It couldn't be Gloves. As far as I knew, Peters and Gloves always used the back door.

I crept towards the noise.

Standing in the doorway to the passage across from the hallway, I listened as a man rammed his fists and then his shoulder against the doors. They shook and rattled but, fortunately, did not give way.

'Ares, you cretin, I'm going to strangle you! Where's my bloody money? Cough up you bastard!'

This was not the police officer I had hoped for.

What did he mean his money? I didn't think Gloves kept money in the house and why was he asking for Peters?

The man stopped, probably assuming that there was no one in the house. I hoped he wasn't going to leave; if he managed to find a way in, then I could find a way out.

I ran over to the door and put my hands against the frame. I was too fearful to say anything; this guy could be dangerous. He heard me at the door and stepped forward, slamming his hands against the wood once more.

'Ares,' he yelled.

Frightened, I gasped and took a step back; so did he.

'Not Ares,' he said slightly surprised, his voice muffled from beyond the door. The letterbox rattled and cautiously I bent my knees slowly to look back at the curious dark eyes observing me. He peered through the letterbox at an angle, as if he was bending over.

'Hi,' he said, raising an eyebrow. 'Do you know who Ares is?'

His voice was calm and friendly. I didn't trust him. I had witnessed rage turn quickly to friendliness and back again once or twice before.

I nodded.

'Is he there?' he asked politely. He might have been asking if my mother was home.

I nodded again.

'I'm 'H',' he said conversationally. 'You must be Athena.' He must be Hephaestus.

'Could you let me in?'

I shook my head. The request was politely made but impossible to action. I saw a flash of annoyance cross his eyes before he spoke again.

'Would you please tell Ares that I'm here?'

I nodded and stepped away from the door.

If I found a way to let Hephaestus in, I knew that he was unlikely to go away peacefully. Perhaps I'd be able to make an escape during the ruckus that was sure to follow. Peters was already keen to break out of his room upstairs, so I knew that he was awake and alert. He'd have nothing to gain by agreeing to meet Hephaestus, especially if he owed him money. I would have to find a way to lead Peters to the door.

I hurried up the stairs and stood outside Peters' room. Would Peters assume that Gloves was still in the house?

The other room still had the door open and the pink folder still on the dressing table. I had an idea, and crossed my fingers.

I checked the door of this second room and was relieved to find that it had a key on the inside. I took the key and stepping back into the hallway I closed and locked the door as quietly as I could and tucked the key in my right pocket.

I held my breath as I approached Peters' door and turned the key slowly trying not to make any noise, then hurried back down the stairs and into the passageway opposite the front door. There was little point in trying to find a hiding place upstairs in the back of the house. Nowhere was safe up there any longer. Gloves hadn't succeeded in constraining me and so now, I guessed, he was limiting the places I could hide. I tucked myself behind the passageway door, peeking through a crack.

I heard a rattling as doors were shaken upstairs and footsteps as Peters bounded down the stairs and into the hall. I closed my eyes. He looked as if he was heading my way.

'Ares!' yelled Hephaestus from the letterbox. Peters froze mid-step and clenched his jaw. He turned towards the voice. 'Ares, get here now,' ordered Hephaestus through gritted teeth, 'or I'll get my car and bloody smash it through.'

Peters' shoulders stiffened as he walked to the door, fishing in his trouser pockets as he did so.

He didn't like being told what to do, but was clearly scared enough of Hephaestus to obey.

Peters unlocked one of the doors and keeping the key in the lock, opened it for his visitor. Another key swung from the ring it was attached to.

Hephaestus limped through, shuffling on his left leg. He carried a smart looking cane which was pressed into his left palm as he walked. His soft shoes slid silently like slippers on the wooden floor. Hephaestus was in his mid-thirties I would have guessed with a subtle Mediterranean look about him. He gave Peters a long, hard look. Peters returned the gaze and the pair stood like boxers staring each other down before a fight.

Peters closed the door and locked it again, returning the keys immediately to his pocket. He wasn't taking any chances. Gloves must have given him a hard time over the mobile phone.

Peters stood with his back to the door and folded his arms. His fingers were twitching slightly, as if he was impatient. Hephaestus noticed it too.

'You've been sampling the merchandise again, haven't you?' He shook his head slowly, clearly thinking Peters was pathetic.

'Well, if it's not fit for purpose, at least it's good for something,' Peters snapped back.

'I can't believe Hermes forgave you for that.'

'He hasn't. Well?' he demanded. 'What are you doing here?'

'I've come for my money. I still haven't been paid for the last batch.'

Hephaestus stood with his back to the stairs and his free arm loose by his side. Peters' body language revealed that his confidence was just bluff, but Hephaestus wasn't bluffing and looked ready to strike out if provoked.

'You were supposed to deliver the cash yesterday. Where is it?'

Peters laughed scornfully. 'We don't pay for inferior work.'

Hephaestus leant forward and with narrowed eyes raised a threatening finger to Peters' nose.

'I did the work and I expect to get paid for it.' The muscles in his arm flexed beneath his thin shirt as he held his finger up. His body looked tense and I could see that he was lean and strong. I wondered what had happened to him.

'Hermes takes care of the finances,' replied Peters flippantly. 'I have been unavoidably detained.'

Immediately, Hephaestus' hand formed a strangulating collar around Peters' throat.

'You're the delivery boy. The cash comes through you. Where is the money?' he whispered.

Any pretence of control that Peters had was gone and he tried to cough.

'With Hermes. He's here,' he gasped, tugging at Hephaestus' wrist. 'Spoke to him through the door.'

'Only Athena's here, you pillock,' spat back Hephaestus, tightening his grip.

'He said he was going to visit Herse today.' Peters staggered forward slightly, desperate to give Hephaestus something.

Hephaestus couldn't hide his surprise. 'But, she's one of my recipients,' he responded, releasing his grip. 'I have Herse and Aphrodite.'

'Only artificially,' replied Peters, coughing, and he couldn't resist a smirk as he spoke.

Hephaestus answered with a strong right punch, catching Peters across the cheek and spinning him round to hit the floor face down.

'I swear, Ares, if I find out that you've been messing with Aphrodite, I'll kill you! I'll rip your head off.'

I clasped both my hands over my mouth as I watched Peters clamber up on to his knees.

'I haven't touched her.'

Hephaestus checked Peters' pockets and removed the keys. My shoulders sagged with the weight of the world. How was I going to get those keys now?

Hephaestus ran a hand through his dark hair as he seemed to ponder where to go.

He shuffled quickly towards me and I backed away from the door into the darkened passageway, but he went into the living room.

Peters lifted his head slowly as if trying to regain his composure. He pulled himself up and rubbing his face, walked swiftly up the stairs.

I forced myself to take controlled breaths through my nose as I pressed my back against the wall and turned my head towards the living room doorway at the back of the house. Hephaestus was rummaging through boxes, swearing aloud and moving things about.

Noisy footsteps came jogging back down the stairs and into the hall.

'Ares!' yelled Hephaestus.

I couldn't move. I was trapped between two dangerous men and moving in any direction would reveal my location. Peters walked into the living room and Hephaestus started yelling and cursing.

'It's not here,' interrupted Peters. 'He's taken it with him.'

'I only have contact with Hermes by phone,' said Hephaestus. 'You're the one who's supposed to deliver the payment. I had to come here to find out why you didn't turn up.'

'Not the bloody money!' exclaimed Peters. 'The sample, he's taken the sample! I've got nothing left.'

'I don't care about samples,' shouted back Hephaestus. 'Where's the cash?'

'There's nothing upstairs,' said Peters, starting to sound desperate. 'I'll go and meet him. He's got something we both want.'

Suddenly there was a loud bleeping.

'It's the clinic,' said Hephaestus, presumably reading a text. 'Herse's miscarried.'

There was a moment's silence as they absorbed the bad news.

'Where's your mobile?' asked Hephaestus.

'Hermes took it.'

Hephaestus laughed. 'He should have taken your keys as well. Maybe he thought he didn't need to ground you too.'

'I need a drink.'

'Later,' ordered Hephaestus. 'There are more important things to take care of first. Let's go.'

I heard them walk out into the hallway, whispering. The front door was opened, closed and locked. All was quiet again. I counted to fifty before I dared to sneak a peek into the living room.

The boxes that Gloves had tidied were now jumbled and pamphlets scattered everywhere. A couple of boxes were on their sides on the floor; damaged by Hephaestus' fury and impatience.

I walked back through the passageway and cautiously tiptoed into the main hallway.

Confident that I was now safely alone, I tried the handles of the main doors. They were locked and I cursed.

The only thing I could think to do now was to find out what was in the pink folder. I went upstairs with the key at the ready. I put the key in the lock, but as I was about to turn it, I sensed movement nearby.

I turned and gasped as I saw Hephaestus standing in the doorway of Peters' room, leaning casually against the frame.

'Hello, Athena,' he smiled.

Chapter 14

'There isn't any money in the house,' I blurted, talking too quickly. 'And I don't have any.'

'I've figured that much out for myself,' he replied. 'You're very clever, by the way.' He nodded at the door behind me. 'I really did think that you were in there, briefly.'

'What do you want?'

'Something even more valuable than money - information.'

'You want the pink folder?' I asked. 'It's in here.' I reached my left hand behind me and fumbled for the lock. Feeling the key beneath my fingers, I turned it, twisting my wrist in an unnatural direction.

Hephaestus smiled again as he straightened up and hobbled towards me.

'Oh, the information I want isn't in the folder,' he whispered, fondling the smooth, polished head of his cane. 'It's in you.'

He reached out a hand and gently tucked a strand of my hair back behind my ear. I had to admit, Hephaestus was a good-looking guy; If I had met him in a bar I might have thought he was attractive. Now I thought he was seriously creepy and I was very scared.

'What kind of information?' I could hear a tremor creeping into my voice and hoped that Hephaestus didn't notice. His fingers lingered behind my ear as he answered.

'Your age? Boyfriend? Any plans for children...' He lent forward to whisper seductively. '... Favourite position.'

His breath was soft and cool against my ear; as gentle as a lover's.

I turned my head to the side and swallowed the disgusting taste taking over my mouth.

'None of your business!' I stated, far more confidently than I felt. 'I'm happily married, thank you, so you can just leave me alone!' I gave him a little shove.

Hephaestus laughed; a deep, throaty chuckle.

'You shouldn't be so fast to say no, Athena,' he chided gently. 'A woman as beautiful as you shouldn't restrict herself. After all, there's only so much a man can resist.'

The fingers that were behind my ear, traced a line along my jaw. I swallowed again and continued to reach for the key behind me.

'Besides,' he continued, 'if you give me a little something, I'll give you something. Call it 'a professional agreement'.'

I pushed my right hand into the centre of his chest firmly. He may have carried a cane, but he was clearly strong.

'No!' I yelled. 'Do you understand that? No!'

Hephaestus simply smiled benignly as he shifted his cane and held up his right hand. Dangling from his middle finger was the ring of two keys he'd taken from Peters' trouser pocket.

Very briefly, I wondered if I could do this; could I endure the worst of all crimes for the promise of freedom? A chill ran over me and I realised that emotionally, I just wasn't that strong.

'Never in a million years.'

Swiftly, Hephaestus brought his cane to my throat, pushing the rounded head into the soft hollow under my jaw.

'I insist you reconsider.'

I pulled on his arm, trying to move the cane choking me, but Hephaestus barely noticed as he dipped his head again, this time to nuzzle against my ear.

At last, I managed to get a grip on the key and pulled it free.

I pulled my arm from behind my back and not letting myself think about what I was doing, I slashed the jagged tip, like a knife across his cheek.

Hephaestus yelled and immediately lifted his hand to his face. Already red spots of blood were forming a dotted line towards his mouth.

I pushed against him as hard as I could and he staggered backwards, trying to maintain his balance.

'Agh! You bitch!'

I ran towards Peters' room and removed the key. Inside, I slammed the door and lent against it as I turned the key in the lock. I just managed to do so, before Hephaestus slammed his fists against the door and rattled the handle.

I backed away and sat on Peters' mattress, hugging my

knees to my chest. I remembered I still had the butter knife in my left pocket and held that between my hands in front of me. If Hephaestus managed to break through the door, it would be as good as useless. Its only purpose was to make me feel more confident, but confident was the last thing I felt.

Sitting there huddled in the gloomy room defiant words were running in circles in my head.

'No way. Never in a million years.'

Hephaestus stopped his banging and tried talking to me through the door. I knew why. Now that Herse had miscarried, they would need to try again, maybe with a new recipient.

'You're making a huge mistake, Athena,' he said. 'You could be a heroine, destined for great things.'

I silently begged him to go away.

Suddenly his mobile phone rang with a shrill tone that made me jump. I crawled on my hands and knees to the door and pressed my ear to the wood.

He seemed to listen carefully for a few seconds before bringing the conversation to a close.

'Ok, I'm on my way. No, locked in Ares' room,' he said. 'She's untouchable.'

Untouchable? Did that simply mean that I wouldn't be manipulated?

'I'll be about twenty minutes.'

His voice was fading away, presumably going downstairs. I sat with my back against the door and rubbed my stiff neck.

I was tired and had a headache. I couldn't even remember what day it was. I felt slightly giddy and massaged the back of my head with my fingers. As I did so, I noticed again the slight bulge in the wallpaper that I had seen the last time I was in here.

I crawled over to the wall and ran my hands over the uneven wallpaper. The loose paper seemed not to be stuck to whatever was behind it; just hiding what was there, like a curtain.

I knelt before the wall and using the tip of the butter knife, scored a line into the brittle paper. I followed the outline beneath and the paper started to flake as a jagged tear appeared.

When I'd cut three sides of a square, I used my fingers to peel back the wallpaper, revealing what looked like a rough, miniature cupboard. A flat piece of wood had been pushed into a square opening and crudely papered over. I sawed the butter knife into the dust, dirt and debris that filled the edges and didn't bother to worry about any of it falling on to me.

I worked desperately, as if I were digging for buried treasure, and tried to lever the knife behind the piece of wood.

After a little while, I managed to dig my fingernails into the gap at the top and, after levering backwards and forwards, I eventually heard a crack as the old plaster gave way. The wooden door fell back on to my lap and I had to cover my nose, coughing as a cloud of ancient dust engulfed me.

The inner space seemed a lot smaller than the door

suggested. But there inside, wrapped in an old and faded cloth, covered with brick dust, was a neat little bundle, never expecting to see daylight again.

Gritty dirt coated blue-tinted paper where the cloth had fallen away. I ran my fingers across the surface and displaced a handful of grime. I laid the bundle on the floor as if they were jewels. To me, they were precious: documents that Gloves and Peters couldn't possibly have known about. I unfolded two giant sheets that rustled loudly as if complaining about being woken from a long hibernation.

These were building plans, old fashioned blueprints showing the layout of a large and possibly handsome house. I had been handling documents and paperwork all my working life, but had never seen a layout as beautifully portrayed as this. Whoever had built this house had put a lot of love into it.

I looked at the bottom right hand corner of the page, squinting at the writing and cursing the lack of light. This was where the address and architect details would be. Written in neat and stylish print was 'plot 30, Badger Hill Farm'.

That name sounded familiar. Badger Hill Farm; I was sure that was a local place. The architect was Simpson & Co (1935) Limited.

I carried the prints over to the door and pressed my ear to the wood. Hoping that I was alone, I unlocked the door and opened it a crack. The light from the hallway shone a narrow triangle on to the rough floor. Laying the paper down in the light, I knelt before the plans and studied what I saw.

Then I pulled out the bottom sheet and laid it on top. This blueprint looked the same as the one before and I was just about to turn my attention back to the previous sheet, when I noticed that some of the lines drawn on this one looked as if they were in the wrong place.

Lines had been drawn across a passageway and stairways. I studied the image more closely and saw that this drawing was dated much later than the other. The reference number on this sheet was HJS15061989. Assuming that HJS was the architect's initials, the rest of the reference number could be the date. That would mean that this drawing was amended on 15th June 1989.

I checked the previous sheet. That looked different. The lines were clearer and sharper, drawn with precision but also with an artistry the second sheet just didn't have. The referencing system did look the same, however. This one said JPS12091949, so the date would be 12th September 1949. I noticed another difference here too. I couldn't see an image for a bathroom in either drawing. Presumably, in 1949 the toilet would be outside. Over the last few days, I had become used to peeing in a bucket.

I was feeling a little sick. These could be the original drawings for this house. If these blueprints were for this house, was it really local to where I lived? Exactly where was I?

I wondered if there was any way I could throw the blueprints out of a window. Maybe someone would be able to identify the house and come to my rescue. But no helpful passing stranger had yet come by the house. I couldn't remember when I'd thrown the cigarette packet outside. Was it yesterday or the day before? Besides, the blueprints were too big and obvious. Peters or Gloves were bound to see those and that would redirect attention back to me.

I wished I'd locked myself in the other room. There was very little light in this one and I could be here for a while.

I heard movement downstairs and quickly pulled the blueprints back into the room and locked the door. I refolded the drawings and returned them to their hidey-hole. Someone was outside the door again. Items were being put on the floor. I opened my mouth to yell out and then remembered that Hephaestus had left. There was only one person who left things on the floor outside my door, but he had left too. I'd chased him from the house and he'd left a steaming cup of coffee on the kitchen table. Hadn't he?

Chapter 15

My throat felt dry. I was in need of a drink, but more than that, I needed to know if Gloves had been in the house when Hephaestus had tried to attack me. Had he known? I banged my hands against the door and called out again.

'Wait! Please wait.'

I didn't hear any footsteps, or even know if anyone was actually there. I could have been talking to an empty hallway for all I knew, but I couldn't risk opening the door. I coughed and tried again.

'Look,' I said, trying to be reasonable. 'If you were here while Hephaestus was here, you'd know what he tried to do, right?' There was no answer. 'Was it you who called him and saved me? I don't know if you were going to punish him, but I'm OK. Well, I'm OK now.'

I was still scared that Hephaestus might return, but I didn't want to think that Gloves was going to kill him. This wasn't because I wanted to protect my attacker, but because if there was a Mr Big behind all this, I'd want to protect my protector.

'Will you just think about it?' I ran my fingers over the paintwork on the door while I tried to think of the right words. What did the ancient Greeks say? 'Will you consider clemency?'

I had to leave it at that. I didn't want to beg for mercy for Hephaestus, or anyone else.

I walked over to the door and pressed my ear against it. I couldn't hear anything and decided to risk opening it to see what Gloves had brought me.

On the floor was a mug of tea and a saucer with a cheese sandwich on it. I wasn't sure if this was lunch or dinner; I no longer knew what time of day it was. I was grateful for the food just the same and ate it inside the room with my back against the door. When I had finished I left the mug and saucer outside the door and decided to have a lie down.

Dust and dirt from the wall had left tiny pieces all over the pillow and mattress on the floor. I shook out the pillow and blankets and it was while I was doing this that I heard movement outside the door. For one heart stopping moment I wondered if I had remembered to lock it, but Gloves made no attempt to enter. I simply froze and waited. After a few moments I unlocked the door as quietly as I could and opened it a crack to peek outside. There was no-one there, but on the floor I noticed that the empty mug I'd left had gone and in its place on the saucer were two ginger-nut biscuits. I love ginger-nuts.

I wondered what I had done to deserve this additional treat. Maybe Gloves had thought about what I'd said. Maybe he had thought about clemency.

Muffled voices and heavy footsteps seeped up through the house. It sounded as if Gloves had brought Peters back with him and they were having another argument. Maybe, with luck, Peters would be out of a job soon. It was clear that he was becoming unreliable and therefore a threat to the project.

I lay down on the mattress and tried to close my eyes, but now that I knew that Peters was in the house, I couldn't rest. He was probably drunk. After a few minutes, all had gone quiet; too quiet. Curious to know what was happening I made the terrible mistake of thinking that it might be safe to open the door.

I turned the key slowly and only pulled the door ajar, but that was enough for Peters to quickly step away from the wall and barge through the door, pushing me backwards and down on to the floor. He came at me with such a menacing look I thought he had come to finish me off.

I shuffled backwards, but Peters was quickly down on his knees and soon had his right hand around my throat.

'Hermes,' I whispered, gasping.

'He can't save you,' sneered Peters. 'He's gone out on one of his important visits. In the meantime I thought you and I should have a little chat.'

There was nothing for us to talk about. I could guess what had happened. Peters had left me alone with Hephaestus and lost his keys. If Hephaestus was going to be in trouble, then Peters would be too and Gloves must have made that clear.

'Ares can't hurt Athena,' I gasped desperately. I was wracking my brains for school time Classical Studies. As far as I could remember, although Ares and Athena were enemies, Ares didn't attack her.

'Hermes says Athena is untouchable,' replied Peters clenching his left fist. 'But Hermes isn't here.'

He pushed harder against my neck and as my elbows gave way, I toppled backwards, banging my head against the floorboards. I barely felt the knock, as Peters held me down and raised his fist above my face.

'Is she pregnant?'

I was gasping for breath but had to say something, anything to distract him.

'Is who pregnant?' Peters did not release his grip, but looked confused.

Distant memories were coming back to me from my schooldays and I vaguely remembered that Aphrodite and Ares had an affair.

'Aphrodite. Is she pregnant?' I was throwing wild guesses in the air. I had only briefly heard Hephaestus speak of Aphrodite.

'Not yet,' smirked Peters, letting his fist drop. He kept his hand against my throat. 'H only went there a few hours ago.'

'H is not the father,' I said, pulling on Peters arm. 'Ares and Aphrodite had a daughter.' Peters' smirk faded and his face seemed to pale.

'You did sleep with her didn't you? She was supposed to be one of H's recipients.'

I risked trying to sit up. I hoped that if I could keep talking, I could distract Peters and maybe give him bigger things to worry about.

'If H has gone to see her, maybe he has found out about your affair.' I pulled Peters fist away from me and watched his face as he swallowed hard.

'That wasn't part of the plan, was it?'

If Hephaestus still had Peters' keys he might come back to look for him, but Peters was worried about something else. 'H will tell Hermes and I'll be reported to Zeus.'

Peters looked like he was starting to sweat. To me, the solution seemed simple enough.

'If you don't want to see him, you'll have to leave, just disappear.' I was not only trying to sound helpful. I'd be very happy if Peters just disappeared.

'No keys,' responded Peters, irritably. 'I'm stuck here, like you.' He ran a hand through his hair and licked his lips nervously. Peters was starting to look like a caged animal.

'Look,' I said, starting to feel nervous myself again, 'only you and I know each other's real names. If we can break out of here together, nobody else needs to know who we are.'

'Hermes knows where to find me,' replied Peters twitching his fingers. 'Nobody leaves The Company.'

Peters rose to his feet and hurried through the door.

I rushed after him, worried that he might lock me in, but Peters ignored me and jogged down the stairs. He marched straight into the kitchen and started searching with growing frustration, opening cupboards and pulling drawers from their housing, cursing all the while. There was nothing useful with which to pick a lock in here. He opened yet another empty drawer and with a yell, hurled it at the wall above the sink, crumbling a handful of damaged plaster and revealing an arch shape where a window might once have been. Cracked wood and lumps of dusty plaster crashed down on top of a couple of mugs.

Peters ran past me and up the back stairs.

'You're wasting your time; there's nothing up there. Or anywhere else. We need the keys.'

I pottered about the kitchen looking for the things I'd need to make a cup of tea, while Peters was crashing and banging upstairs.

There was only one small chair up there; the one that had been in the first room I'd occupied. The kitchen had a table, but no chairs around it and even if Peters could break through a window, how was he going to get down to the ground? He would have to throw all the mattresses out of the same window and risk a jump.

The likelihood of being able to smash through a window was small. In the movies, when a hero fires his gun at a lock, the door magically springs open. In reality the lock and frame are the strongest parts of a door; the weakest part is the centre, so the hero would be better off holstering the gun and smashing at the centre of the door. Peters had nothing to smash at the centre of the window and even if he were able to find something, success would take a lot of time and Gloves could come back at any minute.

I'd found a half clean cup and a tea bag and had just poured in water from the kettle, when Peters came running back down the stairs. I stood close to the door, knowing that my need for an escape route would be likely.

Peters stood, breathless, in the kitchen and rubbed the back of his neck. He simply lifted his head and looked directly at me.

'You are the reason we're both here.' He said. 'You were the one we were instructed to monitor and you've slowed our progress and wasted our time.' I instinctively took a couple of steps back and Peters took a couple forward.

'Now you're going to have to give us what we want.'

I threw the cup at him and a hot brown splash landed flat across his chest. He yelled and was momentarily distracted while he tried to pull the scorched fabric away from his skin.

I turned and ran out into the passageway, into the main hallway and up the stairs. I headed towards the second room. I was already at the door when I realized that Peters wasn't following me. I paused for a moment with my hand resting on the handle and the lock before going inside; obviously Peters had found something more interesting to distract him.

Once safely inside the room, I saw that the pink folder I had ignored earlier was scattered across the floor, as if someone had dropped it and the paperwork had flown everywhere. Perhaps Hephaestus had vented his anger when I had escaped him. I needed to find out what was in this folder. Something about it had to be important.

I knelt before the folder and started to tidy the papers. These were supposed to be dispatch orders and payments, but on nearly every piece of paper the delivery was to be made to the same person at the same address every time. I was used to sending paperwork all over the world, but here it didn't seem to matter what language it was in, it was all going to me, Kim Anderson, at an address I didn't recognise.

I put my hands over my eyes and took a deep breath. I was so tired and my hands felt rough. I'd lost the makeshift bandage I'd put on my damaged finger. It was still disgustingly discoloured.

I sat back on my heels and wondered what was to become of me. I didn't know what else I could do to get out of here except give Gloves what he wanted.

Soft footsteps were coming up the stairs. I held my breath and waited. This was neither Peters nor Gloves and whoever it was had arrived on foot; I hadn't heard a car. Maybe Peters had seen someone coming towards the main door. The only person who had used that door before was Hephaestus, so Peters would have been wise to hide. But, I didn't think this was Hephaestus either.

A few moments later there was a gentle rap on the door and a woman's voice called 'hello?'

I was so shocked at hearing a woman speak that I toppled over from my crouched position on the floor.

'Hello, yes, I'm here,' I answered. 'Don't go.'

I had no idea who this person was, but I had to hope that she would help me.

I unlocked the door and opened it a crack. I don't know which one of us was more surprised.

The young woman was about twenty-two or twenty-three and looked like summer personified. She had long wavy golden hair with two strands plaited from the temples and tied back. Her light skin was rosy and her blue eyes shone like a moon under water. She was wearing a pastel lemon shirt and a white cotton skirt that reached almost to her ankles. She looked as if she ought to be standing in a meadow of daisies.

'Are you Aphrodite?' I asked, making an educated guess.

She raised her eyebrows.

'Yes. You must be Athena.' She had obviously not been expecting to meet me. I wondered if she had the keys Hephaestus had taken from Peters.

'Is H with you?' I asked, as casually as I could.

'No.' She lowered her eyes to the floor at the mention of his name and I thought my suspicions about her and Peters must be correct. 'He just dropped me off at the bottom of the road. He said Zeus wanted to see me.'

I swallowed hard and with all the bravado I could muster, said; 'He'll be here soon. You better let me look after your keys for you, just so they don't get lost.' I held out my hand encouragingly.

Aphrodite might have looked like an innocent little thing, but she wasn't stupid. Her face paled and she took a step away from me. I was desperate to get my hands on those keys and if there's one thing I'd learned, it's that desperate people will do anything to get what they want. I opened the door and made a grab for her arm, but she was too quick for me and ran back down the stairs and into the hallway.

I raced after her and saw that she was already fumbling

with the lock on the main door. From out of nowhere, Peters stepped in front of me blocking the path between me and his lover.

Chapter 16

I skidded to a halt and immediately started stepping backwards.

Peters was still wearing the tea-splattered shirt and his eyes narrowed as he glared back at me.

Aphrodite smiled and a knowing glimmer shone from her eyes like moonbeams. She walked over to Peters, draping her arms around his neck and hugged him from behind. She lifted only her eyes to look at me.

'Ares!' she said.

Peters kept his eyes on me when he spoke to her. 'How did you get here?' It was not a polite question.

'H drove me.'

'Did you bring anything?' Presumably he meant either drink or a sample.

'No, but I can get you some.'

I doubted this was possible. Aphrodite wasn't carrying a bag or a jacket and she only had soft canvas shoes on her feet; she wasn't planning on going out. This must mean that Hephaestus had smuggled her out of the clinic and bundled her into the car. He'd be back.

I turned and hurried back up the stairs with Peters' eyes burning holes into my back. I'd have to rethink how I was going to get hold of those keys.

I locked myself back in the room with the folder and knelt on the floor with the paperwork once more. Thinking things over, I knew Peters wouldn't leave. If Aphrodite could persuade The Company that she had successfully become pregnant, like she had in the legends, then Peters would be rewarded, as Ares had been, regardless of Hephaestus' fury. Now all I had to do was sit tight and wait for something to happen.

I rummaged in the folder and found the regulation ballpoint. Slipping my jogging bottoms over my hips I scribbled on the inside of my thigh and copied the address that was on the dispatch sheets. I had no way of knowing if it was important, but just in case, I didn't want to rely on memory.

A little while later, I heard a car pull up to the front of the house. As this room was above the hallway, I ran over to the window to see if I could recognise the visitor. I had to squash my cheek to the glass and peer down my nose as the car was parked too close for me to get a suitable view.

Hephaestus got out of the car first. I had assumed he'd return, but he had brought someone else with him.

This second man stayed in the back of the car and waited for Hephaestus to walk around the side and open his door for him. When he stepped out, all I could see was a black balaclava mask above a smart business jacket. The rest of him was shielded by the car. He lifted his hands and pulled a leather driving glove a little tighter towards his wrist. As if sensing that he was being watched, he lifted his head and looked up at the window.

I was too shocked to move and simply stared back. I knew I was being appraised and guessed that he knew I was doing the same.

The main door opened downstairs and diverted his attention. Hephaestus strode into the hallway and proceeded up the main stairs towards me. I darted across to the door and made sure that it was locked.

'Hephaestus! Leave her.'

The sharply barked order came from a stern, well-educated voice, calling the bad dog to heel.

'They're not here,' said Hephaestus from outside the door.

I waited for a few moments, trying to give Hephaestus enough time to search the other rooms before I followed. I was hoping that if they were sufficiently distracted by Peters and Aphrodite, I could sneak in behind them and locate the keys.

It was crazy of me to think I could get away with any of this but I felt like I was going mad in this place. I had no idea what time it was, and no longer knew what day it was. I was permanently tired and constantly hungry.

I crept down the stairs and into the passageway. I paused for a moment by the kitchen and could hear angry voices above.

Peters and Hephaestus were hurling insults at each other like stones and Aphrodite's voice was pleading and tearful.

I tiptoed up the back stairs and stood outside what was once Gloves' room. The door was ajar and unable to stay shut without its lock. I held my breath and peeked round the frame.

Hephaestus had Peters pinned against the wall, caught wearing only his boxer shorts. Aphrodite was kneeling on the bed, clutching her clothes, trying to preserve what was left of her modesty.

'H, c'mon, you've got to let him go. Please...'

Her pleas were falling on deaf ears as Hephaestus continued to rant.

'You'll be punished well for this, you bastard. Just couldn't resist trying them all out, could you?'

'It wasn't like that, H. He's been good to me.' Aphrodite was wasting her time, but at least she was trying to restore a little calm.

Hephaestus sneered as he looked Peters over, his lip curling in disgust.

'Not even sending you here could keep you away. Forbidden fruit, isn't it?'

My eyes scanned the floor and I saw them! The keys were there, halfway under the end of the bed.

I knelt down on all fours and slowly pushed the door. The fight continued and I remained unnoticed.

Lying flat on my stomach I stretched out my arms and reached towards the keys. They were about three inches out of my reach. I shuffled forward, swimming with my shoulders and my hips and excitedly breathed out as I wrapped my fingers around them.

'I'm afraid I'm going to have to take those from you.' The voice was calm and softly spoken. I didn't detect any malice, but there was a tone of authority that wouldn't have tolerated disobedience.

The man in black stood perfectly still. He was in the hallway, just a foot or two behind me and would have been out of sight from Hephaestus and Peters, but even so the sound of his voice brought everything to a stop.

Peters struggled free from Hephaestus. 'You set us up, you git!'

The man was wearing an expensive looking business suit and polished black shoes. I guessed from his manner and neat appearance that he might have been a little older than I had first presumed. He held out his hand towards me.

I sat up to face him and gripped the keys even tighter. Now that I had my hands on the prize I wasn't willing to let it go.

Hephaestus turned his head to look at me. Aphrodite was hurriedly getting dressed. The voice behind the door remained calm.

'You're very resourceful, Athena. I'm sure you will be an excellent asset.'

'Over my dead body!'

'That could be arranged,' quipped Peters. Hephaestus gave him a spiteful look.

Zeus interrupted sternly. 'The two of you were required to fulfil an obligation.'

'It has been.' The whispered answer from the bed cancelled the need for Zeus to ask any more questions.

'I knew it! You bitch!' Hephaestus' fury had returned and forgetting about Peters, he lifted his right arm and slapped Aphrodite with a forceful backhand, full across her face. With an agonized squeal, she fell sideways, burying her head in the bedclothes.

'I told you they had betrayed us,' continued Hephaestus, his tone almost triumphant.

Zeus walked slowly into the room, taking well placed, methodical steps.

'I forgave your attack on Athena, on one condition,' he said quietly.

Hephaestus was shocked, his eyes wide. 'But how did you...'

'Now that the condition has been met by someone else, I shall have to give you a new task.'

Hephaestus opened his mouth as if to speak, but there really wasn't anything he could say.

'You will take Ares and Aphrodite back to the clinic. Wait in the car.'

The two men did as they were told and left the room.

Zeus knelt in front of me and held out his hand to take the keys. I pulled my hand further away and almost laughed.

They were my keys now. Except that they weren't. Zeus reached towards me and gripping my wrist, squeezed hard against the two protruding bones under the skin. A stab of pain shot up the inside of my wrist and into my hand and I dropped the keys.

With a slight smile, Zeus bent to pick them up, and then turned to Aphrodite.

'Tidy yourself and go to the car.' He spoke softly and not unkindly.

Pausing in the doorway to look back at me, he went back downstairs.

As soon as Zeus was out of sight, I ran over to the bed and tried to comfort Aphrodite. I put a hand on the back of her shoulder and she lifted her head.

Already I could see the swell of an angry red mark running from the top of her cheek to the side of her bloody nose. I pushed her hair back from her face and gently cupped her head in my hands.

'I don't think you'll be making the cover of Vogue this month.'

Aphrodite jerked her head away and gave a scornful look. 'You don't look so hot yourself.'

'Look, you're only bruised. If you can get dressed quickly, we can jump the fence towards the back and follow the road to the next town. It can't be more than a couple of miles.'

Aphrodite shook her head. 'They said you were smart. They'd shoot us both before we got that far. Zeus keeps a gun in the car. Once the Company decides who they want, they won't let go. Nobody leaves The Company.'

'But we have to at least try.'

'I'm alive. At least, for now. I have no desire to get shot in the back.'

'Who takes care of you?' I asked, nodding at her wounds.

'Who takes care of you? Look, they only want you for your intelligence and initiative. The Company always gets what it wants. Do yourself a favour and don't ask questions and don't try and make friends. Everybody works for The Company. Including you.'

'There's really no escape?'

'A few of the other women tried; they were always brought back. And punished. Besides, we signed an agreement. We're committed.'

'Not to this!' I was incredulous. 'What the hell were you thinking?!'

'I signed up to a drug trial, a reproduction programme. None of us knew it would be like this.' She lifted a finger to her nose and sniffed gently. The bleeding seemed to have stopped.

'What can I do to help you?'

'Nothing. And there's nothing anyone can do to help you. Once they transfer you to the clinic, there'll be no way back.' She looked over her shoulder to make sure no-one was there.

'I overheard two guys talking at the clinic. The police found your car in the barn.'

My heart leapt and I was suddenly breathless. 'They're looking for me, they've found a lead. That's wonderful!'

'No, it's not,' said Aphrodite, pulling me back down to earth. 'The barn was a private enough place for them all to meet. Now that it's been discovered, The Company will have to find somewhere else.' She looked at me as if I was being a bit slow. 'Somewhere like here,' she added.

'Why can't they just meet at this clinic?'

'Only a privileged few are invited into these meetings; apparently that's when they discuss their next steps.'

I swallowed hard. 'How many people?'

Aphrodite shook her head. 'I don't know, I just heard talk; maybe twenty, maybe thirty. They call themselves something like the elite.' She tided her clothes and stood up, ready to leave. She smiled humourlessly. 'Good luck.'

'Aphrodite, wait.' I had just one more question. 'Who is The Company?'

Aphrodite seemed surprised I didn't know.

'Fireflight,' she said, and then she was gone.

Chapter 17

I sat on the bed quietly for several minutes thinking about what Aphrodite had said. She was sufficiently scared to warn me that I had to find a way to escape.

Unfortunately, she already thought it was too late for her. I wanted to believe that if I could find a way to end all this and get out, I could rescue her too.

I shivered and rubbed my arms. My skin was goose pimpled and already a dark shadow had descended on the room. In another hour it would be night.

I wondered if I was hungry. Maybe I was but fear and dread were halting my appetite. I'd heard somewhere that knowing that you were hungry and thirsty was a good thing; failing to recognise your appetite was a danger signal.

The fear that had accompanied my thoughts since I arrived was slowly being replaced by dread, and that was something even worse. Dread was the fear of fear; the feeling that something really awful was going to happen.

Aphrodite, and God knew how many other women, thought that their dreams were going to come true, but what of their future?

I climbed beneath the covers and curled up into a ball. I closed my eyes, pulled the blanket over my head and tried to sleep.

When I woke, the first thought to enter my head was that I needed to go downstairs to try the doors; I had forgotten to follow Aphrodite and check them last night. The items I saw in the room told me that someone had saved me the trouble. There was an empty bucket and a washing-up bowl of hot water. On top of the dressing table were clean clothes.

The door had been left standing ajar. I sat up in bed and took a good look around the room, trying to recall every detail to see if anything had changed. The lock on the door was still missing and the window was still bare.

The dressing table was in the same place, but while I was looking at it, I understood what was different. I had been given clean clothes the last time I was in this room, but they had been put away in the drawers. This new set of clothes was sitting on top. There were two possibilities here; either someone other than Gloves had put them there or they were an afterthought, arriving after my wash bowl. Or else, just as likely, I was being paranoid and going slightly crazy.

I went over to the wash bowl and dipped my hand in. It was still fairly hot, so couldn't have been there for more than a few minutes.

I washed carefully and tried to avoid the address I'd written on my leg yesterday. Getting dressed, I suddenly guessed what the address on the dispatch sheets was and why it was so important. It was so obvious now and I was surprised to realise that Gloves had tried to send me a warning. This was the address of the clinic. It was clever of them to choose a location in the Home Counties; close enough to be in convenient travelling distance to London, but also far enough away so as not to attract attention.

I would not have expected Gloves, or anyone else, to be so careless as to let me see the address. He was the only person who might deliberately let me see it and only because it was relevant. I shuddered slightly at the thought that I might be moved there.

I finished dressing and again tried to think who would wear clothes like this. They smelt clean like washing powder, but none that I recognised. I was grateful to notice I'd been given a clean pair of socks. I attempted to use the bucket but was unsuccessful. That was unusual for me.

At the bottom of the stairs I tried the back door before entering the kitchen. On the table there was a fresh plastic bottle of milk, a box of cornflakes, a loaf of bread and a jar of coffee. Gloves had been out shopping and compared with what I'd seen before, this was a feast.

I helped myself to coffee and cereal. Unable to finish the whole bowl, I left it on the table and took my coffee cup out of the kitchen and into the living room.

I gripped my cup tightly, warming my hands as I mentally complained about the absence of heat in this wretched place.

I nearly dropped it when I looked up and saw Zeus standing in the middle of the living room waiting for me. He appeared to be wearing the same balaclava hood as yesterday and the same tight black driving gloves. He wore a dark, thick woollen three-quarter length coat, beneath which I could just see dark suit trousers and polished shoes. He looked immaculate.

'Good morning, Athena,' he said.

I said nothing as I took in the image before me and hoped that I wasn't displaying the shock that I felt.

Zeus lifted a hand towards one of the armchairs. 'Sit down, please.'

'Where is Hermes?' I asked, staying where I was.

'He's here,' replied Zeus. He nodded behind him towards the door that led into the main hallway. 'Sit down.'

I did as I was told, but kept my eyes on Zeus all the while. 'How is Aphrodite?' I noticed a suspicious tone in my own voice that I hadn't wanted Zeus to hear, but I was genuinely worried about her and last night's feeling of dread had not abated.

'She's fine. She has a black eye, but other than that she's very well.'

'And Hephaestus? What about him?'

Zeus stretched out the fingers of one hand and clenched a fist, stretching the leather across his knuckles, but when he spoke his voice was quite calm.

'Oh, you needn't worry about him. He will be assigned a new obligation.'

I guessed that he was expected to be a donor for a new recipient. Tentatively I said, 'You knew he tried to... attack me?'

'Had he succeeded, I would throw him from an even higher window.' Zeus pulled sharply on the glove and looked back at me. I returned his gaze, stubbornly, but his image was just too dark for me to identify. I couldn't even see what colour his eyes were. I felt fairly certain he knew what I was trying to do, but he didn't turn his face away.

'He's been here before, you know,' I said. I felt no pangs about betraying Hephaestus and inadvertently lifted my hand to my face as I remembered the blow he'd inflicted on Aphrodite.

Zeus stood still and said nothing.

'He came to the house to load boxes into the back of Hermes' SUV.'

Zeus took a deep breath and remained silent. I guessed he hadn't been aware that Hephaestus knew about the house before he came looking for his money. Hephaestus had a grievance with Peters and knew where to find him.

I then realised something I hadn't thought of before. 'He came to the front door to talk to Ares.'

Zeus tilted his head slightly. I don't think he knew what I was talking about. If Hephaestus was already familiar with the house, why had he come to the front door when claiming his payment? Why hadn't he just come to the back door like Peters and Gloves always did? And then I realised. He had been calling for Ares. By coming to the front door, he'd be less likely to bump into Gloves, who might have refused payment for the faulty batch, and that might be another reason why he hadn't gone with Peters when he left the house.

'Why are you here?'

Zeus adjusted his feet and stood squarely and upright. He came straight to the point.

'I want you to join the reproduction programme to test a new procedure.'

Immediately there was a loud thump from the hallway as Gloves banged his fist against the door.

Zeus' shoulders flexed slightly, clearly annoyed at Gloves' disapproval. Zeus expected compliance, he didn't need approval. I said what I knew Gloves was thinking.

'Hermes considers Athena to be untouchable.'

Zeus suddenly shouted, firing his words down upon me like sharp shards of glass.

'I decide who is or is not to be untouchable!' The rage in that one sentence was absolute and Zeus' chest was heaving slightly. He had been very careful not to lose control in front of me but a challenge to his authority was something he would not tolerate. The outburst was frightening and I took a couple of deep breaths before I spoke.

'If you have already decided that I am to be a part of this procedure, why are you bothering to ask my permission?' My voice was quivering and there was nothing I could do to hide it.

'I'm not. I expect you to comply.'

I guessed that this sentence was directed as much to the man behind the door, as to me.

'You are no kind of man, you know that? You have no honour.'

Zeus laughed. 'Honour? I have an honourable army. In

the legions of charitable do-gooders, we are the Special Forces. In order for any global health reform to be effective, it must be properly controlled and targeted.'

'And what about those outside your targets? Those who can't or won't be controlled?'

'Then they cannot be considered worthy of the necessary health reforms.'

'That's unfair. Good health care should be available to everyone.'

'A pathetic and unrealistic fantasy,' he stated. 'The Hellenistic world understood that better than this one. Modern life is an utter shambles. People contribute nothing and society gives nothing. How can it? You're fed a diet of junk food, doped by reality television and lied to by the news. Nothing changes unless we change it.'

'And who are you to say what is and what isn't worth changing? You can't arrogantly impose ancient values on to today's world.'

'You're not being very kind, Athena. Especially as I have given you my protection.'

'Kim! Kim! My name is Kim.'

'Do you actually know what that name means? It describes a safe and elevated piece of land. An important and revered location.'

'It's the name my mother gave me.'

'Still, an inadequate reflection of the one I gave you. It was Athena I gave the aegis to.'

'The what?'

'The aegis. A symbol of my protection. I've been looking after you for years. I expect you to be grateful and therefore compliant.'

'You offer me no protection! What the hell are you talking about?'

'I'm protecting you from the future and, right now, from those around you. Be careful, Athena. Aphrodite is not your friend.'

'What if I refuse your protection?'

Zeus readjusted his feet again and lent forward slightly on to his toes. 'Don't.' I had been warned. Punishment would be forthcoming if I did not conform.

'What exactly is this new procedure?'

I saw Zeus' shoulders relax a little and his voice continued polite and calm.

'It's called Ovarian Tissue Transplantation.'

'You're going to put bits of another woman's ovary into my body?!'

'The tissue will have been perfectly harvested and cryogenically preserved.'

'Did you request volunteers for that, too?'

'Of course.' Each response Zeus made was supposed to inspire confidence in me, but made me increasingly uncomfortable.

'How can you be sure it'll be successful?'

'We have developed a unique enhancement,' boasted Zeus.

'Persephone,' I interrupted.

Zeus couldn't hide his surprise. 'What do you know of Persephone?' he demanded.

'I know it's unsafe. I overheard Hephaestus talking.'

'Persephone is perfectly safe, it's been rigorously tested.'

Zeus' body language made him look like a company director who had just been caught lying in a board meeting. I guessed the analogy was fairly close to the truth.

'Hephaestus was talking to Ares. He said that there was a problem with the last batch and that if it couldn't be fixed the only outcome is from Thanatos.'

Zeus bristled and slowly breathed out through his nose. There was no way for me to judge his expression, but he must have been fuming. Hephaestus couldn't have told him the truth, perhaps thinking that this would have affected his payment. I suspected that Gloves knew and had stolen samples to have them tested. The temptation was too much for Peters and he'd drunk the evidence along with his Jack Daniels.

'I shall look into this,' he announced.

'You can't,' I responded flatly. 'It's gone.'

'It won't have been destroyed yet,' said Zeus coolly.

'It may have been used up. Persephone would enhance the effects of alcohol too, wouldn't it?'

Zeus knew whom I was talking about and I hoped Peters had left the country. I suddenly remembered something. When Hephaestus came looking for his money, Peters had unsuccessfully searched the rooms upstairs for more Persephone. There must have been another sample that

Gloves had kept on him. I kept that thought to myself.

Another memory floated briefly to the surface of my brain. I was sure Hermes was the god of thieves. Perhaps Gloves would try to protect Peters.

Chapter 18

'Ares,' he whispered darkly. 'He will be made to pay for this.'

I tested him with another question.

'Will you put that option before the Elite?'

There was brief moment of silence while Zeus absorbed this second surprise.

I was desperately trying to force my brain to put two and two together, but it was like trying to piece together a jigsaw puzzle without seeing the picture.

Aphrodite had given me a glimpse of the inner world of The Company and I was pretty sure Zeus was the Mr Big controlling a network of people. The Company must be quite large if, as the name suggested, only special members met and numbered about thirty.

Zeus slowly leant forward until his face was close to mine and lifted my chin with his right hand. I shut my eyes tight. I didn't want to glare back at him, I was too scared. I was letting my mouth run away with me again and silently chastising myself I swallowed down the fear.

'This afternoon,' he whispered, 'it will be you we'll be talking about.' Zeus turned to leave.

'Wait!'

Zeus stopped but did not turn back. He simply waited for

me to speak.

'About Aphrodite,' I began. 'She needs looking after - I mean, protection.' I swallowed, trying to find the right words. I was asking a favour from a man I feared and couldn't trust.

'I want you to promise that she'll be taken care of properly. Respected and protected.' That was my request, for all the good it was worth.

Zeus tilted his head to the side as he listened to me and appeared to consider my request seriously. He nodded.

'You have my word.'

I breathed out a long ragged breath and looked down at the coffee cup I was still cradling. My coffee was now as cold as I was.

Zeus closed the door to the living room carefully behind him and I heard whispered voices beyond, but couldn't hear what they were saying.

Someone as powerful as Zeus would not want to risk the dangerous batch of Persephone. It was clear to me now that this wasn't just a back-street operation.

Somewhere out there, The Company had a respectable face and its own support system. The network of members would need to include doctors, surgeons, anaesthetists, lab assistants and accountants. And then there was me.

I considered it unlikely that Zeus would get rid of Hephaestus, despite this mistake; he was necessary and if he was holding a similar job elsewhere, questions would be asked if he suddenly disappeared.

Zeus himself must be a man of some standing, a figure in his local community. I was going to have to be a lot more careful what I said in front of Zeus, especially as I now knew he had keys to the house.

I remembered that both Gloves and Peters had their own sets of keys. As far as I knew, Gloves kept his keys on him at all times and he didn't sleep here at the house, so never left them anywhere. Hephaestus had stolen the set Peters held and had given them to Aphrodite. Zeus took them yesterday, but that was after he managed to gain entry to the house. He must have had another set that Hephaestus used to open the main door. So, there were three sets of keys. Gloves was in possession of one set and Zeus had the other two.

There was no way I could get hold of Zeus' keys, but I might be desperate enough to try to steal Gloves' keys.

I heard the front door open and close and then all was quiet. I guessed that Gloves was driving Zeus back to the clinic and I now knew where that was. No, that wasn't quite right; I knew the address, and it was disturbing to think it was less than an hours' drive from my own home.

I closed my eyes as I tried to think. I would need something of Gloves' to exchange for help and protection.

I took my coffee cup back to the kitchen and went up the back stairs to Gloves' room. I thought, briefly, that if there had been anything in the room useful to me, I would have noticed it, but I could no longer be sure. I could be missing obvious clues and opportunities for escape without realising it; my brain felt full of porridge.

I stood as close to the middle of the room as I could get, and taking a deep breath, tried to clear my mind. I then turned, slowly walking in a tight circle, letting my eyes drift over the objects in the room and trying not to focus on one thing.

I stood still and took another breath. Then I looked back at the dressing table. I had handled Gloves' things before. There had been a shaving mirror and a pair of cufflinks, both now conspicuous by their absence, but there had also been a hairbrush and that was still sitting on top of the dressing table.

I smiled as I picked it up. This was perfect. The brushed hair caught in the bristles would have hair follicles still attached; necessary for DNA identification. Gloves had taken the other things away, but left this behind.

I took the hairbrush back downstairs and ran along the length of the house and then up the main stairs to the room with the pink folder. I rifled through the pages until I found a couple of pieces of paper that wouldn't be missed. These were additional sheets of notes sent through with the invoices, and to my mind, disposable. I laid them on top of the dressing table, slightly overlapping and put the hairbrush on top. I wrapped it up like a portion of chips and hid it in Peters' top drawer.

I dug around inside the folder and found the ballpoint pen. Tidying the folder, I turned it over to write a message on the back.

'To Hermes,' I wrote. 'I will agree to join the reproduction programme if you will free the women you are holding.'

I knew I was in no position to demand anything, but I had to try something. 'I have your hairbrush, which is likely to have your DNA. I'll return it in exchange for their freedom.'

I wanted to sign it 'Kim', but I wasn't even sure if he had any idea who Kim was. I reluctantly signed the message 'Athena'.

Now all I could do was wait for Gloves to read it.

I took the folder back downstairs and left it on the kitchen table. I had no idea when Gloves was likely to return, but to busy myself in the meantime I started to tidy the kitchen as best I could. I looked for a cloth to wipe the table and filled the kettle to provide hot water.

I thought I'd read about this somewhere; to make the best of bad situations, we alter our surroundings to make them more homely.

I immediately stopped myself. I didn't want to be at home here. I stepped back and eyed the grubby surroundings. They were disgusting. I felt sick. It was all revolting: the dirty mugs and saucers in the sink, the unwashed floor, the peeling paint, the filthy chairs in the living room, and the exposed floorboards in all the other rooms. Where the bloody hell was this place, anyway?

I dragged my hands down the front of my clothes, fruitlessly attempting to wipe off the stench of years of neglect that invaded every room. I remembered my grandmother had always insisted that houses were alive with the echoes of the children who grew up there, but this house was dead. I couldn't imagine any children ever living here. The house might have been beautiful once but now it looked dead and it smelt dead, as if whoever had loved this house had turned their back on it and left it to rot.

I backed out of the room and into the hallway. I checked the back door. It was locked. I rubbed my hands over the skin on my upper arms, imagining creepy crawlies infesting the house. I ran to the front door and shook the handles. That too was locked.

This was unbearable! I was suffocating in this hell hole. I stood in the hallway with clenched fists and stifled a scream of frustration. I took a few deep breaths and tried to think. What did I know? What was I learning? How could I use it? My ability to remember things and recall details seemed to be diminishing. Each time I tried to think of something, the image crumbled before my eyes and details disappeared as if written in invisible ink.

I sat on the last step of the stairs with my eyes closed. I thought about Nick at home. Was he looking after himself?

Was he looking after the house? Nick and I had been married for five years, but he still couldn't tell the difference between a floor towel and a bath towel.

He tolerated my OCD with infinite patience, even though I knew it drove him crazy.

If he put a sticky jar of jam back in the fridge, I'd have to find a new, fresh, cleaning cloth and everything in the fridge would have to come out. Every jar, bottle or Tupperware tub would have to be checked, wiped and checked again before being returned to the fridge in its rightful place and the cleaning cloth binned.

Once, Nick had left half a can of rice pudding in there. I would normally have insisted that the contents should be transferred to a tub, but just this once, I wanted to pretend that I was in charge of my OCD; it was not in charge of me.

While we watched TV that evening, I thought I was doing quite well. I managed to stay suitably distracted until Nick went back to make me a cup of coffee. I couldn't drink it. I can't explain why, but I couldn't shake the feeling that somehow the milk had been contaminated by the open can.

I managed to continue distracting myself with other tasks until I went to bed. I tossed and turned for most of the night until at 1.30am I could stand it no longer.

Nick came downstairs at 2am with his cricket bat held high to find me scrubbing out the salad drawers with bleach.

'I thought we had burglars,' he said.

Once I knew the fridge was clean, I could finally sleep. But I couldn't clean my mind. Here in this filthy house, with its filthy walls and its filthy floors, my imagination was making me believe that everything else was filthy too.

I had to believe that, somehow, I'd get out of here, but how could I go back to my neat, tidy and structured life after this? My whole world centred on everything being ordered, but I didn't have an ordered life to go back to. Not now that he had confessed.

It was a month ago. Nick had been distant with me for several weeks when he finally sat me down with the words, 'Kim, there's something I need to tell you.'

Chapter 19

He and an ex-girlfriend had bumped into each other in a pub after work one evening. She'd had too much to drink, and Nick, being the gentleman he was, had poured her into a taxi and taken her back home. He said goodbye to her at the door to her flat, but she had kissed him and pulled him inside. It was all over very quickly and both agreed it was a terrible mistake and should never be mentioned again. The guilt had been eating away at him and he loved me far too much to keep such a thing from me.

'All I can do now is beg for your forgiveness,' he said.

'Ok,' I said. I could feel the tears on my face and my cheeks getting hot.

'Are you angry?' he asked.

'No.'

'It's OK if you are. I'll go to counselling with you. Anything you want...'

'That won't be necessary,' I interrupted. I had enough difficulty acknowledging my feelings to myself, let alone revealing them to anyone else.

Nick had wanted to see proof of passion. He wanted to see my anger and fire. But I was too shocked to respond that way. I felt as if every ounce of oxygen had been sucked out of the room. The weight he'd been carrying on his chest, he'd simply transferred on to mine. All I felt was an overwhelming sense of sadness. I didn't have enough strength to express anger and passion.

Nick was still waiting for our relationship to return to normal, but what was normal? I let him kiss me; I let him make love to me, but I couldn't let myself forget the pain he had caused me.

'I'm sick of feeling like I'm being demanding,' he yelled during yet another row. 'I'm sick of you making me feel like I'm being demanding. It's not like I force myself on you every night. I don't see why it's necessary to make me feel dirty every time I want to get close to you.'

'You make me feel dirty every time you want to get close to me,' I responded. 'We've talked this over a thousand times. What more do you want from me? I let you have me when you want me.'

'Yes, very kind of you. What I want is a loving and responsive wife.'

'I've always told you I love you. I've told you I forgive you. What else can I say?' I had run out of words and was feeling exhausted.

'How about saying 'I'm angry and I feel like screaming'? At least that would show me some emotion.' I think Nick probably would have been happier if I had threatened to poison his coffee. The reaction I gave was one he hadn't anticipated.

The man whom I knew, without any doubt, I loved more

than any other, had betrayed me for nothing more than a drunken encounter. Actually, he didn't even have that excuse; he wasn't drunk.

I hadn't dared speak of this to anyone else. I really didn't have any close girlfriends I could confide in and both his parents and my father thought Nick and I were the perfect match. In fact, all his mother had been talking about lately was how lovely it would be to welcome a new arrival sometime soon.

I blamed most of our emotional discord on myself. If I were more demonstrative, more amenable, then perhaps Nick wouldn't have been tempted. But he knew what I was like before we married; he knew what he was getting into. When we first met, he saw me as a challenge. It was only when he witnessed a panic attack that I think he truly realised how real my anxiety was.

We had been introduced by a friend and later that month, invited to her house warming party. Some of Nick's old uni friends were there. Nick later told me that their behaviour was unpredictable at the best of times, but especially so with plenty of beer to go around.

A group of us were in the kitchen when a couple of Nick's friends started jostling each other. This was nothing more than the friendly roughhousing of mates, but as their noise grew louder, so did the tension in my neck. I asked them several times to calm down, but they goaded each other into increasingly juvenile taunts and started a food fight.

'How'd you like to try some dip, Pete?'

'Yeah, very nice. Have some salad dressing.'

Their faces began to swim and merge into monstrous shapes. I moved suddenly and my wine glass flew out of my hand. My heart was pounding and I started to sweat. I gripped the edge of the counter top for support and tried to focus on my breathing.

'That's enough.' With those two words, softly spoken, order was once more restored. Nick placed his drink on the counter and ignoring the broken glass, led me into the garden.

I managed a weak, grateful smile for my rescuer and saw an apology in his eyes. We sat on the steps facing the tiny back yard and talked until the dark blue sky turned black. When the warmth of the late spring evening had gone, Nick lifted his jacket over my shoulders and promised me it had only recently been dry cleaned.

Our marriage gave us both exactly what we wanted and I gained the position I needed in the profession I chose. Everything was engineered to make me feel safe, or perhaps it's more accurate to say that I engineered my world to make me feel safe and Nick tolerated it. Because he loved me. Because he understood that's what I needed. Or because it was easier than arguing for what he wanted. Had we become one of those god-awful boring couples who only said 'yes dear' over the cornflakes?

A car drew up, going too fast. I heard the engine stutter to a halt. The back door slammed and a waft of cigarette smoke infiltrated the house. I was scared, but also angry. I stayed where I was.

'There yoμ are,' said Peters when he found me. He grabbed my arm and yanked me up. 'Get moving.'

He dragged me back up the stairs and pushed me into the darkened room.

'What's going on? Where's Hermes? I want to speak to Hermes.'

'Wait here. We'll let you know if we want to speak to you.' He pulled the door shut without further explanation and locked it, leaving me alone in the dark.

There was much kerfuffle downstairs and I paced the room as I wondered what was happening. There was a lot of noise and I had heard cars approaching the house for several minutes. Many voices spoke over one another but none that I recognised. Who were these strangers? Oh, God. What did they want with me? There was nothing in the room that would have served as a suitable weapon and, strangely, I started to pray. I'd never been particularly religious before, but I honestly thought that this was the day I was going to meet my maker. Regardless of the talk I'd had with Zeus, he could easily have changed his mind about me.

'Please whatever comes, make it quick. Find a way to let Nick know what's happened.' I wondered if other people who found themselves in dangerous situations, prayed.

Footsteps approached the door and the figure who marched into the room was wearing a balaclava mask, but this wasn't Zeus. I could tell from his silhouette that this man was a stranger to me.

He was carrying the hood, taken from my former cell and when I saw it, I screamed.

I tried to make a run for the door, but he was fast and strong. He gripped my arm roughly and pulled me back. Despite my attempts at a struggle, he quickly had the hood over my head and my arms behind my back, which he restrained with another of those wretched plastic ties.

'Where are we going?' I yelled. 'What do you want with me?'

The man didn't speak. He gripped me tightly as he guided me back down the stairs and across the hallway. Soon he turned me around and sat me in a small chair.

'What's going on?' Panic was rising in my voice. 'Why have you brought me down here?'

My voice was lost among several others as I heard men whisper, 'that's her, that's Athena.'

Suddenly, someone clapped their hands and the background chatter faded.

'Thank you Mr Secretary.' This was Zeus. 'I call this assembly to order.' His voice seemed to come from the centre of the room and there was slight shuffling of feet as a few stepped back from the great man. 'We have three items of business to discuss. Firstly, as most of you will have heard, the location of our previous meeting place has been discovered, along with Athena's car.'

Aphrodite was right! She had warned me of this.

'I will ensure that we need not meet here again. My contact assures me that the authorities are still a long way behind us, but it remains essential that the on-going project stays on schedule.'

'Your controlled reproduction programme,' I butted in. 'That can't be going too well if you want me to be involved in the new one.'

A strong hand suddenly grabbed at my throat and I gasped, realising too late, that I'd let my big mouth run away with me again. A hoarse voice hissed close to my ear, 'shut up.' I knew I wouldn't get another warning.

'Now that our previous venue is out of action,' continued Zeus, 'We will have to find a better, more secure and larger meeting place. A few of you have already suggested that we meet at the clinic. That is a bad idea. Not only must we maintain a professional distance between our private conversations and our public image, our on-going work exposes us to personnel who are not involved in our greater aspirations.'

I translated this to mean that there was public face and a private reality; there could be hundreds of employees, legitimately employed, with perfectly altruistic intentions, who had no idea what this faceless Mr Big had planned for their work.

'Zeus, I have an additional property. Please consider it to be at your disposal.'

'Thank you, Hephaestus. I was hoping that we wouldn't have to consider a property in that area, but it will do temporarily. Secondly, one of our personal employees has just recently admitted an indiscretion which will need very careful handling.'

I almost cheered. Ares would have to reveal his affair with Aphrodite. If I was to survive this situation, Peters was going to have to leave.

'We will open the court in a moment.'

Court?

'Lastly, we are now launching our new proposition, which initial reports have indicated will be worth £500 million.'

A general sound of approval rippled around the room.

'Trust me gentlemen,' continued Zeus, 'this is only the beginning.'

The beginning of the end for the freedom of choice for thousands of women, I thought. My conversation with Aphrodite suggested that once caught up in this web of deception, their lives wouldn't be their own. They were unknowingly gambling their dreams on a questionable product with unproven benefits.

'I would like to introduce to you our newest acquisition. This is Athena, and I have decided that she is to be the heroine of our latest procedure.'

Suddenly, there was a loud thump from my right; the same noise I had heard earlier when Hermes told Zeus that he didn't want me involved. Was he protecting me or saving me for something else?

Zeus bristled; I could hear it in his voice and sense it in his manner.

'The decision has been made,' he stated sternly. 'This is what the future will be. It is up to us to decide how that future is shaped. Nothing must interfere with the nature of our work. It is essential that Mankind not only maintains its status as the dominant species, but that the correct people are suitably equipped and educated to fulfil that potential.' Zeus spoke with clarity and conviction. This wasn't just a speech, he was declaring his beliefs.

Another murmur echoed around the hall. I wasn't sure if these people were converts or disciples. Did they choose to believe, or were they persuaded to believe?

'Now that humans are the guardians of Earth's potential, we, the Selected Elite, are the guardians of mankind's potential. We will not go the way of the dinosaurs. We will have safeguards in place to protect not only our status, but also our future success, from the whims of nature. The future of the human race depends upon it.'

I was now convinced I was in the clutches of a megalomaniac. Was this eugenics? Human engineering?

'I will now open the court and hear the case of Ares first.'

There was more than one case?

Chapter 20

Zeus moved across to my right, to the furthest end of the hall. I thought I heard him sit. There was a shuffling of feet as people moved back towards the edges of the room. People walked past me towards Zeus and came to a stop. The person closest to where I sat spoke first.

'Zeus, it came to my attention that Ares has had an affair with Aphrodite, when it was made clear to the Elite that she was my recipient.' This was Hephaestus speaking. 'I respectfully request that he be removed from the programme and that I be permitted to apply for his position as Ares.'

'Thank you, Accuser,' said Zeus. 'And now, Defender?'

An unfamiliar voice spoke. 'It has become known to several of the Elite that although their affair was unauthorised, the result is a successful outcome for our purposes. Aphrodite is pregnant and, with her attributes of beauty and sexuality and Ares' attributes of determination and battle readiness, the resulting offspring will be a unique and useful addition to the programme.'

What programme? I wanted to yell out, to scream, to lash out at somebody. Anybody. Wouldn't the child be able to stay with its mother? What was to become of this baby? What plans did they have for this child?

'Thank you, Defender,' said Zeus. 'As Aphrodite is known to be pregnant, Ares' position in the programme will remain unchanged. He will, however, be relocated to another clinic and assigned a new purpose to run alongside this one. There will be no further contact between him and Aphrodite.'

'But she's my recipient!' exclaimed Hephaestus. 'He abused his position.'

'You still have Herse,' replied Zeus calmly. 'Which brings us neatly to your situation. Herse's pregnancy was not as stable as hoped and therefore the attempt between you and her was a failure. This missed opportunity has lost us the possibility of gaining a Cephalus to the Elite membership.'

Who was Cephalus? Was that a child of Herse?

'That's hardly my fault!' he complained. 'She's the one with problems.'

Zeus was losing his temper. He had already made the major decisions. He was expecting quiet compliance, not arguments.

'This is what will happen,' he shouted. 'Herse will be the first donor of the new procedure. Athena will be the first recipient. I will be the first male donor. You will be tasked with a new appointment. Hermes will give you the details of your new location.'

Hephaestus was indignant. 'I have always been faithful to the company.'

'Your loyalty is not in question, but your competency is.'

'What?!'

'The last batch of Persephone was faulty and now we find

that it is good only for six months' worth of treatment. After that it becomes a redundant product. We will have to redirect those batches to the less fortunate countries.'

'No!' I yelled, completely forgetting that I wasn't permitted to speak. 'You can't possibly palm them off like that! You can't!'

'I make the decisions about what can and can't be done,' Zeus replied, 'but that is not open to discussion. What is to be discussed is that this batch will lose us money, therefore there will be an alternative price to pay.'

'But I've corrected it now,' said Hephaestus.

'What you have done is substituted one problem for another. Now instead of being dangerous, it's simply ineffective. Perhaps we should substitute one developer for another?'

A small ripple of sniggers went round the room.

'It's fine now,' he insisted.

'It's not fine,' responded Zeus, 'It simply doesn't work and won't generate profit.'

'But, as soon as I discovered the fault, I reported it...' Hephaestus trailed off, realising what he was about to say.

'To Ares, yes, but you spoke to Athena instead,' said Zeus, summing up the situation. 'As usual, talking too much and risking even more.'

That was the real reason Zeus wanted me in the programme. I'd already learnt too much. There wasn't any point in their hiding these discussions from me; I'd already figured most of it out. It's like Capone once said; you keep your friends close and your enemies even closer.

'But, my property, the new address I gave you....' he persisted.

'The Selected Elite are most grateful.'

Hermes thumped against the wall again.

'Hermes has announced he has feelings for Herse,' Zeus informed the room. 'He also considers Athena to be untouchable.' My guard sniggered again. 'Herse's emotional condition has already been documented. Athena's contribution is therefore essential. I expect that to be clearly understood. Time is racing and we have work to do. Hermes, you will take Ares to his new location. We will meet again at the new site in two days. Thank you.'

People started moving around me. Everyone began to make their way to the main door. My guard gripped my arm and led me back towards the stairs.

'Who is Hermes?' I asked him as he led me back to the darkened room. 'Do you know him? Is he trying to protect me?' The guard ignored my questions and pushed me into the room ahead of him. I heard the click of a flick knife and he freed my hands. The door closed and locked, leaving me alone in the dark once more.

I pulled off the hood as quickly as I could and ran to the door. I banged my fists against it and shook the door in the frame. Not eliciting any response, I pressed my ear to the door and listened.

'No, she's fine, just annoyed. You better get moving, Hermes, if you need to be at the clinic tonight.'

His voice faded as he went back down the stairs.

Hermes. Who was he? I had to find out. I remembered the AB monogram on the handkerchief I'd seen when I first arrived here. The only AB I knew was my boss, Andrew. But even he had to answer to somebody else and that person was Tony, his uncle and owner of the company.

Tony Brownlow was a charming and charismatic businessman. He had a reputation for not wanting to shake hands with anyone, but other than this single quirk, he was as honest and as hard-working as anyone I knew. He must have been in his mid-forties, but had a persistent worried expression that often made him appear a little older. His calm and controlled manner encouraged you to work harder without him having to ask more of you. He did seem to smile a little longer at me than at the other female workers. I hadn't ever thought of him as a flirt, but I was flattered by his attention and the way he didn't expect me to be like the other women who worked there.

Tony was kind and undemanding. That certainly wasn't enough of a reason to have an affair of my own. Tony was principled and likeable, a man I felt proud to work for.

'We need to reorganise the payments system,' I said one morning when he was just passing through. He hadn't even taken his coat or gloves off yet. 'When payments come in, it can take several days to appear in our account. Even with direct payments the money is always extremely slow to get to us. If we could arrange a separate accounting system for payment orders, our major customers could call off whatever print they wanted on demand. It would be cheaper for them and cost effective for us.'

Tony tugged on his shirtsleeve and his gold cufflink winked at me under the office lights.

'What does Andrew say?'

'He said I could arrange whatever I want.'

He smiled more with his eyes than with his mouth. 'You do too much of his job for him,' he said. 'By the way, Andrew and I are working on a separate project that might necessitate reopening accounts you've already closed off. We'd need your passcodes for that.'

I thought for a moment. 'Well, why not let me have the paperwork and I'll reopen them for you? I'd be happy to help you with your project.'

'I could apply to Finance directly for these codes.'

'Yes, you could. But they're supposed to be confidential.' Tony didn't reply.

'So what do you think about reorganising the payments system?'

'I'll think about it.'

'Do you think that I push too hard?' He'd been frowning a lot more than usual in the last few days. 'I trust your judgement, I hope you trust mine.'

'No,' he said, smiling. 'I don't think you push too hard.'

I pretended that I hadn't seen Angela raise her eyes to the ceiling. Apple pie Anderson was making changes again.

'It'll be a whole lot easier to process the urgent requests,' I told her at lunchtime, trying to justify myself yet again.

‘Oh, I understand all that,’ agreed Angela, smiling. ‘But,’ she added, nodding her head in the direction of the gossips at the photocopier, ‘you’ve got to remember to be a little more tolerant of us lesser mortals. Not everyone has a five year plan, or thinks one is necessary.’

‘Is it inappropriate for me to tell Tony what I think in the office?’ I asked.

‘No,’ she responded, cautiously. ‘But you do have the boss’s ear. That’s a great advantage to have in the workplace; not something the rest of us can share.’

I was careful after that conversation to be sure that any suggestions I made, I put to Tony in private and were more likely to benefit the employees, not just the company. But still, I never really made true friends at work.

‘Go out to lunch with them,’ suggested Nick. ‘Ask their advice about things.’

‘But they eat sushi and want advice about dieting. I hate both.’ Nick just laughed.

As the sound of retreating cars faded, I strained to listen for others in the house. Zeus had told Hermes to take Ares to his new location straight away, but I could still hear movement downstairs. I sat with my back to the door, hoping that if anyone came up the stairs, I’d hear them approach. It was only the faintest of creaks that told me who had come this time. If Hermes had already left, then this must be...

‘Athena,’ whispered Hephaestus. A gentle click sounded in the door and a slip of light inched across the floor. I’d moved just a foot to the right and crouched as small as I could but H wasn't intent on attacking me; nothing quite so honest.

'Come on out, Athena,' he said, beckoning with a finger. 'I've got something to show you.'

Hephaestus was already making his way back down the stairs, placing both feet on each step one at a time. I wondered for a moment how hard it might be to rush up behind him and push him down. By the time I'd caught up with him, he had already reached the bottom and was walking towards the door to the living room. I followed him as far as the doorway and stared at the new stash of boxes lined up against the wall.

'Do they look familiar?' Hephaestus waved his cane towards the display of cardboard. 'Our new delivery and ordered especially for you.' He smiled as if he had just presented me with a gift. 'You and the other women like you. Let me open one for you.'

He stepped forward and leaning his cane against one box, he pulled another towards him and tore away the tape across the top. A large pack of polystyrene came out and when that was pulled away, I saw what looked like a picnic cooler box. The medical snake and sword logo on the side told me I was wrong.

'They're organ transplant boxes.'

'Very good. Do you know what they're going to transport?'

I pushed my hair back from my face and gripped the sides of my head to stop it from exploding.

Hephaestus smiled. 'I have to admit, I had no idea how

important you were until I found out about your mother.'

'My mother died many years ago.'

'Yes, but how much do you know about her?'

'I know that she was smart and brave and that she loved me.'

'So, not very much then. Did you know that she worked for us?'

Chapter 21

'You're lying! I can't believe that any of my family would have anything to do with you. My mother would have been horrified at the things you're planning. Do you even know what you're doing? It's bullshit! You're just trying to get inside my head. You're megalomaniacs, the lot of you!'

Hephaestus chuckled. 'We might be intent on taking over the world,' he said, 'but everything we do is planned for the greater good; our greater good. It really doesn't matter how altruistic anyone tries to be, some men will always be more equal than others.'

'It's cruel and terrifying. You're stomping on women's dreams and you're not even sure that the drug you have is safe. You're nothing but corrupt drug smugglers.'

'The women signed a contract. And you will, too.'

'I'll never sign anything to do with this. It's evil.'

'It's not things that make people evil, it's people who decide what's evil. What if we were smuggling kitchen knives? You could be up in arms saying that we're contributing to the culture of street crime. Would you feel guilty the next time you cut into a steak?'

'This is entirely different. It's horrific!'

'It's realistic.' Hephaestus picked up his cane and started

towards the main front door.

'I have evidence,' I shouted after him. 'I have the means to connect you, or at least Hermes to this place.'

Hephaestus turned slowly to look at me.

'He left his brush, mirror and cufflinks behind. They're all things he handled; all will have his fingerprints on them.' Hephaestus gave the kind of smile he might have given to a simple child. 'The brush and mirror are new. The only fingerprints will be yours. Hermes requested permission from the Elite to buy them for you.'

'The cufflinks are his. They'll be linked back to him.'

'How, exactly? They're no use to you unless you can get them out of this house, and trust me, you can't.'

'I might. Why would someone like Hermes take such a risk?'

'Hermes doesn't take risks.' Hephaestus turned back towards the door. 'By the way,' he called back at me, 'there's something else for you in the kitchen.'

I closed my eyes and took a breath. I could run after him and attempt to batter him with his cane in the hope of getting out of here, or I could go into the kitchen and find out what had been left for me. I went to the kitchen. There, sitting in the middle of the kitchen table was the folder on which I had written my message to Hermes. An extra line had been added to the bottom in plain nondescript block capital print.

'There will be no negotiation.'

I leant against the door frame and ran a hand through my

hair. I closed my eyes and breathed deeply through my nose. Hephaestus was lying. Mother would never have worked for them. It was just a sick game he was playing.

I was desperate to get back home. The best way to do that was to work my way through this situation and manufacture an escape. But how? I'd done everything I could to alert others to my incarceration and no-one had come for me.

Bloody Hermes! Bloody Ares! Who the hell were they? Maybe Hephaestus had lied about the hairbrush, too. Maybe it could identify one of them.

I ran back up the stairs to Peters' room and retrieved the little package from the drawer. I raised the window once again. With a wish and a prayer, I sent the package soaring and hoped that it would find its way to the hands of a kind person; someone who would take it to the police. Someone who realised that I needed help. Someone who could tell my husband where to find me. Nick would find me. Someone would come.

I tried to remember the last conversation I had with my husband. It was Tuesday; the morning I was kidnapped. I'd just used up the last of the cornflakes again and he was complaining that there wasn't enough milk. I wondered what he was thinking now. Was he out looking for me? Disjointed thoughts returned to me which my mind couldn't place in the right order.

That morning, I was feeling rushed again. There were a million and one things I had to do when I got to the office. I'd just put my coat on and was about to say goodbye, when he suddenly asked, 'Have you ironed my dark trousers for me?'

Two pairs of pale coloured ones were hanging in his wardrobe.

'No,' I replied, frowning at him. 'But you know where the iron is kept, so if you want them, you can iron them yourself.'

Nick looked horrified. 'I'll have to do it?'

'Well, you think you wear the trousers in this house,' I said, 'so you can wash and iron them, too.' I pointed to the ironing board and iron standing in the corner of the dining room.

Nick eyed the strange contraption suspiciously. 'How do I turn it on?' he asked.

'Try stroking the heat dial,' I suggested, heading for the door. 'If you feel a slap, then that means 'no'.'

'Everyone's a bloody comedian,' I heard him mutter as I ran for my getaway car.

Maybe marrying after the standard three year courtship wasn't the logical succession to my life I thought it was. I didn't marry Nick believing I was pursuing love's young dream; I wasn't the kind of girl who was swayed by romantic notions, but I did love him. It just seemed the most appropriate time. Nick was level-headed and tolerant and, most times, ensuring that I remain calm and happy was enough to make him happy too. Or was it?

Nick had been trying to teach me reflective meditation, and although I didn't really have the patience for such things, I had to admit my panic attacks were much less severe.

In order that I could cope, nothing in our lives was spontaneous, everything happened in a pre-arranged order at a pre-arranged time.

I would never go anywhere unfamiliar just to explore. Attending university had been very carefully organised and meticulously planned. I found suitable accommodation, but I had to journey to campus. Before I'd even packed my case, I knew where I was going, what bus I needed, what time it was expected and where it would drop me. The journey from digs to campus was exactly forty seven minutes from door to door.

My life revolved around places and in each place in my life, home, uni or at work, I had learnt that relationships were transitory. Most friendships, even close ones, are not designed to last. Someone might call themselves a good friend, but that doesn't mean that they want to be too fully involved in your life. I had never expected anyone other than Nick to say 'I love you'.

I never missed anything I left behind from any place in the past. The past was gone and the only place where I felt content, and therefore happy, was in the present. I never concerned myself too much with the future, because what will happen is largely influenced by what happens in the present, which was under control. Or was before control was taken from me. To influence the future I needed to influence the present.

I pressed the heels of my hands against my eyes to try and push the tiredness away. I had read an article a couple of months before about scientists who were studying the figures released in the news following terror attacks. The scientists had discovered a power law; a formula to show how a change in one area can influence an equal change in another.

I hurriedly cleared the table and shoved everything to one side. I hunted out the pen and hoped that this would work.

Into the sticky and grubby surface I scratched a right angle. I marked it big and bold, covering as much space as I could. I then scratched markers, about half an inch apart, along both edges. The pen was having more success lifting grime from the table rather than leaving clear markings, but at least they were visible.

I then drew a curve stretching from the top of the diagram and sloping down in a long arch across to the far edge. Along the bottom of the diagram I wrote: Chance of Success. Along the left edge of the diagram I wrote: Strength of Rebellion. Scientifically, this Power Law Diagram was nothing more than a child's picture. Personally, it seemed the only way I had of being able to stick a pair of fingers in the air.

Tired and homesick, I trudged upstairs to lie down for a little while. Boredom and loneliness were sucking away my energy, but thinking of the diagram made me smile, if only a little.

I might be the only one who understood it, but I hoped it would be enough to worry them. I hoped there were other women out there who were willing to rebel. I hoped that I would live long enough to find out about them.

Chapter 22

I was six when I realised there were different kinds of facts of life. There were the kind that explained how mummies and daddies made babies, and then there were the kind that explained how fairy tales could be true. There were cruel, rich kings, evil queens and monsters with magical powers; they just hid in plain sight.

'You're a special girl, Kim,' my mother told me. 'You have magic inside you.'

'Am I a princess? Will I have a kingdom?'

My father laughed, but my mother looked serious. 'God, I hope not.'

'Melissa, don't. She's just a kid. Let her have her fairy stories.' Dad gave Mother a warning look, but smiled at me. 'Eat your porridge, Kimmie.'

Breakfast table conversations seemed to be the way Mother and Dad solved their problems, which meant that soon I could be sent to my room to play.

Mother flung that morning's paper across the table. 'They've made a move, Tim.'

I silently started to count my fingers and toes. I had to ensure that I ended on an even number, or else I'd have to start again.

'Mel, we said we'd never speak of these things in front of her.'

Mother kissed the top of my head. 'Take a look.'

'Isn't this what you were doing?'

'Not quite. But check out the lead scientist. It's Max Alex. It has to be.'

I took another spoonful of porridge and started counting again. It always surprised me how grown-ups assumed that children wouldn't be interested in their conversations, but I was. Especially as I seemed to have difficulty conversing with other children.

Mother sat down heavily and sighed. My parents were having a conversation over the top of my head that should have been conducted in private.

'They want us back, Tim. They want both of us.'

Dad banged the table and knocked over his coffee cup. 'God, Melissa! No! No, you can't. Don't even think about it.' Dad's voice sounded panicked. 'How long will it be before they find out?'

I'd counted up to twenty-one. That was bad. I needed an even number. I started again.

'You could be walking straight into a war zone,' said Dad.

Seven. Still bad. 'Can I go and play now, Daddy?'

'Finish your porridge, Kimmie.'

One, two, three...

'Melissa, don't. Please darling, don't speak..'

'But I have to. I need to go.'

'I might not be able to get you out this time.'

Mother smiled. 'Eat your porridge, Kim.'

I looked up at my father's stricken face. 'Daddy, don't be sad.'

I ran over and sat on his lap. At that moment I hated my mother. How could she be so mean as to make my Daddy cry? But as I sat hugging my father, he reached across the breakfast table to take Mother's hand and there was only their silent communication.

I thought of my mother now. Dad described Mother as a kind and gentle person, but the woman I remembered was sharp and clever.

God, Mother. What were you up to?

Hephaestus' suggestion that Mother had worked for the company was ridiculous – nothing more than a twisted mind game. Could it really be true? Mother had died in a work accident; there had been a fire in the lab where she was working. I had never really grasped the whole story, but I didn't seek to know all the details. When Nick and I first started dating, he'd wanted to know everything about me, where I had gone to uni, what my parents had done for a living, and I had been flattered by his attention. Now in this God forsaken hell hole, I was starting to question everything, including the loyalty of the people I loved most.

Nick had always said he was completely fascinated by me. I thought that was romantic.

If my mother had been involved in The Company's schemes, could Nick be a part of their operations, too? I imagined him calling our friends, talking to my Dad, being questioned by the police. Why hadn't they found me yet? Did they even know where to start looking? Or was he misleading them? Surely my colleagues could give them some information. I was a planning princess and so particular about ensuring that the jobs were ordered, I was never absent unless I was ill. Nick had to practically order me to go on holiday.

I usually started to panic if Nick had booked somewhere before I had a chance to vet it, but Nick was fascinated by foreign culture and treated every holiday as an adventure. He couldn't wait for the plane to land so he could eavesdrop in a local café. He could placate me by taking me to a museum, but Nick had always found people uniquely interesting.

Nick had studied ancient languages at university and seemed to have a natural aptitude. He could speak Greek, Latin, French and Italian. He'd enjoyed his university days so much, he'd immediately applied to work in one as soon as his studies had finished.

'There's more to language than just the way people speak,' he'd said while we were making a lasagne together one evening. 'It's inflection, nuance, culture, tradition. Even slang. What we say and how we say it affects what we write and how we write it, what we project and how we project it. And this also affects how we view history.'

'You can make the cheese sauce this time,' I said. 'Mine always ends up like flavourless custard. Isn't academic archival work horribly boring?' I asked, only half joking.

Nick pretended to look horrified. 'How dare you!'

'You'll have to start wearing horn rimmed glasses and tweed jackets with leather patches at the elbows.'

Nick laughed. 'Actually, I've always thought tweed jackets look quite distinguished. My boss certainly seems to think so.'

'Now you just need to earn enough to be able to buy yourself one.'

'Well, I don't know if what we've discovered is going to lead to more funding, but we do have something that we can use to apply.'

'Oh, yes?'

'We found a text that we had to verify before sending it to be digitised.'

'Was there a suspicion about it then?'

'Unfortunately, yes. We found another layer of text beneath the writing, and when we analysed it, we found that it was a couple of hundred years earlier.'

'So, the top layer of text was a fake?'

'No. Producing text was so expensive and materials in such short supply, that paper and vellum from this era was regularly reused. Both layers are equally authentic.'

'What do they say?'

'They're both recipes for medicines to treat battle wounds. The oldest is a mixture of honey and lavender written in ancient Greek.'

'Would that have even worked?'

'Perhaps not as well as they might have hoped. Both honey and lavender are antiseptic, so I suppose it would depend on whether the wounded was expected to live. Fighting infection means that the soldier lives to fight another day. We need more parmesan.'

'Well, it all sounds very interesting.'

Nick kissed the side of my head. 'You said that very diplomatically, darling. Thank you. But, yes; I'm really enjoying this. I can't wait to see what else there is. Maybe I'll find an ancient cure that will work for mankind. Other than medicinal honey, I mean.'

Unable to sleep, I stared with unseeing eyes at the wall and tried to sort my thoughts in a logical order. I'd never before felt so ridiculously foggy; it was like a form of mental constipation. I couldn't think clearly and the harder I tried, the more unfocused my thoughts became. Nick hadn't come. I didn't know if anybody would. I had to leave a message behind; provide some evidence that I had been here.

I remembered the pen on the kitchen table. I ran back to get it and took it into the darkened room. I knelt in front of the concealed hidey hole and released the wallpaper covering it. Scribbling in a corner to be sure the pen would work, I wrote on the loose paper everything I could about myself. I started with my name and address, followed by all the contact telephone numbers I could think of.

I then wrote everything I could about my kidnappers; what Peters looked and sounded like, what he smelled like, how tall he was. I had little to offer about Gloves. I could only guess at his height, but I could describe what his gloves felt like, what his soap smelled like.

Chapter 23

I coughed and spluttered as I woke. I didn't know how long I had slept. My mouth felt like sandpaper and I really needed a drink. I paced the floor and stared out of the window. The day was miserable and cold and so was the house. I half hoped that I would see a car, not so that I could uselessly try to attract attention, but just so that I could curse it and the unobservant drivers ignoring this place.

I went over to the door and pressed my ear to the wood. Not hearing anything, I unlocked it slowly. Through a crack, I saw that the door to the darkened room was closed.

I hurried downstairs, still dressed in the clothes I was wearing previously and walked straight through the house into the kitchen. On the table there was a packet of ham sandwiches and some supermarket muffins. I opened the sandwiches and wondered what we were celebrating. Was this breakfast, or was it lunch? I no longer knew. I was a little suspicious, though. I didn't get good food without some sort of purpose and I was trying to guess what that was when I saw a sheet of pink paper under a mug.

It was a pastel tinted sheet of A4 folded into quarters. A scrawling hand had filled one side with a message to me.

'Dear Athena,'

That wasn't a good start. Whoever wrote this didn't know my real name.

'I know you must be worried at the moment, but do be brave. Good things are just around the corner. Just when I was about to give up, I discovered I was pregnant and you will too.'

She must have assumed that I was on the reproduction programme. Maybe I was. Zeus had decided that I should be and I'd even hinted at it myself, when I'd written a note on the back of the folder, in the hope of receiving a letter like this.

'We are being looked after very well and have everything we want. I can't wait to welcome a new sister to the clinic. Anytime I want something all I have to do is ask for it. I can have new clothes, and Hermes even bought me new make-up last week. The food here is great. It's all cooked for us and we don't have to shop for it ourselves. A couple of days ago a hairdresser visited us, too.

'I've been told that in a couple more weeks I can go back home to my husband and I can't wait. In the meantime I have to stay here for monitoring. But that's expensive. Don't worry; if you just tell Hermes the account codes, the money he'll get will be used to look after all of us, including you, and don't you think we're worth twenty-five million?

'Take care; hope to see you soon, Gaia.'

I refolded the paper thoughtfully.

Aphrodite must have told Gaia about me and so she must have assumed that I was a volunteer too. Either she hadn't experienced the same things as Aphrodite, or else she was delusional. The belief that she could go back to her husband soon, worried me very much. I nibbled cheap bread nervously and tried not to think about what might happen to her or her baby.

But as I ate, I realised, there was something else troubling me. At first I couldn't figure out what it was, but something Gaia had said was wrong somehow. I opened the letter and read it again.

Twenty-five million? Was that right? But how could it be? The account codes I'd revealed were only worth twenty-five thousand. I did a quick mental calculation.

If each account code was worth £25,000 and there were four codes in the first folder, five in the second and another four in the pink folder, then that still only equalled £325,000.

I didn't think that anyone who had access to this information could have altered the value of the accounts themselves, unless they had done so after I had signed off the invoices and forwarded them to Tony. If I had noticed the accounts were overloaded, I would have reported it immediately. The idea of £25million staggered me and I wondered what work I could have done that would be worth that much money.

Was this correct, or was there more to come? Was Brownlow Print laundering money for Fireflight? I was starting to think so.

I understood why I had been misled over the value of

these accounts. This was the kind of money a client account was worth over several years, not the price of one project.

The question I had to ask myself was, is £25 million enough to finance a drug launch, and if it's not, where is the rest of the money coming from?

I closed my eyes and took a deep breath.

'My mind still feels foggy.'

Did I say that out loud? I had to force myself to think clearly and logically; that was the only way I was going to get to the truth. Did I really want to know the truth, about what happened to Gaia and the other women? With a slight sense of foreboding, I realised that I did. I've never believed that there are things best left unsaid. The hunger for the truth is a persistent craving. That is the curse of the logical mind; to always pursue the truth, even at the risk of discovering what you don't want to know.

I refolded the paper and decided to hide it. Perhaps there was something on it that a forensics team might find, a clue to where she was. I would conceal the note in the hidey hole where I had discovered the blueprints.

With purpose I walked out of the kitchen and into the passageway, where I paused for a moment, listening. Hearing nothing, I walked through to the front of the house, up the stairs and tried the handle of the darkened room. I felt the door click open.

I left the door open, so that I would hear approaching footsteps and looked at the hidey hole again.

The paper was just as I had left it and when I peeled it

open, I was relieved to find my writing untouched. I slipped the note inside the hole and replaced the board as before and smoothed the paper over the front. This time the paper appeared to be unco-operative and wouldn't stay in position as it had done before. Regardless of how many times I ran my hand over the paper, it kept falling back and I could see that the brittleness of the paper, which had helped conceal the hole previously, had been lost with my handling it.

'Stay back. I need you to stay back.'

I stopped and sat back on to my heels. I held my hands out in front of me to see if they were shaking. They didn't seem to be, but then they didn't look much like my hands any more. These were rough and dry hands with rough and dry nails, scaly and uncared for.

I abandoned the hidey hole and went back down stairs, this time walking into the living room. It really didn't seem important that I try and avoid Gloves any more. I had more or less assumed that I was going to become a 'volunteer'. I had no idea why Gloves was trying to protect me from what seemed an inevitable outcome.

In the living room, I saw that Gloves had been busy while I had been asleep upstairs. There were only two boxes lined up against the wall today, along with one that looked a little different. This was a white plastic box with a hard lid, the kind I had used occasionally at work.

Unable to ignore it, I knelt before it and lifted the lid; the curse of the logical mind sitting like a devil on my shoulder whispering, 'Open it, open it.'

Inside I saw everything I had previously thrown out of the window; the cigarette packet and its contents, the blueprints and the hairbrush. All the clues to my whereabouts had been gathered up and stored away.

I started crying. I couldn't help it. I'd held back tears for too long and now they just came flooding out of me. It was all too much. Every attempt I'd made at protecting or freeing myself had failed, the only protection I had was that which was given to me by someone else. I was going to die in this God forsaken hell hole, or worse, was going to be a lab rat for a group of mad scientists.

Eventually, I rubbed my fist against my eyes and wiped the back of my hand across my mouth. I needed a glass of water. When I reached the doorway to the kitchen, I immediately stopped. Leaning against one of the cabinets, facing the doorway, was Peters.

'Hello Athena. Miss me?'

'What the hell are you doing here?'

'Now, that's no way to speak to an old friend.' He reached towards the table. 'Here, have a drink. Let's celebrate your promotion.'

'But it's still morning,' I protested. 'Isn't it?'

'What does that matter?' Peters poured a slug of Jack Daniels into a mug. He'd already helped himself to some food. He nodded towards the living room.

'I thought you needed some alone time,' he said.

'How thoughtful. How did you get in?'

'I borrowed some keys.'

'Who from? You were banished, sent away.'

Peters laughed. 'Banished? I'm a hero, a father to be. Any punishment is nothing I can't handle.' He took a gulp. Maybe he was being bold and brazen unnecessarily.

'Besides, I'm still working for The Company,' he added.

'Yes, of course, how silly of me, I forgot. Nobody leaves The Company.'

Peters gave me a mean stare, but said nothing.

'Where is Hermes?' I asked, starting to feel nervous.

'Not here,' he replied shortly. 'He's paying a visit today.'

I guessed that this meant Peters had been watching the house, waiting for Gloves to leave.

'So, why are you here?' I reached over to take a muffin, but it was already stale and rubbery.

'You received a letter from Gaia this morning,' said Peters, coming to the point. 'We want it back.'

I didn't respond straight away, but the hairs on the back of my neck stood up and warning bells rang in my head.

Chapter 24

There was only one reason I could think of why The Company would want the letter back, and that was the slip of the pen that told me the accounts were worth more than twenty-five thousand pounds each.

Peters must have entered the house while I was crying in the living room, leading him to assume that the letter was nearby. If Peters had written it himself, he'd made a mistake and that explained why he was here.

'Gaia didn't write that letter, did she?'

Peters pulled his mouth into a hard line but didn't speak.

'Does she even exist?'

'Yes, she exists. Now, where is it?'

'I destroyed it.'

'You did what?!'

'I used a lighter you left behind and dropped it in the sink.'

Peters lent over the sink and peered over the grimy mugs and saucers.

I was lying through my teeth, desperately. I started to question the necessity of keeping the letter, but perhaps it was worth all this trouble; there still might be a way to trace the paper back to the clinic and the women.

'Is twenty-five million enough to finance a new drug?' I shot the question out of the blue. Peters kept his hands astride the sink and glared at me over his shoulder.

'It's very expensive.'

'So, you don't know, then.' I was pushing him, but that logical little devil was whispering to me again and I knew that whatever was to become of me, I needed to know the truth.

'That's only a fraction of what's needed, legally.'

'And, illegally?' I prompted.

Peters smirked. 'That's only a fraction of what's wanted.'

'So, where does the rest of the money come from?'

Peters left the sink to stride over to me and I instinctively backed off. 'Why all the questions?'

If only some of the money was coming from Brownlow, maybe there were other businesses, or they were charging the volunteers.

'I'll need all the facts to give to the police when I escape from here.'

Peters threw back his head and laughed. 'You're not going anywhere. The new heroine is to be restrained and cared for until moved to a new home. These are the latest instructions.'

'Where has Hermes gone today?' I asked.

'None of your business.'

He didn't know. I had a horrible feeling that Gloves had been called back to the clinic or to Zeus. He had stood up to the Selected Elite and had been threatened with punishment for doing so. Today he would find out what that punishment was.

'Where am I going?' I asked.

'What?' Peters was irritated and I was pushing my luck. I was inconvenient and he wasn't supposed to be here. He'd only come back to get the letter.

'You said I would be moved to a new home. Where is that?'

'A new place. I'll be promoted.'

'From 'hired heavy level two' to 'hired heavy level one'?'

Peters gripped my throat and pushed his face towards mine. I knew he couldn't risk killing me; The Company would not forgive that.

A shrill beep sounded and Peters reluctantly let me go so that he could search his pockets for his phone. Peters read the text and frowned.

'That must be from Hermes,' I said.

He looked up unable to hide his surprise.

'Let me guess. Herse is in trouble and he needs you to meet him.''

Peters continued to remain silent, frowning at me with a worried expression. No doubt he was concerned that he would give himself away, but I had already guessed that if a promotion had been hinted at, he would be looking for ways to impress The Company. What better way than to be the one who made me reveal the last set of account codes and what better way to do that than to write a fictional letter from one of the women I was so concerned about?

'He doesn't know you're here, does he?' I continued. 'But

he'll guess when he can't reach you at your hideaway. You must have thought that he was just being kind when he gave you your phone back.'

The look behind Peters' eyes hardened.

'Don't you think that it's possible that you might have been set up?'

'No,' insisted Peters immediately. 'I would not have been betrayed.'

'Not by Aphrodite,' I agreed. 'It's in her interests to stay on your good side until after the baby is born. She might have known that you wrote the letter, but apart from you coming here yourself, there's only one other person who could have delivered it.'

Peters swallowed and tried to resist looking at the table. He desperately needed another drink, but didn't want to take his eyes from me.

'Did you let Hermes read the letter before you asked him to deliver it?'

It didn't really matter if he did; there was no envelope that I could see and Gloves probably read it anyway. If so, he would have noticed Peters' mistake and left it.

If Gloves was now being threatened with punishment, he would be telling The Company about the letter.

Peters finally gave in to the need for a drink and turned his back on me to refill his mug. I involuntarily looked towards the passageway that would take me back through the house and to the hidden letter.

After replacing his mug, Peters patted his pockets to

search for his cigarettes. Previously Gloves had made him smoke outside, but there really wasn't any reason for him to obey the rules now.

Peters flipped the lid of the pack with his thumb and a light thump within the pack told me that I was in really big trouble. I couldn't see what Peters was looking at, but I guessed that, in common with many other smokers, to avoid losing his lighter, he placed it inside the pack with the cigarettes.

Peters lifted the lighter from the pack and held it up for me to see. It was an expensive looking gold lighter, slim and stylish. I had made the mistake of assuming that Peters wouldn't miss a disposable one. But a man like Peters wouldn't use a disposable lighter, appearances were too important to him.

'Is this the lighter you used to destroy the letter?' he asked. I didn't think an answer was necessary. I turned and ran through the passageway, up the stairs and into the darkened room. I knew that I was practically leading Peters to the letter, but if I got there first, I might have a chance of saving it.

Peters was fast behind me. I raced into the room, tripping over the mattress and pillow in my haste to get to the precious hiding place. But the hidey hole was no longer a discreet location. The wallpaper hung down like a gaping mouth revealing the board.

Stretching across the floor, I grabbed at the board, knocking it over. I fumbled for the paper and almost immediately, Peters was on top of me, gripping my wrist. His other arm flew over the top of my head as he tried to reach over and tear the paper from my grasp. I threw my left hand back, trying to hit him and although I thought I had made a connection, it made very little difference.

Peters pulled on my wrist and dragged me up on to my feet, swinging me round to face him. He still had hold of my arm and again reached over with his left hand to make another grab. Desperate, I twisted my wrist in a circle under his arm, to free myself from his grip. Already, angry red marks were appearing on my arm like a Chinese burn.

With his left hand free, Peters went to strike me, raising his hand to deliver a forceful slap. Barely a second before, I remembered that Peters was left-handed and just managed to duck my head down as his hand swung across the back of my head, glancing off my skull and tearing at my hair. I dipped down under his arm and stumbled for the door, the precious piece of paper still clasped as if my life depended on it.

Terrified, and fighting for breath, I gripped the banister as I ran too quickly down the stairs. Peters was no more than three or four steps behind me and made a grab for my tee shirt, tugging at the cloth and almost pulling me backwards. I yanked myself free and tripped at the last step, landing heavily on my knees. I screamed as I went down, and the letter flew across the hall like a leaf in the wind.

Peters jumped the last couple of steps and stood in front of me looking like he was going to kick me in the face. I cupped one hand behind his heel and pushed the other against his knee. Pushing and pulling both at the same time, I toppled him over flat on to his back. Peters hit the floor with a yelled curse and I took the opportunity to deliver a blow of my own, giving him a swift kick in the crotch.

Peters squealed as he instinctively curled into the foetal position. "You bitch! I'll make you pay for that!'

I would have loved to have delivered another kick but instead, ran to retrieve the letter and took it through the door into the living room.

I spun around in a circle hoping that a new hiding place would reveal itself to me, but the only place I could think of in time was the plastic box with my other clues. I quickly lifted a corner of the lid and slid the paper inside. I hurried through the other door into the passageway and through into the kitchen, where I scrabbled around looking for a knife.

I was breathing too fast and my chest was burning. I pressed my lips together and tried to force myself to take a few deep breaths through my nose. Plunging my hand into the filthy sink, I came up with a smeared dinner knife that would have lost a fight with a cooked steak and stood no chance against a crazed bully.

Peters staggered in through the kitchen doorway, still bent over. He lent against the frame to catch his breath and laughed when saw me holding the knife.

'What do you think you're going to do with that?'

'Anything I can to hurt you.'

Peters laughed again. He lurched forward and grabbed my tee shirt. I swung at his face with the knife, but he butted my hand away like an annoying fly and the knife clattered to the floor.

'No,' I cried, but Peters didn't even hear me. The last means of defence had gone and with it all hope that I would survive this.

Peters dragged me back into the living room and sneered at me. He smelt like market stall aftershave; sickly sweet and I could see his pupils were already enlarged. I wondered how much he had drunk before he came here. I hadn't seen him take any Persephone, but that didn't mean he hadn't.

'What is the major account code we need?' he demanded.

'I don't know.'

'I know you know. What is it?' Peters was tugging against my tee shirt, trying to make me look at him.

'Tell me, or I'll beat it out of you,' he threatened and I knew he would. The only thing I could think of doing was making him work hard for it.

'Go screw yourself,' I said and closed my eyes.

Chapter 25

I already knew that Persephone with alcohol would speed up its effects and lead to erratic behaviour, but then even before the details were known, I'd been expecting this.

Peters grabbed at the neck of my tee shirt and held it tight in his fist while his other hand was left free to rain punches down upon me.

He pulled against the fabric and lowered me to my knees as I raised my arms to protect my face. Too late, I realised, as a stinging blow across my cheek brought tears to my eyes and swung my head so forcefully, I felt my neck click.

Suddenly, a square bottle crashed against the back of Peters' head, connecting with a stomach-lurching thud. Peters didn't make a sound as he slithered to the ground, landing in an untidy heap on the floor.

I looked up, unsurprised, at my unlikely hero. He'd been protecting me from Peters all along, but the time for secrecy was long past. The handkerchief he'd given me that first day was his and I should have guessed it earlier. The only other person who could have gained access to my desk files apart from my boss, Andrew Brownlow, was his boss and uncle, Anthony Brownlow.

'Hello, Tony.' I said.

Tony eyed my face carefully and assessed the situation. Obviously, he hadn't wanted to reveal himself, but I was grateful he had chosen to save me. Peters' behaviour had grown increasingly unpredictable.

'Can you stand?' Tony was calm and direct, trying to make the best of a bad situation. His Manchester accent was one I'd recognise anywhere. A self-made man, he was famous in the company for having a strong sense of right and wrong and I wondered if that would influence how he saw me now.

Tony helped me as I stumbled clumsily to my feet. My face was throbbing and I could taste blood in my mouth. I had a ringing in my ears and my vision was fuzzy. I collapsed into a chair. I couldn't speak; I thought I was going to be sick.

Tony hauled one of Peters' arms around his neck and dragged him, like a scarecrow, through the passageway and back into the kitchen.

'I'll decide what to do with him later,' said Tony, as he came back in the room. A frown deepened the ridge between his eyes. 'In the meantime, I have to think what to do with you.' He offered me a damp rag. Another handkerchief squeezed out with cold water. I pressed the cool cloth against my throbbing temple.

'Is this it then?' I demanded, my voice sounding much weaker than I hoped. 'Make it quick. You won't have to try too hard. I'm halfway there already.'

Tony gave me a don't-be-stupid look. 'I'm still waiting for you to finish your final task,' he said, taking the other chair.

'After all, that is why I brought you here.'

‘Couldn’t you just have invited me away for a weekend in the country?’

‘Even if I’d managed to persuade you that what we’re doing is for the greater good, would you have come?’

I couldn’t answer. Even if the whole of mankind was depending on it, I would have baulked at the idea of betraying the company I worked for or breaking the law.

‘Why choose me, anyway? It seems an unnecessary risk that you would have someone like me holding the passcodes to your money.’

‘This isn’t just about the money, Kim. It’s about you. You really don’t know how valuable you are, do you?’

‘Valuable? In what way? You should have shared that with Peters.’

‘There’s no ice or antiseptic,’ he said, sidestepping the question.

‘I’m not valuable to you. Your pathetic project is more important than I am. I’m just…’ I struggled for the right word. ‘Useful.’

‘That’s true,’ replied Tony. ‘But that doesn’t mean I don’t care.’

I remembered when he had washed my feet. I pressed the cloth to my bruised cheek.

‘You know nothing about me, how can you say you care? Fancying someone isn’t the same thing, you know.’

Tony laughed as if we were simply having a friendly conversation. ‘I’ve always fancied you,’ he stated unashamedly. ‘And I’ve always cared. Don’t you remember your interview with Andrew and the yearly appraisals? They're always recorded.'

I remembered them well and had been annoyed that Andrew had neglected to warn me the first time. I had assumed that this was merely a corporate imposition and would go no further.

'I was impressed from the beginning and learnt all I could about you.'

'Like what?' I asked, my voice wavering.

Tony looked relaxed in his chair. He leaned back and took a deep breath before counting off on his fingers.

'Anderson, middle name Jane after your maternal grandmother. Married for five years, no children, but your husband would like a child.'

This was news to me, but I didn't interrupt. I wanted to know what else he knew about me.

'You are a creature of habit and hate it when your routine is disrupted. You lunch at Peggy's Tea Shop every Thursday, which is when you shop in the town during your lunch break. You prefer to treat yourself to cosmetics rather than clothes or shoes and your favourite wine is Italian white.'

'If you've been following me or had me followed, then that would have been fairly easy to discover.' I swallowed hard, trying to calm myself. 'Now tell me something CCTV can't tell you.'

I had to try to convince him that he didn't really care about me. If I could somehow break that belief, then there would be no need for him to keep me here.

'Your favourite colour is green,' he stated confidently. 'It makes you feel calm and comfortable.'

That was true. 'It's blue, actually.'

Tony laughed that easy laugh again, not even bothering to acknowledge my lie. He was enjoying this.

I glanced nervously towards the door.

'Is he....?' I asked, not knowing how to find the words.

'He's fine. Or at least he will be, apart from a serious headache.'

'What are you going to do with me?'

Tony rubbed his fist against his chin as he thought about this.

'I haven't decided yet,' he said frowning. 'But I'll have to decide by tonight. We're, er, moving house.'

There were only two boxes left stacked against the back wall. Everything else had already been taken.

'Where are you going?' I asked, as casually as I could.

Tony laughed again and didn't answer. He just smiled at me.

'What happened to the other women?'

I hoped my question would startle him, but Tony looked confused.

'What do you mean?'

'The other women,' I repeated impatiently. 'The ones you've been forcing to take drugs. Are they dead?'

Tony raised his eyebrows and smiled.

'No one was forced to take drugs, Kim. The women who participated in the trial, signed up freely. They were very well looked after.'

'Are they still alive? Are they going to remain alive?'

'Of course,' Tony replied, trying to sound reassuring. 'Only one has been unsuccessful.' He frowned, looking concerned. 'That was unfortunate. I should have been watching her more closely.'

'Unfortunate?' I was incredulous. 'Is that what you call an overdose?'

'She didn't overdose; she miscarried and then found out that Gaia had conceived.'

'And this Gaia,' I said, trying to remain on track. 'Is she alive and well?'

'Yes, she's alive and well. We think she'll have a boy.'

'Oh, congratulations,' I replied, sarcastically. 'Maybe she'll call him Tony.'

'Or Ericthonius,' he suggested, but I didn't understand.

'We'll have to keep monitoring her,' he murmured thoughtfully. 'She's a little older.'

'What do you mean?'

Tony seemed to feel free to reveal more information, but I still didn't understand what he was up to or why it had been necessary to keep so much from me.

'Gaia is in her mid-forties. We'll be monitoring her pregnancy carefully.'

'What about the father? Won't he be looking after her?'

Tony gave that quizzical look and smiled again.

I felt myself blushing and looked down at my hands and rubbed my bruised and battered finger.

'Call me old fashioned, but from what I understand, someone somewhere must have made a donation'.

'Let's just say; he's no longer a part of the picture.' A hardened look had taken over Tony's eyes and something about that situation clearly didn't sit comfortably with him.

A crazy thought had entered my mind, but I decided to test it out and see how Tony reacted.

'Is it Hephaestus?'

Tony didn't answer straight away and he continued to stare ahead. That look frightened me and I hoped that I wasn't going to experience what it felt like to be on the receiving end of it.

Tony closed his eyes to help clear his mind and dropped his head as he smiled.

'I've underestimated you, Kim. Yes, it's Hephaestus.' He noticed my alarmed expression. 'Oh, don't worry, she's quite safe. He won't get anywhere near her.'

'What if he does?'

'He knows that if he does, he'll be eliminated from the project.'

I wasn't sure I wanted to know what that meant, but Tony was talking as if he was entirely confident in the Company's ability to take care of things.

'Are there other women like her, like Gaia?'

'Yes, of course; many women of all ages and many children.'

'And all owing their existence to Uncle Tony,' I replied cattily. I knew Tony wasn't a benevolent man; there was still a lot to feel uneasy about.

'Nobody owes me anything, Kim, just as long as the women are fit and strong enough to undergo the trial.'

'And presumably, the right age,' I added, trying another prompt.

Tony didn't answer but kept his expression neutral.

I looked down at my hands and wondered about myself. How long would it be before they started to give my age away? Already the skin looked dry and flaky and my nails were brittle.

I ran a hand through my hair. That felt rough and brittle too.

I felt Tony watching me. He balanced his chin against the first two fingers of his hand as he studied me.

'I'm not the kind of woman you want to experiment on,' I said, trying to pre-empt his thoughts. I picked at the dry ends of my hair. 'Not very feminine.'

He laughed, but not unkindly. 'Femininity is not measured in years, Kim. I know a lady in her eighties. Her hair may be grey, but her eyes are sixteen and always have been.'

My mouth fell open in shock. 'Surely you can't be suggesting pregnancy for a woman in her eighties!'

Tony shrugged as if to say, 'why not?'

'She was and always will be a wonderful mother. The fact that she's in her eighties doesn't make her less of a mother or less of a woman.'

'You're talking about your own mother,' I stated, making

an assumption.

Tony's response was blunt.

'My mother is dead.'

Chapter 26

'Oh.' I sat back, surprised. 'She must have been older than I thought, maybe she...'

'She was forty-five and finally succeeded in taking her own life.'

'Finally?'

'It took her several attempts.'

Tony sat forward with his elbows on his knees and slowly started to remove his gloves.

'Every miscarriage, every failed pregnancy, every month without hope; they all took their toll and when she'd made the decision, for the last time, she made sure there wasn't any way I could stop her again.'

Tony dropped the gloves on the floor and held his hands out for me to see.

'It's not just a touch of OCD that prevents me from shaking hands, you know.'

For the first time, I saw the matted scarring of serious burns. Office legend gossiped about his hands but nothing had ever been confirmed.

'What the hell did she do?'

'There was a narrow stream that ran across the bottom of our garden. She sat on the bank with a carry can of petrol and a bottle of vodka and lit a match. I tried to save her, but she was already dead by the time I found her.'

'But why? Why would she do such a thing? She had you.'

Tony shrugged. 'I was adopted,' he said simply.

I leant forward in the chair and let the cloth fall to floor.

'Oh, dear God. I can't imagine what that must have been like to witness. My mother died in a fire, too.' I dropped my face into my hands which were already shaking.

'I know. Not the nicest thing for us to have in common.'

I felt a rough lump the size of an apple in my throat, which I tried to swallow down.

I spoke very quietly. 'This doesn't mean that you can prey on my sympathies to get what you want.'

'I'm not trying to coerce you into anything, Kim. I'm just trying to make you understand the benefits of what we want to achieve.'

'So you think you can play God and if you can't change the past, at least you can influence the future.'

'Well, why the hell not?' Tony wasn't bothering to hide his frustration. 'You haven't seen what I've seen. You haven't witnessed what I've had to witness.'

'You can't change the world...'

'I can bloody well try!'

I looked in Tony's face and maybe believed for one moment that if there was someone who thought they could change the world, it was him.

I opened my hands in a questioning gesture.

'So, what do you want?'

Tony looked me straight in the eyes and this time he was the one to speak very quietly.

'You know what I want.'

I did. I got up and walked over to the boxes and in the one that contained my escape attempts I found the pink folder and a pen.

It took just a moment to find the necessary sheet and I filled in the major account code; that last little piece of precious information I'd guarded for so long. Not wanting to look at the paper I simply held it out towards Tony.

He rose from his chair slowly and taking the paper, put everything neatly back into the folder and returned the folder to the box. He stood before me without pride or victory on his face.

'Thank you,' he said.

I nearly laughed. 'For what?'

'For the code; it's the last one. This money will pay for the children's education...'

I held up my hand to stop him and turned my face away. I no longer wanted to know. He'd beaten me, he'd won. It wasn't about the money anymore. He'd got what he wanted. I clenched my fists as hot, humiliated tears spilled over my cheeks.

I briefly thought about attempting an attack, but dismissed the idea almost immediately. I didn't really have the energy to inflict a blow, exhausted more with emotion than tiredness. Besides, Tony was stronger, both physically and emotionally. He gripped my hands and now I was able to take a concentrated look at the matted lines covering both of his.

Tony looked up from his hands to my face. 'It's lunchtime and you need a drink,' he stated. 'So do I.'

He picked up the discarded bottle from the floor and left me to stand breathless in the living room, wondering what the hell was going on, while he walked into the kitchen.

I can't explain why I didn't run away then. Maybe I wanted the drink. Maybe I didn't want to run away.

Tony came back with two mugs, each with a generous slug of Jack Daniels. I gulped mine almost in one, like a desperate cowboy before a gunfight.

Tony didn't drink. He slowly bent his knees to put his mug on one of the boxes, his eyes never leaving my face. He walked purposefully towards me and gripped my shoulders. His fingers played at the edges of the sleeves of my tee shirt. I opened my mouth to argue, but there really wasn't anything I wanted to say. I think Tony already knew he had won the fight. I looked at him, trying to judge what he was thinking. Tony gazed back. Words were unnecessary. He slipped his fingers under the sleeves of my tee shirt and stroked my skin up to my shoulders and back to my elbows.

I could have turned and tried again to run away, but at that moment I didn't want to.

Tony suddenly gripped my chin in his right hand and studied my face as if he could read undeniable truths there. He probably could. He kissed me hard and I let him. There was no tenderness; this was not a loving embrace. This was stupid and potentially dangerous and I didn't care.

Tony ran his fingertips over the top of my shoulders and down either side of my spine, stopping at the waistband of my joggers. I reached out my hand as I kissed him back and felt the firm, cold leather of his belt against his hip.

Tony hooked his thumb into my waistband and tugged at the elastic. The joggers were baggy and badly fitting and didn't need much persuasion to fall to the floor. When he slipped his hand just inside my underwear, I thought I was going to faint.

I kissed him again and tugged at his shirt, trying to pull it loose from under his belt. Tony pushed against me, making me walk backwards like a dancing partner, stepping over the discarded joggers, and guiding me towards the armchair. I thought that he was going to push me into it, but he turned me around and sat down himself. I stood before him, anxious that he may have changed his mind, but seeing his expression, I realised he wanted me to make the next move.

I slipped one finger into the top of my underpants and wriggled them over my hips. They dropped to the floor. I stepped out of them and towards Tony's lap. Sitting across him, I fumbled with his buckle and saw that my hands were shaking as I undid his belt and lowered his fly. Tony didn't lift a finger to help me, but now his breathing was deep and audible. When I placed my hand against his chest I could feel his heart beating strongly against the thin cotton of his shirt. My own heart was beating a lot faster than his.

He cupped my face again and this time let his thumb run

across the surface of my lips. Before his thumb could escape me, I turned my head slightly and caught it in my mouth. As I sucked, I smelt his body respond with a sent warm and soft, filling my head like a song. He smelt like clean earth in a forest. I flexed my feet, spreading my toes, imagining I could feel the leaves beneath us.

Tony gripped my hips, pulling me forwards and when he entered me, I closed my eyes and crossed my wrists behind my back.

I woke up in the same armchair I'd fallen asleep in.

I was still naked, except for a blanket Tony had wrapped around me.

I could hardly believe that the woman who had thrown caution to the wind and behaved so brazenly was me.

The truth was that what we had done wasn't about sex, it was about power. Tony had demonstrated the power he had over me simply by sitting in a chair and doing nothing. But, I'd realised as I was standing in front of him, ignoring my last chance to escape, that what he found attractive about me was that he thought of me as some sort of equal. He recognised in me similarities to himself and although that made me uncomfortable, I knew that if I had run away, he would have seen that as a weakness; I'm the kind of person who would stay and fight. I had sacrificed a battle to win a points war.

Why had I done that? What had compelled me? Perhaps I had been attracted to his conviction. Perhaps overpowered by his personality. I had no answers and frankly, didn't want any.

My head was pounding and the fuzziness felt familiar. He'd drugged me with the second drink. I sat up and took a few deep breaths and took another look around the room. It looked different today.

The familiar boxes had disappeared, but something else had reappeared. My blouse and skirt were hanging up in a plastic wrapper on the back of the door. Against the wall were my shoes, neatly standing and smelling of polish. Balanced on top of them was a new packet of nylons and my underwear, clean and fresh. Placed next to the shoes was my handbag.

Everything I had entered the house with had been given back to me.

I quickly rifled through my bag. Purse, credit cards and lipstick; all were there. They'd taken nothing. My mobile phone was there. I pressed the buttons and anxiously looked at the screen. It was dead.

Hurriedly I dressed on the spot, behind the door. Could they really be giving me my stuff back? Was I getting out of here?

My skirt felt loose. I could now spin it completely around my waist, the waistband bagging out at the edges. I had been on a crash diet and my clothes were the proof.

I left my handbag where it was and ran through the living room and up the main stairs. If Tony were still here, he would have locked me in another room. I wanted to see if Peters was still here.

Both of the bedroom doors were open and deserted. I

wandered into the bedroom Peters had last used.

The camp bed had gone and the floor looked as if it had been swept.

The chest of drawers was still there, so I quickly opened one drawer after the other to find them all completely empty.

Running along the hallway, I entered the other room and found it an empty shell.

The mattress that had been on the floor, the blankets and pillow were all gone. Also missing was the boarding that had been up at the window.

The patch on the wall where I had found the house plans was still hanging open and was just as I had left it.

I suddenly felt very vulnerable. I felt very alone.

I walked slowly back down the main stairs and back into the living room. It was then that I noticed the only thing brought into the house that was still here was the blanket I'd been wrapped in. I had to check the other rooms.

I was nervous about climbing the back stairs. It was the first time I had walked up those stairs without the fear of someone coming after me, but still I could feel my heart beating hard.

The broken door of the room that had once been mine was still hanging in place, but the room behind it was no more than a box. The primitive amenities provided for me had disappeared.

Tony's room was the same as Peters'. The chest of drawers and bed frame were still there, but everything else, including the bedding had gone. They'd truly left and taken everything with them.

I walked into the kitchen and for the first time, it was clean. There was no rubbish; no washing up in the sink and the kettle had gone too. There was no food and the grubby table had been scrubbed. The diagram I'd scribbled before was a faded memory; nothing to suggest that anyone had ever been there – except for one thing.

In the middle of the kitchen table, where Tony had left me bread or coffee before, there was a ten pound note. It was simply lying there as if a kind spouse had just pulled it from a wallet so that the other could pop to the shops.

I reached over to take it, but stopped. I realised I had three things I could use; not accidental things, but items Tony had left me.

The ten pound note would have his finger prints on it; the blanket had come from somewhere and might be traced back to him and I had... Well, I had his DNA. I couldn't help smiling. Had that been a deliberate gift?

I went back to the living room and retrieved my handbag and the blanket. I took the note from the table and with only my fingertips, dropped it into my bag.

This was my exit; time to leave.

I walked to the back door and stood in front of it, bracing myself to give the handle one last try.

I took a deep breath and closed my eyes. The door opened and the soft brush of mid-afternoon wind caressed my face. A laugh escaped me as I stood there, relishing the moment.

I was almost fearful that if I opened my eyes the illusion

of freedom would vanish, so I kept them closed as I took that first precious step into the outside.

PART 2

Chapter 27

Outside the grounds of the house, I was unsure which way to turn, so I decided to follow the road and head towards the overhead railway lines I saw in the distance. I thought that when I was closer to the tracks, I'd be able to follow the line of the railway back towards the town. The idea filled me with hope; people, cars and shops. After days of isolation I actually wanted to see crowds.

The pavement was quite narrow and in some places disappeared into a grass verge. Cars whizzed past, some even honking at the inconsiderate idiot trying to get herself run over.

I must have walked for ages, but time meant nothing to me. Why should I worry about what the clock said?

Eventually, the road widened out and I came to a roundabout. To the left, and furthest from me, there were more cars and noise. To the right the road sloped to a dip that then went under a bridge with the railway line on top. If I turned right, I might reach the train station and get home.

The waft of an enticing smell changed my mind. I crossed the road and took the left-hand route, soon finding myself surrounded by bustling bodies, noise and confusion.

The local market was busy as stall holders shouted reduced prices to their afternoon customers. All the life that had annoyed me before, now welcomed me like an old friend. I'd missed this badly.

A distracted mother fumbled for change as her toddler stole an apple. A teenage boy let his hand slip a little too far from his girlfriend's waist and received an elbowed rebuff and several elderly couples hobbled arm in arm, exchanging smiles and nods with acquaintances whose names they couldn't remember.

The smell came again and I saw the shop front no more than four doors away.

I wandered in and stood behind the waiting customers, a few of whom stepped sideways when I walked in. Most looked bored, but I felt excited. Of all the wonderful experiences I'd had, most of which I'd barely noticed, this one was going to be the best. But, it required a sacrifice. Would I sacrifice something I knew was important for a selfish reason or could I hold out for justice?

The assistant raised her head and blew a strand of hair up and away from her hot, flushed cheeks.

'Yes please?' she enquired, looking directly at me.

I pulled out the ten pound note.

'Haddock and chips please, and could I have a diet coke with that?'

I found a quiet bench at the edge of the market square and sat to observe the whole of human life. Going home or to the police wasn't immediately important any more.

I unwrapped my fish and chips slowly as if opening a present. The first three chips barely touched my sides as I gobbled them down. I was brought up to believe that eating anything other than a sandwich with your fingers was bad manners, but as I broke away a piece of fish, nearly burning my fingers with it, my childhood ethics vanished. That first bite was one I'd remember forever; a million calories and full of fat, guaranteed to glue itself to the top of my thighs for the rest of my life. I'd never tasted anything as delicious.

I rarely had any trouble with eating, but I was surprised to find that I couldn't finish my fish. After less than half of it, I was incredibly full. My stomach had shrunk and now I felt a little sick.

Dumping the remains of my meal in a public waste bin I glanced up to see a shadow looking back at me. I was immediately startled and almost cried out; they'd found me and come to get me. Then I realised that the shadow was mimicking me and what I was really seeing was my own reflection in a shop window. I looked at the stranger before me. Who was that haggard, old looking woman?

My skin was dull and drawn, my hair was sticking up all over the place.

I knew then exactly where I was going next.

'Yeah?' he enquired, before lifting his head.

I said nothing, just looking back to see if he recognised me. It took a few moments for the penny to drop, along with his jaw.

'Waitin' for anover train from London, are ya?' Mr

Attendant asked.

I had to smile. It was so nice to see a friendly face. He left his chair and a little door in the partition wall opened.

'Bin 'ome? Bin to police?' He looked shocked when I said no.

'Ya gotta call 'em,' he insisted. 'Bin swarmin' all over 'ere lookin' for you. Even 'ad me in and checkin' all the tapes. They found your car, an' all.'

I reached out for his arm, just to stop him talking.

'I need a favour,' I said.

Mr Attendant grinned a nicotine smile.

A short walk later and we were at his flat, which was surprisingly neat and tidy. The curtains and tablecloth were made of matching fabric and artificial flowers sat in a shallow bowl on the window sill beneath a frilly net.

'Dolly always liked 'fings to look nice,' he said by way of explanation. 'Couldn't bring meself to change anyfink when she passed on.'

I had only wanted to use Reg's bathroom and he had listened without interrupting when I explained why I hadn't wanted to go home. I couldn't risk letting Nick see me like this and my Dad would have fussed and called the police anyway.

Reg found me a black sack to put the blanket in. I copied the address from my thigh on to a scrap of paper and added that to the sack. Reg went to make tea while I had a shower. He called out that there was a new toothbrush in the bathroom cabinet, and as I scrubbed my mouth under clean running water I swore that I'd never take such a privilege for granted ever again.

I borrowed Reg's phone and while we were having a second cup, the doorbell rang.

Strangely, I felt quite nervous as I went to answer it.

Nick just stood on the doorstep, looking very out of place.

His clothes were clean and he smelt of his regular deodorant, but otherwise he looked a mess; much like me, I imagined.

A shaggy beard threatened to take over the lower half of his face, with the possibility of strange creatures nesting there. His eyes were red-rimmed and wide with incomprehension. I wondered when he had last slept.

'You're here...' he gasped. 'You're back... God, you look awful.'

All other words were lost in a bear hug and I could feel Nick's shoulders shaking beneath his coat.

'I'll take you shopping,' he whispered, pretending he hadn't been crying. 'Get you some more clothes, a hot meal.'

He pushed me from him to look at me.

'Some soup,' he announced. 'Do you want some soup?'

'No!' I cried, raising my hands in mock horror. 'I never want to eat soup ever again!'

Nick barely heard me, as he swamped me in another hug.

'God, I can't believe it. You're here.' Every doubt I'd had about him melted away.

'I'll get anover cup, then,' muttered someone.

Nick drove me home and I immediately changed out of

my skirt and blouse and stuffed them into the same sack as the blanket. I never wanted to see them again.

While I was changing, Nick called the police and two plain clothes detectives arrived on the doorstep less than ten minutes later.

'We've been very worried about you, Mrs Anderson,' said DCI Little, as if I'd been a naughty girl.

He politely declined to sit and stood before me as he scribbled notes, occasionally pausing to readjust the knot of his tie. He was extremely neat, as if an orderly appearance assisted in maintaining an orderly mind. He looked to be about five years from retirement. It would be a very difficult goodbye for him when the time came.

'We were most concerned when we found your car and not your handbag.'

'They must have taken that,' I said, trying to remember. 'I didn't have it while I was in the house.' When I had turned my phone back on, there had been over thirty messages from Nick.

The female officer, DS Kelly, was very sweet and quite maternal in her manner. She sat beside me and held my hand as she asked me about how I had been treated, her serious blue eyes absorbing everything.

'You'll have to come back to the station with us to make a full statement.' The DCI gave a discreet, slightly embarrassed cough. 'But that can wait until you've been to the hospital.'

'But I don't need to go to the hospital,' I insisted. 'I feel fine and I haven't been injured.'

The DCI smiled at me over the top of his glasses and gently scratched his balding brow with the top of his pen.

The Detective Sergeant patted the top of my hand, patronisingly.

'It's OK,' she soothed. 'I'll be with you the whole time.' Then I understood what test they wanted.

Nick looked pale. 'Oh, God.'

'Nick, it's all right. This is just procedure.' I looked at DS Kelly. 'Right?'

'Right. In all instances of violent crime, a swab test would be taken.'

'Violent crime?! What happened to you?'

'Nothing. I'm fine.'

DS Kelly's eyes switched from Nick to me and back again.

'Kidnapping is classed as a violent crime. With Mrs Anderson's assertion, this case has moved from being a missing person enquiry, but we can take your statement later.'

I returned from hospital with a feeling of slight embarrassment, a dressing on my hand and a prescription for hydration powders.

'Aren't you going to keep her in?' asked Nick.

'He's spent so long without me, he thinks I'll be in his way,' I joked.

'Don't, Kim. I'm just worried, that's all.'

'I'm just a little dehydrated. I've already drunk enough to float a navy. And every time I need to pee I'm not shown to the loo, I'm given a cup.'

DS Kelly took the black plastic sack from me, and I heard that the police had followed my directions and were now swarming all over the house.

Evidence of my incarceration would be everywhere; blood on the floor outside my prison where I had scrapped my ankle, my blood and hair in other rooms and my writing in Peters' room where I had found the blueprints.

I relayed my story and DS Kelly made copious notes. 'It won't be long before we have them all locked up,' she announced confidently.

I doubted that they would have any success, but refrained from saying so. The Company was an army and Tony and Peters were foot soldiers. Even if the police found and arrested them, there would still be many willing to fill their shoes and advance the next project.

DCI Little arranged for us to be picked up and taken to the police station straight away. I was asked to wait alone in the interview room. When Little entered, he dropped a thick manila file on the table and sat in the uncomfortable looking steel chair opposite.

'We need to ensure that all details are captured while they're still fresh in your head, Mrs Anderson.'

'That's an awfully big file, considering that I was only gone for a few days.'

'A file is created on the same day a person is reported missing. What can you tell me about Brownlow Print?' he asked.

'Don't you need to know about the kidnappers, first?'

'I'm hoping that what you say might lead us there. How long have you worked for the company?'

'About three years, I guess. When can I see my husband?'

'He's here. You'll see him presently. About three years? You can't be more precise?'

'Three years, four months and two weeks. Why have you separated us? Am I going to need a solicitor?'

'We need to speak to each of you independently, and then we can arrange for you to go home. During your time with the company, have you ever noticed anything unusual about the payments or costs that you dealt with?'

'Absolutely not! All my paperwork was in perfect order.'

'Your paperwork, yes. But the company's paperwork is another matter.' Little opened the file in front of him. 'When we discovered that you'd gone missing on Brownlow Print's time, we started looking a little closer at the company. Andrew Brownlow has provided a statement, but Anthony Brownlow has disappeared. So have most of the company assets.' Little paused here a moment to let me absorb this information. 'You were the Finance Manager, correct?'

'Correct.'

'And other than a black eye and a swollen finger, you're quite well?'

'Yes...'

'You're sure? You weren't molested or raped?' Little stared at me sternly.

'No, I wasn't.'

'But you did recently have sex?'

'I was kidnapped!'

'Were you? The forensic evidence in your car suggests that it was moved by someone else, but the only fingerprints we found belonged to you and your husband.'

'Just what are you trying to suggest?'

'I'm suggesting, Mrs Anderson, that you had the means and the skills to illegally transfer large sums of money, and make your own paper trail appear innocent, while your lover absconded with freshly laundered drug money.'

'That preposterous! I would never have done anything like that!' But it was starting to look like that's exactly what had happened.

'Who was responsible for managing the company accounts above you?' asked Little, 'Was that Andrew?'

'No, Andrew is the Production Manager. Tony had overall control. I always thought very highly of him. At least, I did.'

'Yes, well,' Little coughed discreetly and straightened his tie. 'Tony, about whom you thought very highly, is nowhere to be found, leaving Andrew and you behind.' He flicked his thumb through the thick wad of papers in the file. 'As you can see, my colleagues in the Fraud department have been very busy.'

'Well, if you're not going to arrest me, why not let me see the paperwork. I handle financial documents daily; if there's anything unusual in them, I'll find it.'

Little nodded and slid a few sheets across the desk. 'These are copies of emails sent by Tony Brownlow to someone outside the company. The receiving email address no longer exists.'

'Hmm. Fire and feathers.'

'Pardon?'

'It's an image I had in my head that I just can't shake.' I said. 'These emails are talking about investing money in a single high risk venture. This is an Icarus project.'

'And what does that mean, exactly?'

'In business, an Icarus Project is one that is typically launched with a lot of fanfare and the chance of success is good, but dependant on more than one thing. The risk of failure is small, but if failure occurs...'

'Then everything goes down in flames,' Little finished for me.

'The investment in this paperwork looks pretty ordinary at first glance,' I said, 'but if one part fails, the whole project will tumble like a line of dominoes. There was a senior manager at Brownlow's who was working on minimising the risk of such projects.'

'Do you know what kind of project? The emails don't specify.'

'I can't tell, but it could be anything. It's not unusual for any business to make outside investments.'

'But what kind of high risk venture would a printing company like Brownlow be interested in?' Little took the paperwork back to look at it himself. 'Drug production?'

I felt myself bristle under Little's gaze. 'I kept perfect paperwork. I can promise you, if the company was involved in money laundering, I would have known.'

Little adjusted his tie. 'Your perfect paperwork appeared to justify what could have been illegal activity. My colleagues and I have been working on tracing the owners or directors of Phoenix companies. Is that term familiar to you?'

I shook my head.

'Phoenix companies are businesses that have been disbanded by a court, usually because of financial irregularities, but then reappear under a different name, often with the same senior members.'

'That can't apply to Brownlow Print; they're a traditional family firm.'

Little gave me a sympathetic look. 'Actually, no, they're not. We believe that Tony Brownlow's name is Anthony Bridges, or Andrew Brown, or perhaps Tony Barge. And Brownlow Print has only been trading for twelve years.'

I could only open and close my mouth like a goldfish.

Chapter 28

'You're very loyal, Mrs Anderson.' Little leant back in his chair and let out a breath. 'I'm very sorry to be the one to tell you that your loyalty has been misplaced. Your dedication and attention to detail has been used against you. I appreciate that this is difficult to hear, but we will need to discuss this further. I'm sure that there is something you saw that may help us. In the meantime, I recommend dinner and sleep,' he rubbed the back of his neck, 'for all of us.'

I woke up at about two in the morning to an empty space beside me and the sound of muttering coming from downstairs.

I sighed and threw back the covers. Usually when Nick was busy with a project, I was happy to leave him to it. Often he would work through the night, but this time was different. He needed to find the answers I didn't have. There was no point in trying to sleep while both our minds were whirring.

As I descended the stairs, the aroma of strong coffee greeted me from the dining room. Nick was standing at the table, which was covered with open volumes and a pile of notepaper held down by a near empty cafetiere. When Nick was looking for an answer, he went back to his books to find it.

I pulled my robe around me and dropped into a chair. 'Any luck?'

'I think I understand now.' Nick put down his pen and looked up, his eyes shining.

'Understand what? What are you talking about?' I rubbed my face and yawned.

'I understand what the legend means. It's what you saw in the paperwork at the police station. The Icarus Project set up. You said that the architect's name on the blueprints was Simpson & Co, right? It seems that the place where you were held was built by this architect. But he wasn't just an architect, he was also a businessman. I traced an article online by someone of that name.'

'One of the senior managers at Brownlow Print was working on a strategy to reduce the possibility of Icarus Phenomenon in company projects. That's the phenomenon of sudden and dramatic failure after a period of outstanding success. I mentioned that to Little.'

Nick nodded. 'It's his article. If Brownlow Print was just a front for The Company, it was very careless to publish a paper online. But then, this Simpson guy probably didn't know...'

'But what does that have to do with the Icarus legend? Why was it important to Fireflight?'

'I wondered that too. Then I remembered.' Nick lifted a heavy book from the cluttered table to show me a picture. 'Icarus' father was Daedalus, a gifted Athenian craftsman. He built the Labyrinth for King Minos of Crete to imprison the Minotaur. Minos imprisoned Daedalus himself in the labyrinth because he gave Minos's daughter, Ariadne, a ball of string to help Theseus, the enemy of Minos, to survive the Labyrinth and defeat the Minotaur.'

I had to think about that carefully. 'You're suggesting that if there was a project about Icarus phenomenon in Brownlow, then there was also a Daedalus in The Company and Simpson could be him.'

'It makes sense to me that they'd need someone to monitor such a project.'

'I'm glad it makes sense to you. I'm still not sure it makes sense to me. There's no way for us to know if there was a Daedalus in The Company. Do your books say how Daedalus died?'

Nick shook his head. 'The myths don't say, but he lived and worked successfully in Sicily and it's thought that he lived to a ripe old age.' Nick reached under a pile of papers and pulled out a large sheet. 'Look. I've been working on an Olympian family tree and filled in the names you know.'

'It looks like an organogram.'

'Well, it is. In a way. But The Company aren't going to make theirs known, are they?'

'But organograms aren't meant for public use,' I said, handing the sheet back to him. 'It shows the staff who reports to whom. Now that really would be information worth knowing.'

'Well, I'm afraid the best I can do is put a few names in the right places.'

I went into the kitchen to fetch myself a cup and finish off Nick's coffee. 'I have a nasty feeling about this.'

'Well, Little seems to have nasty feelings about it, too. We can relate what we've found to him later today, but I don't know what use this will be. We can't even be sure that Icarus or Daedalus are people.'

'Well, drugs, people or projects, I don't think it really matters at this point. Whoever is managing all of this, the Elite, whoever they are, will want to protect their money. This wasn't just about thousands of pounds, but many hundreds of thousands of pounds.'

Nick puffed out his cheeks with a breath. 'Just imagine. If they had companies like this all over the country, how much money would they really be making?'

'I still can't believe that Brownlow was a front. We don't know who Fireflight Healthcare are. Could it be that the company I worked for really belonged to Fireflight, and operated by the Elite?'

Nick smiled humourlessly. 'What service would you like today, Madam? Dry clean or intense scrub and rinse?'

'I don't know how much this will help the police. If they want to actually stop what's going on, they need to find the transferred money. Would Daedalus or Simpson even know? These are just more names we've thrown into the ring.'

Nick put his arm around my shoulder. 'Let's sleep on it. Things will look clearer in the morning.'

I returned to bed and when I opened my eyes later that morning I knew that it was Tuesday. Just to know what day it was seemed like a wonderful achievement.

I lay very still in bed looking at the familiar surroundings of my bedroom and moved only my eyes as I saw my bedside clock, the ceramic pot I dropped my earrings into each night and the way the morning sun tickled the walls with shafts of light as it inched its way around the room.

I remembered how I always hated the way this room was decorated and how I hated that we couldn't afford to change it yet. Now, it didn't offend me quite as much and I felt perfectly happy just to lie there.

When we arrived at the police station, DCI Little was less enthusiastic than we had expected.

'Thank you for the additional names', he said, 'but this morning I received an instruction from the Chief that the investigation has already achieved its aims and is now officially closed.'

'But I thought you were the senior investigating officer in this case,' protested Nick.

'Everyone answers to someone else,' said Little. 'The requirement of the investigation was to ensure the wellbeing and safe return of Mrs Anderson. Mission accomplished.'

I stared at Little with my mouth open. 'But what if I'm in danger? They could come after me again!'

Little observed me carefully over the top of his glasses. 'There is no evidence to suggest that you are still being pursued, or will be in the future. We haven't even been able to find any evidence of the persons you called Aphrodite, Hephaestus or Zeus.'

'But they were there, in the house. There must be traces. There must be! And what about the boxes? With everything inside? Have you found them?'

'We have not found any boxes of any description in the property, at the clinic address or at your former place of employment.'

'They were planning another programme. I've already explained this.'

'I believe you,' said Little calmly, 'but with nothing left to examine, we can't take this any further.' He started tidying papers on his desk. 'I have already spoken to the Drugs Unit of your suspicions.'

'My suspicions?!' I had to hold on to the edge of his desk for support. Nick put a hand on my arm and gently led me towards the door.

'Come on, Kim,' he said, glaring at Little. 'There's nothing more we can do here.'

Little sat in his chair and opened a cardboard folder. 'Thank you for your co-operation in this matter.'

I sat in the car, fuming.

'I can't believe that he would speak to us like that! I thought he was a good guy. I thought he was on our side.'

'He probably still is,' said Nick thoughtfully.

'Oh? And how do you figure that?'

'Well, he's clearly been warned off, but he's already spoken to the Drugs Unit, right?'

'That's what he said.'

'About what, exactly? If the technicians could find no

trace of anyone but you in that house, then either they've got bloody awful CSI or someone, somewhere, is suppressing information.'

I looked over at Nick. 'Do you think he'll find Daedalus?'

'They might have the resources to find a drug of that name.'

I couldn't put into words my worry that this might not be a drug. Nick seemed to understand and lent over to squeeze my shoulder.

'I'll call into work and extend my leave a little longer. Just to make sure that there's no-one out there.'

'There's always going to be someone out there.' I glanced out the car window at the near empty car park and felt a hundred eyes upon me. 'I feel like running away, but there's nowhere for us to go.'

'Apart from Sicily or Crete,' suggested Nick.

I almost laughed. 'You want to go on holiday?'

'I think a holiday would be a good idea. We can start looking for Daedalus in Crete, or look for evidence of his work in Sicily, or look for his grave in Egypt.'

'You really think he's a person?'

'There's no way to know; I'm just guessing, but I think it's more likely than the name for a drug. Why not just take a trip and see if we can find out? But we could be putting ourselves in more danger,' he warned.

'How much danger are we already in? I don't think anything has ended just because we've come to a stop. At least we'd be doing something.' Already I felt happier.

I turned to Nick and held his face in both my hands and kissed him. 'Let's book the tickets today.'

Chapter 29

'I've booked tickets for Crete online,' said Nick. 'I think that might be the best place to start. There's a beautiful looking house close to the sea that once belonged to a retired engineer. And I saw an ad for a Greek coffee bar called Kafes not too far from here. It says it offers a taste of the authentic Greece. Do you fancy giving it a try?'

It was only a half hour drive away, but I was still nervous. Nervous of everything; being alone, being surrounded, being with Nick and being without him. I sat at a table in the middle of the shop, twisting a paper napkin, while I waited for Nick to bring the coffee.

'Your nerves are understandable,' said a bearded old man from behind a newspaper, 'but I promise you, you have nothing to fear from me.'

'I'm not nervous,' I lied. 'I'm just waiting for my husband.'

'I've been waiting for you both,' said the man, lowering his newspaper. 'I have information that you'll need for your trip.'

I stood up, but felt frozen, unsure of where to run.

'What's going on?' asked Nick, suddenly behind me, his eyes moving from me to the old man and back again.

'Please do sit down, both of you.'

Nick slowly lowered the tray on to the table, but still didn't sit. 'Who are you?'

'Oh, I beg your pardon,' said the man. 'I forgot to introduce myself.' He extended a hand towards me. 'Henry Simpson. I believe you've been looking for me.'

I shook the old man's hand and sat. 'Are you...?'

'I no longer use that name,' said the old man, unable to avoid glancing at the door, 'but yes, I once was Daedalus.'

'We've just booked a trip to go looking for you,' said Nick. Simpson smiled benignly. 'I know. That's my house by the coast.'

'I was imprisoned in another of your houses.'

'Were you? Wherever it was, it belongs to The Company, now.'

'Did you follow us here?' I asked, suddenly afraid.

'No, I come here quite often,' he replied. 'The coffee isn't very authentic, but the konafa pastries are very nice.'

Nick narrowed his eyes at the old man. 'How did you know we would be here?'

'I sent you a message.'

'I didn't receive any message.'

'Yes, you did. "For a taste of the authentic Greece..."'

'Daedalus lived in Crete and died in Egypt.'

Simpson shrugged. 'Why do you think I'm still here?'

I glanced across to Nick. 'Should we cancel the flights?'

'Oh no,' said Simpson. 'If you want to put a halt to The Company's plans, then you must go.'

‘What do you know of The Company’s plans?’ I wasn’t sure I could trust this stranger, but he clearly had information I needed.

‘I know that when The Company launch a new project, they always produce two drugs. One supports their efforts, the other closes the operation. They view the drugs like offspring; a good child and a bad child. The bad child I created is in Crete.’

‘Do you think their plans are international?’

‘The Company have enormous ambitions, both foreign and domestic. If what I suspect is true, there could be Fireflight members in every department in the government; Health, the Home Secretary’s office and the Foreign Secretary’s office. And separate cells in foreign governments, too.’

‘That sounds like a ridiculous conspiracy theory,’ scoffed Nick. ‘It’s preposterous.’

‘No,’ said Simpson. ‘It really isn’t.’

I thought back to the conversation I had in the house with Zeus.

‘I was told about the procedure,’ I said. ‘They wanted to do Ovarian Tissue Transplantation. They told me about Persephone. It sounded dangerous.’

Simpson shook his head. ‘It’s not the one they tell you about that should worry you,’ he said. ‘It’s the one they don’t tell you about that’s dangerous. If you want to stop this, you’ll have to find its source in Crete.’

Nick stirred his coffee, angrily splashing into the saucer.

'Why don't you go find its source in Crete?'

'It would be a risky adventure for anyone,' agreed Simpson. He turned to look at me. 'But I am a mortal, and only an Olympian can challenge the Olympians.'

I stared back at him. 'They'll kill me.'

Simpson smiled. 'But you are Athena, my dear. A goddess of Olympia. You would only be assassinated if you were stripped of your goddess status and relegated to mortal.'

'Who the hell decided that I was going to be Athena?'

'Zeus, of course. You need to have a conversation with your father. Ask him about Tcells. We both have a history with Zeus.'

I could hear my blood pulsing through my head. 'My father couldn't possibly be involved in anything The Company was doing,' I said.

I closed my eyes, but couldn't supress that annoying little whisper in the back of my head which hinted that if my mother had been involved with The Company, my father, a research scientist, may have been involved, too.

'Clearly there is much he has kept from you. But when your car was discovered, he guessed that you weren't just missing, you had been kidnapped. He reached out to his contacts, including me.'

'Zeus is in London. What is the point of going to Crete now?'

'Zeus was in London. Daedalus lived in Crete for a while and I was there while working for the Elite. That's where the answers will be.'

I stirred my coffee, but no longer wanted it. 'You were one of the Elite?'

'Yes, but I have since outlived my usefulness and am mortal once again.'

Nick returned his cup to the table and pushed it away. 'Well, this mortal has heard enough rubbish for one day. We're leaving.'

I held up my hand. 'Not yet. I need to know more.' I turned my attention back to Simpson. 'What is the difference between the Olympians and the Elite?'

'The Olympians are the twelve men and women in positions of high power, who meet to discuss the social and political matters in the news.' He fixed me with a stern stare. 'And act to change its direction. The Selected Elite are about thirty people who carry out the wishes of the Olympians. They could be anyone; doctors, judges, professors, politicians. The mortals,' Simpson paused here to look over at Nick, 'are people like you and me. Up to 400 ordinary people who might be of future interest to The Company.'

'They wouldn't be interested in me,' Nick said.

'Don't be so naive,' responded Simpson, sharply. 'You're married to a goddess who didn't have a recognised consort. Of course they'd be interested in you.'

'What you're telling me,' I whispered, my voice already wavering, 'is that I will have to be Athena and address the Olympians directly.' I reached out for Nick's hand. 'It's the only way to find out what they're up to. I can then appeal to them to stop. But what if my appeal is denied?'

Simpson let his eyes drop to the table. 'I don't know. You'd be relying on your goddess status to avoid assassination.'

Nick gripped my hand and pulled me to my feet.

'It's not happening. I'm cancelling the trip. If you want to stop this,' he flung his paper napkin towards Simpson, 'then you can go.'

Simpson rose, reaching for his coat and newspaper. 'I'd probably be assassinated as soon as they found out I was in Crete. I'd need to travel with you; hide under your shadow, so to speak. But I would still need to go.'

'Even knowing you'd risk assassination?' I didn't understand. 'Why?'

'You remember I told you that there would also be a "bad offspring"? It's mine.' He smiled sadly. 'I called it Iapyx. And I'm the only one who can kill it.'

'What the hell is Iapyx?'

'It's a closure compound. I'll need you to help me find it.'

We'd promised Simpson nothing as we left the café. Nick wanted to head straight home and cancel the tickets immediately, but I asked him to wait until I'd spoken to my father. I had some serious questions to put to him and needed more information before we rushed into a decision.

When I called and told him we needed to talk, he insisted that I allow him to buy us dinner that night.

'If this is going to be the conversation I think it is, then a public place might be safer. And besides, when was the last time you treated yourself to a nice meal?' He had a point. I never knew what to eat anymore.

'Yes, all right. We'll come.'

'I'll pick you up at 7.30.'

'Dad, why didn't you call me when you knew I'd returned home?'

'I wanted to give you time to rest, darling. I spoke to Nick almost every day.'

'But not to me.'

'We'll go to The Harrington. Wear your pretty pleated dress.'

'Dad...'

'And your nice shoes...'

'Dad! What were you up to?'

'I had to make enquiries. I wanted to make sure you'd be properly protected.'

'What does that mean?'

'Tonight. I'll answer your questions tonight.'

Chapter 30

The Harrington was the only place in North London where asking for beer, champagne, oysters and steak all in the same meal would be encouraged. In many other well-to-do restaurants, the waiters would sniff at such a request. At The Harrington you'd be applauded, not for being anti-establishment or bohemian, but because The Harrington could provide it. Even during the war, the bar still stocked four different types of gin. It was the kind of place where the concierge would offer you a tie if you arrived inadequately dressed. The Harrington's front door was scarlet and the lights over the bar were bright. The only thing that was understated was modesty.

I pushed away my plate and looked up at my father.

'Don't you like your meal, darling?'

'Dad, when I was missing, did you know that I'd been kidnapped?'

He paused before answering. 'No. I didn't know, but I suspected. I was calling every contact I knew. I still am.'

'What do you know about Tcells?'

Nick coughed, embarrassed, but Dad kept his eyes averted. 'What's brought this on, Kimmie?'

'Dad, you promised you'd answer my questions tonight.'

'Did your kidnappers say something to you?'

'It's what they didn't say that made me concerned. I remembered Mother saying something when I was small. She wanted to attract The Company's attention. How did she do that?'

'Your mother used to say lots of things.'

'Dad!' The diners at the next table were starting to turn their heads. 'Spit it out. I deserve to know.'

Dad sighed and rubbed his face with his hand. 'I've been avoiding this conversation since you were born. We were honest with you about one thing. I'm not your birth father.'

'I know that. That's not why I'm asking.'

He swallowed and started again. 'Your mother was working in a medical research lab when she made a unique discovery. She was part of a team that found a way to combine the actions of two types of Tcells. These are protector cells in the body. They identify and destroy damaged or infected cells. One adhered to the top of infected cells restricting movement and one surrounded the cells restricting growth, like a cap and a cloak. The damaged cell would basically suffocate before infecting any others.'

'But how?'

'Sometimes the body creates antibodies that react incorrectly; they see normal tissue as damaged and the body attacks itself. Your mother's team wanted to combine this knowledge with the new Tcells technology.'

'Why would the Elite be interested in that?'

'This technology had unique potential. The aim was to

engineer a programed cell to penetrate the damaged cells and alter its function. But we were unsuccessful.'

'Programed with what?'

'Whatever information the Elite thought would be useful.'

'You said we were unsuccessful?'

'Your mother was my senior manager.'

I leant forward on the table and avoided my father's eyes.

'Is that Tcell combination when you both became members of the Elite?' I whispered.

Dad glanced around before fixing his eyes on the tablecloth. 'I was only a protector, but your mother was. Yes.'

I slumped back in my chair. 'When the hell was I going to learn this? When were you going to tell me? I could have died in that bloody house! When was I going to find this out?'

Dad shrugged and smiled sadly. 'Your mother wanted to tell you. She wanted you to know, but I was scared that too much knowledge would be dangerous and it was safer for you not to know who we were working for. We had several rows about it.'

'When mother was your boss, what did you call her?'

'Kimmie, don't...'

'It's time I was told.'

'Metis. I called her Metis.'

Nick looked up. 'Metis was Athena's mother.'

Dad apologised with his eyes. 'Kimmie darling, look; I know you have every right to be angry...'

'Angry?!' The bar manager looked up, champagne bottle still in hand. 'I'm fucking furious!'

The lady with letterbox-red lipstick at the next table tutted and I lowered my voice. 'How did all this start? I mean really?'

'Darling, it's a long story.'

'I don't care if it takes all night. We're having this conversation. You say you've been trying to protect me all these years? Well guess what? Time's up. I want everything. Every little detail.'

'Perhaps somewhere a little more private?' suggested Nick.

'No. Here and now.'

Dad started rearranging the remaining silverware; straightening spoons, smoothing napkins and then he stopped. He closed his eyes before he spoke, unable now to even look at me.

'Your mother and I went to the same university, but we didn't know each other then.'

'You told me you met at work, in the same lab.'

'That's only partly true. We both got those jobs because while we were at university we both belonged to the same political students' group.'

'What group was that?'

'The Fireflight Register.'

'Fireflight. Again. Is that where it started? At Uni?'

'Yes. We believed in being radical then. It was all the rage in the seventies.' Dad looked up then and smiled, but I waited.

'The register was a comprehensive list of names of high

achievers who had strong and specific views in common.'

'And you and Mother were both on this list?'

'Yes, but back then she was the girlfriend of the group leader. We moved in different circles.'

'What were these "strong and specific views"?' I took a sip of water and wished it was brandy.

'We were all studying major sciences and all believed that targeted health reform, designed to uniquely benefit future generations, was the best way to strengthen our own country's interests and eventually influence world health.'

I sat quietly for a moment while I tried to digest this on top of salmon and seasonal vegetables. 'Are you saying that you wanted to develop your own eugenics programme?'

Dad kept his eyes on the table. 'Yes.'

Nick raised a finger at a passing waiter. 'Two brandies, please. Large ones.'

'You can't drink that,' I scolded. 'Brandy makes you moody.'

'I'm not drinking,' responded Nick. 'The other one's for your father.'

Dad sat back in his chair and let his eyes roam around the restaurant. 'I've always liked this place. When I was still at university, I promised myself I'd bring a beautiful woman here to celebrate my Nobel Prize.' He smiled sadly. 'Now I'm here with a beautiful woman discussing my demise.'

I felt impatient at Dad's theatrics. 'No one's going to shoot you.'

'No, they wouldn't be that kind. Knowledge is dangerous

Kimmie. Please don't get involved. I should be making you promise that you're not going to do anything with this information.' He smiled again. 'I'd be wasting my time though, wouldn't I? Be very careful, darling.'

We were silent as the waiter delivered coffee and brandy. I thought I'd be better off with the coffee; I was going to need to keep a clear head.

'This Group Leader. What can you tell me about him?'

Dad shook his head. 'Not much. I wasn't even sure of his name. But I do know that the register was governed by a belief in philhellenism, and he was its biggest preacher.'

'What's that? Philhelli something.'

'Philhellenism,' repeated Dad. 'It's a love of ancient Greek culture and a belief that theirs was the perfect way to govern a society.'

Nick frowned. 'It's not that perfect,' he sniffed. 'That belief takes no account that their society was strictly hierarchical. Women had no voice and slavery was practically necessary.'

Dad smiled slightly. 'Well actually, maybe it did.'

'Why me?' I asked. 'What do they want with me?'

'They're crazy,' said Nick with a snort of derision, 'a group of wannabe megalomaniacs. How can anyone know what they want?'

'They want a test subject. They want to know if you're a suitable candidate for their future plans.' Dad swirled his brandy slowly, deliberately not looking at me. 'You have all the required attributes, darling. Above average intelligence, fit and healthy, and the right parentage.'

'How could they be sure?'

'Look back at everything that happened. Think of it as a test. How far did you trust them? How far did you push them? Did you provide any blood?'

I clattered my cup back into the saucer. 'No, I did not provide any blood! I think I'd have noticed if they'd stuck a God damn needle in my arm!'

'Are you sure?' persisted Dad. 'What did you eat or drink?' I thought back to the two times I'd been unconscious when Nick suddenly spoke.

'Kim, what about your ankle?'

'That was just a graze.'

'But it bled, right?'

'Yes, but only a drop.'

Dad dropped his head to his chest. 'A drop is all they'd need. What about hair? Saliva?'

'I used a hairbrush...'

'Whose brush?'

'Oh, for God's sake! Does it matter? If they really are who you say, then everything probably still worked out the way they wanted.' I began to hear numbers in my head, like I had when I was a child. One. Two. Three...

'Not exactly,' said Dad.

'What do you mean, "not exactly"?' I reminded myself to take another breath. Think logically, not emotionally. Emotional thinking overwhelms me.

Dad took a sip of brandy before continuing.

'If you were initiated into a programme, you'd already have been squirreled away to a clinic somewhere. Right now, you're back in the public domain, and that can only mean one of two things. Either the Selected Elite changed their minds about you, or one of them let you go.'

Nick replaced his cup and pretended not to care. 'Well, either way, you're safe now. And if you were let go, well, actually, I don't care. You're here.'

'Yes, but why?' Dad looked thoughtful while he rolled his glass between his hands.

'They let me go. Hermes let me go.'

'You used a brush and left a drop of blood when you grazed your ankle?'

'Yes.'

'Then they know your blood type. They'll extract your DNA. They'll know everything about you.'

'They'll know things I don't know.' I was beginning to realise that being the finance manager was not the only reason I'd been kidnapped. 'You said when you and Mother were working on T-cells that they bound to other cells like a cap and a cloak?'

'Yes.'

'They're a helmet and a shield.'

Dad looked confused, but Nick picked up what I was saying and the look of worry on his face broke my heart.

'They called you Athena.'

I glanced around the restaurant and lowered my voice again. 'How did Mother die?'

'Kimmie...'

'Should I stand up and start screaming?'

Nick added more cream to his coffee and changed his mind about drinking it. 'Kim, do you really want to know? I mean, whatever happened, it's not going to be nice to hear.'

'I wouldn't describe anything that's happened to me lately as nice.'

'It wasn't that much fun for us either while you were growing up. You were only ten when it happened.' Dad pushed the brandy away. 'We were always looking over our shoulders, constantly fearful. When you have children, it comes with the territory, but in your case, even more so. I was so relieved when you got married. It felt like you'd dodged a bullet.'

Nick nodded, understanding. 'Athena didn't have a recognised consort.'

'That's right. And she didn't have children. I was hopeful that they'd lose interest in you when you married, but most women have their first child within five years of meeting their partner. You two have been married for five years. They probably wanted to know your childbearing potential.'

'Now they presumably know all about me, my blood and about Mother.' I stretched my fingers, trying to cool the stickiness on my palms. 'They've probably been watching me all my life.'

'In the Greek legends,' said Nick, 'Zeus feared a son who could usurp him. Metis died when Zeus consumed her.'

I turned to Dad. 'And Mother?'

'You already know that she died in a lab fire. It was at the research facility.'

'You told me it was an accident at work.'

'I was told it was a work accident, but even then, all lab facilities had their own procedures for safe operations. There was no further investigation.'

'You never believed it was an accident?'

'No. It all felt horribly suspicious. She was working on all sorts of projects, but mostly immunisations for protection against potential criminal activity.'

I felt my eyes widen. 'You mean terrorism?'

'Well, that's not what we called it then, but yes. We still had a few friends back then. They found out the Elite had developed a powerful sedative which was deliberately dangerous.'

'That could be Thanatos.'

'Your mother was secretly working on an antidote, something that would halt and stabilise the effects. She was especially excited about one particular compound.'

'Was it destroyed?'

'I've no idea, but I have to assume so.'

'I only have one more question.'

'Go on.'

'What is Zeus's aegis?'

'It's a shield of protection that Zeus gave to Athena.'

The unspoken hint hung between us, heavy, like smoke.

Chapter 31

Dad got out of the car and kissed me goodnight when we reached home.

'Welcome home, pumpkin,' he whispered and brought a lump to my throat.

I walked straight into the kitchen and poured a glass of water.

Nick came up behind me and massaged the back of my neck. He ruffled my hair with his nose.

'Are you OK?'

'Yes. Well, no, not really. But I'll be all right.'

'It's been a crazy night.'

I nodded. 'I wanted the truth out in the open, now I think I've just torn scabs off old wounds.'

'Do you think it's true about the Fireflight register having altruistic beginnings?'

'Sure. But every organisation says that, don't they?'

Nick didn't have an answer; he just sighed and hugged me before he went to change.

The local weekly newspaper was left discarded near the sink, where I had dumped it that morning. Now, I idly flipped through the pages, trying to delay going upstairs, when one article caught my eye. The photo was of a house I recognised.

'Local Demolition of Countryside Eyesore.'

'Nick!' I called, urgently. 'Take a look at this!'

Nick wandered into the kitchen, tugging at his tie.

'Isn't that the place you were taken to?' he asked, his eyes widening. I nodded, reading as fast as I could.

'The demolition of the country house of two wealthy eccentric brothers is to take place next Saturday afternoon. That's only five days away!' I exclaimed. 'I want to go and see it!'

I continued reading. 'The two brothers lived together until a furious row came between them. Each claimed full ownership of the house and each refused to move out. With tensions spiralling out of control, they decided to make the divide physical and had the internal walls constructed. One brother used the front door, the other used the back door and they never spoke to each other again, only entering into the kitchen or living room when the other went out. Neither brother married and both continued to claim that the house was theirs until they died within two months of each other.' I looked up. 'Simpson was the architect. He didn't live there.'

'Daedalus was a craftsman working for others, so I guess that makes sense,' said Nick.

'But we didn't ask him why he hid the blueprints in the house.'

'There's only one possibility that I can think of,' said Nick. 'He hid them so that if something happened to him, whoever found them would know who had built the house.

He was leaving something of himself behind. Now that the Company, Fireflight, have them, they'll have his real name. They'll be able to check if he worked for them.'

I had abandoned the newspaper and was following Nick upstairs.

'He must have. It's just too convenient that they had a spare deserted house available. I told Little about the blueprints. And we told him about Daedalus. The police now have the same clues as Fireflight.'

'But Little can't do anything, can he?' said Nick. 'The higher ups in the police had clearly told him to back off. Mission accomplished.'

I sat on the edge of the bed while I took my shoes off. It was an incredible relief just to be free of them and I couldn't help wondering why women seemed so keen to put themselves through such ridiculous torture.

'Dad didn't mention anything about Daedalus,' I said as I stepped out of my dress. 'Surely if he knew Simpson, he'd mention him.'

'Not if he needed to protect him,' said Nick. 'That's something else to add to the list of things he hasn't told you.'

I fiddled with the clasp of my necklace unsuccessfully and then, giving up, took the combs out of my hair.

Nick was stretched out on the bed, still clothed and with his legs crossed at the ankle and his hands behind his head.

'We're going to have keep to our travel plans,' he said, 'but go to Crete on a different flight.'

'Why?'

'What if this guy we met wasn't Simpson? Daedalus was supposed to live out the rest of his days in Egypt. Why would he want to go to Crete, knowing it's going to be dangerous?'

'He said he's the only one who can destroy the bad offspring,' I reminded him.

'But he's still going to have to escape Crete to get to Sicily or Egypt. If he is Daedalus, he can retire. If he's not, he has a problem.'

'How do I make contact with the Olympians?' I asked. 'What would Athena do?'

'I don't think you'll have to do anything. They'll contact you. As you said, there are clues to follow, and we won't be the only ones following them. Once the house is destroyed there won't be any more.'

I turned to look at Nick.

'You're enjoying this, aren't you? I think you like the idea of unravelling this puzzle.'

'I do,' he agreed. 'But there's something else you should know. If ever I think you're going to be in danger, then I'll do anything to pull you out of it. Even if that means others are at risk or an illegal drug gets released.'

I dropped my head. 'I love you, too,' I whispered, 'but I don't know how I, or Athena, can protect you.'

'Don't you worry about me,' he said. 'We can make a plan tomorrow. I'll go to the library and use the computers there to change the flight time. There's something I want to check while I'm there, anyway.'

'What do you think we should do first?'

Nick kept his hands behind his head and did half a sit-up to view me better.

'I think,' he said, very seriously, 'you should put your shoes back on.'

It took me almost all day to pack, until I was satisfied that everything was as it should be.

We took an afternoon flight, hoping that Simpson had gone ahead of us.

We were counting on the idea that, because we hadn't used the home computer, he wouldn't be aware that we'd changed the time.

It took us just over four hours to get to Heraklion International and we left the terminal just as the sun was starting to dip below the city walls.

I'd read that much of Crete was home to people from all over the world, who had come for a holiday, fallen in love with the island and settled there, but in Heraklion we found that the usual tourist requirements of modern hotels and brightly lit bars had yet to take over the Venetian influence of the harbour.

After a brief, but bumpy, bus ride, we alighted outside a crumbling fort. We followed directions that led us up a steep slope and on to a large area of flat land overlooking the boats, bobbing by the harbour wall. At the far end of the strip sat a squat two storey building with a balcony on the upper level. A patio at ground level led us to a swimming pool behind the house.

Nick tapped a code into the key safe by the door. 'Let's

check it out inside,' he said.

The modern layout within was sparsely furnished, but everything was of the highest quality. A bright, open plan living space led to a small, well-fitted kitchen at the rear, with windows showing a view of the pool. It all looked beautifully clean.

There were two keys on the key ring that Nick was holding. He pulled one off and handed it to me.

'Here. You should have your own key. Just in case.' He put his arms around me. 'You OK?'

I nodded. 'I'm surprised we don't have a welcoming committee.'

'Don't think about it. We can wait until they make contact. Until then we should just enjoy being here. What would you like to do first?'

'I'm hungry. Let's find somewhere friendly to eat.'

'Really? Without vetting the kitchens?' Nick laughed. 'You're going soft around the edges. I should bring you away more often.'

We decided to leave the modern seafood restaurants behind and crossed the ancient circle of defence walls into the old town.

After about twenty minutes walking, the buildings started to regain their old world charm as the traditional interior slowly revealed itself.

We wandered into a leafy square, where we were drawn by the wonderful smells of home-cooked food, to a dimly lit, but welcoming café called Perdika.

'We need to be careful,' warned Nick. 'We've developed a habit of engaging in uncomfortable conversations in places like this.'

'No, not quite like this,' I said.

Back home, I would never have dreamt of entering a restaurant I hadn't reviewed first, but here in this beautiful place, none of that seemed important.

'This reminds me of RendezBrew,' said Nick, speaking about a coffee shop we used to visit. 'That was family owned, too. They used to sell these lovely little pastries. A bit embarrassing, though...'

'They were using the same cloths to clean all the steam nozzles,' I protested. 'I just had to complain.'

'...Might be a while before I can go back there again.'

We asked for a bottle of the Archanes wine, and although our meals were chicken and fish, the wine was a deep, fragrant red, thick enough to coat the mouth. Thereafter, every forkful was enhanced with a rich, berry flavour.

'We'll have to get a taxi back to the house,' said Nick looking at his watch. 'We won't be able to find our way in the dark.'

We asked the owners if they had a number, but the motherly proprietor insisted that her son would drive us back.

A tall and lanky young man in his early twenties hobbled towards us, promising that it would be no trouble. A pronounced limp hindered the left side of his body.

'I was born in this region,' he said, speaking excellent

English. 'It will only be five minutes in the car.'

We buckled ourselves into the back as the young man slid behind the wheel.

'We're staying in the house above the fort,' said Nick.

'I know,' he said raising an eyebrow at me in the rear view mirror. 'I've been waiting to talk to you all evening.'

Chapter 32

Nick instinctively reached for my hand.

'The name of your café is Perdika. That means partridge. Perdix. Daedalus's nephew and apprentice. '

'You can call me Perry.'

'Stop this car immediately!' Nick reached for the door. 'Stop and let us out!'

Perry remained calm and didn't even raise his voice. 'The doors will stay locked while the car is in motion. All I'm asking of you is four more minutes of your time.'

'So this is the Welcoming Committee.' I glanced at Nick. 'How did you get us to come here?'

'All I did,' said Perry, keeping his eyes on the road, 'Is to arrange to have one of our business cards slipped in with your tickets. It is really quite surprising how little persuasion people need.'

I gripped Nick's hand a little tighter. 'What do you want with us?'

'It is perfectly simple,' he replied. 'When you meet with the Olympians, I want you to tell them that I have a better alternative to Iapyx.'

I decided to gamble with my response. 'I think they already know. It's not you they're interested in. They want

Daedalus. They want your uncle. He seemed very keen to disrupt Fireflight's plans, even knowing it would be dangerous.'

Nick frowned. 'How can he be your uncle?' he asked. 'Simpson is English and an old man.'

Perry snorted. 'He has lived in England many years, but he is no more English than you are Greek. And he has spat on my ideas all my life.'

'What did he do to you?' I asked.

'A car crash,' said Perry. 'He tells me he is going away for business. He will be back in a few days, I may have his car. He flies to London. I nearly die and he does not come back. Deilos! Now I work in Mama's restaurant; all my plans, all my education, all my hopes – gone.'

'What makes you think they'll listen to me? I don't even know if we'll make it back to London.' Nick shot me a worried look. 'Now that we're away from the British police, I mean.'

But Perry laughed.

'You are a goddess. They will listen. You are safer here than in London. Here is Greece, here is home.'

'London has always been my home.'

'Here is better. Important people eat at Perdika. They say you are always worried, you are always concerned. Here you sit, eat, laugh.'

'What important people?'

'I am sure you will meet them.'

'I'm surprised you didn't try to poison me.'

Perry raised his eyebrows again. 'You are a goddess,' he repeated. 'You eat the best. Here is home.'

I was about to argue again when I realised we had reached the house. The car slowed to a stop and the doors clicked. Perry turned in his seat to look directly at me.

'You will tell them. He owes me this.'

Nick did not give me the time to reply as he pushed his door open and pulled me from the car. No sooner had he slammed the door, than Perry pulled away into the night. Nick had held on to my hand the whole journey back and was still holding it now.

'Whatever happens next,' he said, 'I'm coming with you. I'm not letting you out of my sight.'

'Do we have some strong coffee?' I asked. 'I think I need some.'

Nick held up a hand to silence me. The front door was ajar. He burst on through, yelling at the top of his lungs.

'Stay right where you are, I'm armed!'

If there was a better way to get shot at, I didn't think I knew it, but the old man at the kitchen counter was holding bread, not a gun. Simpson was standing with his arms aloft, frozen mid-mouthful.

'Oh, dear God.' I put my hand to my chest to calm my heart. 'What the hell are you doing here?'

Simpson looked confused as he swallowed carefully. 'This is my house.' Now, I detected a slight accent that he didn't have in London.

Nick slumped on the sofa and used his toes to push off

his shoes. 'I had hoped to give you the slip,' he said.

'You did, but I still had to come. You were not the late night visitors I was expecting.'

'Our driver didn't insist on coffee,' I said as I moved towards the kitchen. 'If he had, things might be a little different.'

'We've just met Perry,' explained Nick.

Simpson nodded slowly. 'Oh.'

From a tall, narrow pot on the hob came the strong, almost bitter smell of Greek coffee. I looked for the coffee cups. 'Will he know you are here?'

'He will by the time he returns to the café.' Simpson took his cup and sat on the other end of the sofa. 'Which means that we will have to plan tomorrow even more carefully.'

'We?!' Nick turned to face Simpson. 'We? I'm not trusting you as far as I could spit!'

'You don't have to trust me. But you will have to trust Athena.' Here, both of them looked at me. 'You must let the coffee sit for a few minutes before you drink it, my dear. It's unfiltered.'

I took two cups into the living area and, handing one to Nick, sat in a chair opposite the men.

'You'd better fill me in, then.' I said.

Simpson cleared his throat.

'I have been called before the Olympians, myself. This is what happens.' He leant forward on his knees to explain.

'Most Greeks start the day early, before it gets too hot. About seven-thirty tomorrow morning a car will come for you. It will be a nice car, luxurious. The back door will open automatically and the car will not move until you close it. You will not see the driver. The windows are tinted; you can see out, but no one can see in. You will be driven to a business complex or a grand hotel, whichever the Olympians think is most appropriate. An enforcer will be waiting for you when you arrive.'

'An enforcer?'

'A bodyguard. He will open the car door for you and scan you with an electronic wand to check for devices. Don't take your phone. He will take you to your meeting. You will be led through a rear entrance and escorted through the staff areas. The Gods will be waiting for you. After the meeting, the same things will happen, exactly in reverse.'

'Will I meet all the Gods?'

'No. One will have been appointed to meet you, the others will be listening in on a monitor.'

'From another room?'

'They could be anywhere in Crete. Or Greece.'

'I'm going too,' said Nick.

'If you get in the car,' explained Simpson, patiently, 'you won't be going anywhere. The car is for Athena, no one else.'

'She can't go alone!'

'She doesn't have to. I have a rental car parked by the harbour. I suggest that you and I are in it by seven o'clock. When we see a limo leave the fort road, we follow it. Tonight, I will take the second bedroom.'

I stared at the remains in my coffee cup. 'Any advice you

can give me?'

'Be brave. Athena is brave and clear headed. Don't forget that you are a goddess. Stay calm. You have every right to express your opinions and concerns. And of course, gather as much information as you can. I want to find out where Iapyx is hidden.'

'Wouldn't Iapyx be in Athens? You're taking a lot of risks being in Crete.'

'And taking Kim along for the ride,' added Nick.

Simpson took a gulp of coffee. 'Yes. You're right. And I'm sorry for having to ask this of you. But until I know where Iapyx is, we are all in danger.' He dropped his head and spoke more quietly. 'Perry's car crash happened in Athens and I came here to work on Iapyx before leaving for London. By the time Perry and Sofika arrived here, I was already in the UK.'

Nick put down his cup. 'Wow. No wonder Perry's so angry.'

Simpson reached into his pocket and pulled out a folded piece of paper. Nestled within was a shiny black vinyl dot.

'This is a transmitting device. Just in case we lose you. When the enforcer scans you, he'll run the wand over your clothes and around your head, but they never wave it in front of the face. The only place you can hide this is under your tongue. You will have to have this in your mouth before you get in the car, but transfer it to the outside of your body so that I..' he glanced at Nick, '...we can get a signal. That will have to be at some time between the enforcer and the meeting room.'

'What should I wear?'

'Something smart. This is a business meeting.'

I nodded my understanding.

'There is something else that Athena would have, that you don't.'

I looked up, startled. 'What's that?'

Simpson was holding a pretty little diamond and pearl lapel pin.

'A weapon. Don't be alarmed,' he said. 'It's just in case.' Simpson removed the little gold button from the end of the pin. 'To everyone else, it'll look like any other piece of jewellery. But the tip here has been dipped in a powerful anaesthetic.'

'Like Thanatos?'

'No, this is far less dangerous. Athena believed in defence before attack, but if you are attacked, and I mean if, then at least you won't be empty handed.'

Nick ran his hands through his hair.

'I really don't like this. It's all too Mission Impossible for my liking. And I said that I'd never let you out of my sight again.'

'You may have promised Kim,' I said, 'but tomorrow morning I need to be Athena. And she wouldn't put anybody but herself in danger unless it was unavoidable. At least, this Athena wouldn't.'

Simpson smiled. 'Now you're talking like a goddess!'

'Well,' I said, clapping my hands on my knees. 'I suggest

we follow this coffee with some hot milk and see if we can get some sleep. Rest before battle.' I smiled at Nick. He did not smile back.

Chapter 33

At seven twenty-five, before the sun had reached the harbour wall, I was standing outside the house with my eyes fixed on the fort road. The sharp edges of the vinyl dot were cutting into the soft underside of my tongue.

Simpson and Nick had left the house while it was still dark and despite my assertions to Nick that I'd be fine, my stomach was turning cartwheels.

I smoothed down the folds of my white, layered dress. It was the same one I'd worn to dinner with my father. Not having brought any business clothes with me, I could only hope that this was suitable. I tried not to look at the lapel pin on my right shoulder.

Soon enough, the long beams of a car's headlights arced across the front of the house. An executive looking car stopped in front of me and a rear door swung open. As the car reached the fort road, I had to hope that Nick and Simpson were close by. I was too scared to dare look behind.

Within about ten minutes, we reached a smart hotel and drove into the underground car park. The car stopped by the elevators where a stern young man was waiting. I closed my eyes as he scanned me, but he obviously didn't find anything as he turned towards the elevators and said, 'this way, please.'

I quickly lifted the tracker from my mouth and pressed it into the folds of my dress.

There was no conversation on the journey up to the twelfth floor, only the whirring of the elevator gears. Six doors along the corridor, the enforcer inserted a keycard and opened the door for me. It clicked shut behind me quietly and efficiently.

'Come in and have some breakfast,' said a woman. 'I'm sure you haven't eaten yet.'

I walked into a spacious room designed like the parlour of a stately home and couldn't help looking over my shoulder.

A smartly dressed woman in her fifties was sitting at a table loaded with food.

'Clever, isn't it?' she said. 'You'd think that the corridor is the same as any other, with several rooms. But, in fact there are only three on each side. We made sure the corridor remained the same.'

I sat at the breakfast table and watched as she poured me coffee from a similar pot to the one Simpson had used.

'I hope you don't mind that I ordered breakfast without you. You must let the coffee sit for a moment...'

'It's unfiltered,' I interrupted.

'You're learning something about us,' she said, impressed. 'I am Hera.' She paused a moment to let the name sink in. 'And you, Athena, are something of a trouble maker.'

I reached for some thick yoghurt and fruit, willing my hands not to shake. 'You know why I'm here?'

Hera nodded, her black curls bouncing on the top of her head. 'You want to ask us to halt our plans for the use of Demeter and Persephone in our next procedure.'

'Yes.'

Hera laughed as if a child had just told her a joke. 'That is not going to happen. You have no authority in Crete. Perhaps you'll consider Athens for your next holiday.'

'Then why did you agree to see me?'

'I didn't. I was told to meet you. I will answer your questions, listen to your arguments and then discuss them with the Olympians. But you should know that the programme is already too far advanced to be stopped now.'

'Even if it's dangerous, or ineffective?'

'You've already met Hephaestus, I see.'

'Isn't he supposed to be your son?'

'Only in mythology.' Hera smiled as she sipped her coffee. 'None of the Olympians are related by blood.'

'Then how do you choose the twelve?'

'Entry to our circle is strictly by invitation only.'

I threw my spoon back onto the table. 'I'm supposed to be a goddess, too. I wasn't invited, I was kidnapped!'

Hera did not raise her voice. She was doing a better job of keeping her cool than me. 'Athena is not known to have had a child. You have nothing to fear, your name has already been dropped from the programme.'

'But it's not just about me!' I shouted, forgetting all about Simpson's advice to stay calm. 'What about those other women in poorer countries? You're using an uncontrolled drug to experiment on them, so you can further your ridiculous eugenics theory!'

'Ridiculous?' Hera's eyes suddenly looked very dark. 'You think that what we are trying to achieve is ridiculous?' She returned her coffee cup to the table carefully. 'The requirement of better equipped people depends on the creation of better medicines.'

I could feel steam rising off the back of my neck. 'And how much money does this make for you?' I asked.

Hera leant forward slightly, causing me to move back.

'Let me tell you something,' she whispered. 'Every time we demand better medicines for something – anything – someone, somewhere has to sit at a board table and financially justify why it would be in the pharmaceutical company's best interests to produce it. We focus on the creation of the right drugs for the right people; those who can best benefit the population as a whole.'

'But medicine should follow the needs of the people!'

'It does, but business follows the money.'

'Then that is what I will do,' I said. 'I will follow your money and find Iapyx. Unless you can save me some time and tell me now?'

Hera's eyes widened slightly. She obviously didn't know that I'd been told of Iapyx, which probably also meant that she hadn't yet been told Simpson was back in Crete.

'What do you know about Iapyx?'

'I know that you have kept its creation private, and you can't close your operations without it. I'm assuming this means that you can't destroy the evidence of Persephone or Demeter without it. I have also met Perdix. He says he has a better option.'

'And what is this better option?'

'He didn't say, but he made me promise to tell you.'

Hera nodded. 'Do you play chess, Athena?' she asked.

'No.'

'You should. You'd be very good at it. You play standard moves and let your opponent think that they're winning, and then make a surprising one.'

Assuming that our meeting was over, I rose to leave.

'Get away from Crete, Athena,' warned Hera. 'You have no business here.'

Back in the car park, the limo was waiting for me with the door open, but suddenly, a small, red hatchback squealed around the side of the car, blocking it in.

Simpson jumped from the driver's side, running towards me.

'Where is it? Where is Iapyx? Tell me!'

'I don't know. Hera didn't say. Maybe she doesn't know.'

The enforcer jumped in between Simpson and me.

'Get back,' he ordered. 'Stay away from Athena.'

Nick opened the passenger side of the rental and called over to me.

'Kim, are you all right?'

Momentarily distracted, the enforcer let go of Simpson and moved towards the younger and fitter man. Simpson, now free, grabbed hold of my shoulders and started shaking me.

'Where is it? Where is Iapyx?' he yelled.

'I don't know, she didn't tell me anything.'

'You must know something. You don't understand. It's a part of me. If I can't destroy it, I'll never be free.'

Nick and the enforcer were engaged in a fight of their own. 'Get your hands off her,' yelled Nick.

Simpson tightened his grip and shook harder. 'Tell me something! Tell me where to look.'

'You're hurting me!'

He shook me again. I barely realised what I was doing as I tried to defend myself. I pulled the lapel pin from my dress and thought I heard the cap ping as it bounced on the concrete. I stabbed Simpson in the shoulder and he let go of me with a deep, ear-ringing yell.

Everything then seemed to simply stop, as he clutched his shoulder and slid down the side of the car.

Chapter 34

I ran to the driver's door, leaving Simpson slumped against the car. Yanking open the door, I pointed my finger at the terrified looking man within.

'I am Athena. You will take Daedalus and I to the Palace at Knossos.' With eyes wide he nodded mutely and I turned my attention to the enforcer.

'Move away from my husband!' Much to my surprise, he did.

'Simpson must have had a bag and his passport when he arrived,' I said to Nick.

'I need you to go back to the house and find them. Take them to Heraklion airport. We'll meet you there.'

'But Kim,' he protested.

'Please, just do it.' Nick's scared expression broke my heart. 'Go!'

I didn't have time to watch Nick leave as I bundled Simpson into the back of the car.

'I can't believe you stabbed me with my own invention,' he said.

'Isn't that what the Olympians usually do?' I replied.

Simpson smiled. 'Why are we going to Knossos?'

'That's where the labyrinth is supposed to have been built.

I think it's a likely place for Iapyx to be hidden, assuming that we can get there before the other Olympians.' I knocked on the dividing screen between us and the driver. 'Hurry!'

'That makes sense.' Simpson's head nodded and he raised a hand to his head. 'The anaesthetic is starting to take effect.'

'You need to stay awake until we get there. It'll probably be another ten minutes.'

Simpson shook his head. 'I'll be unconscious by then. Listen carefully and I'll tell you what to do.'

'Open your eyes,' I instructed, patting his face. 'Don't fall asleep.'

'No, listen. The labyrinth was a prison system with restricted ways in and out. Iapyx needs to be kept cool, below fifteen degrees Celsius, so it's probably in one of the cave systems. Iapyx is a liquid and a powder which become toxic when combined. It's powerful but can be destroyed easily.'

'How?'

'Vinegar. Isolate the powder and coat with vinegar. Perry would know what to do. Will he be there?'

'Are you expecting him?'

'Always.'

'He blames you for the accident.'

'That was no accident.' Simpson coughed and his head nodded forward again. 'He thinks the other car crashed into mine believing I was driving. But I think Perry was the target.'

'Why do you think that?'

'Perry went to university at a very young age. He was a prodigy. I told him not to brag of his achievements, it would attract the wrong attention.'

'Especially as you had spent so long hiding under the radar.'

'Stupid boy. Those hospital bills... So expensive...'

The car started to slow and already I could see the reconstructed buildings in the complex.

'We're here,' I said. 'Simpson, we're here.' But Simpson had already slid down and was half lying with his head against the back of the seat. I tried patting his face again, but he wouldn't wake. I banged on the partition and the driver slid back the screen.

'Wait for me,' I instructed. 'I'll be as quick as I can.'

At the entrance to the complex, tourist guides were calling out to the visitors, some were attempting to push brochures into the sightseers' hands to encourage a sale. I dodged past the waving arms and pamphlets and ducked into the main entrance. My heart dropped when I saw the queue for tickets.

I knew that the Olympians would be close behind me; I didn't have the time to politely queue. I had an idea. I ran towards the information kiosk and, ignoring everyone else there, leaned across to the flustered lady at the desk. She was taking a call on her headset, tapping on a computer keyboard and answering questions from a tourist, all at the same time.

'You need to stop what you are doing and get me your manager immediately.'

The woman looked up, but gave me nothing more than a withering look. The middle-aged man at the desk started waving his arms and yelling at me in Italian. I reached across the desk and grabbed the lapels of the woman's uniform, lifting her a couple of inches from her chair.

'I am Athena, and you will get him now!'

The poor woman stared back at me, startled and nodded. I released her and she snatched off her headset and hurried to the door at the back of the kiosk. Just a couple of seconds later, a smartly dressed man with a bored expression followed her back to her desk and demanded to know who had called for him.

'Athena,' I said. 'I want you to show me Iapyx.'

The man and woman exchanged a glance and then he looked back at me.

'This way. I'll take you there.'

At the back of the kiosk, a small battery powered buggy sat waiting. The manager sat in the driver's seat and indicated that I should sit beside him.

'I have been waiting for this introduction for many years,' he said. 'I am Mr Janus. It is an honour to meet one of the Fireflight.'

'I'm going to need vinegar,' I said, ignoring his hint at a desire for promotion. 'Lots and lots of vinegar.'

'Of course, whatever you wish,' he replied, as if I had asked for nothing more than a bag of chips to go with it. 'We have an excellent catering kiosk very nearby.'

'How fast can this buggy travel?' I asked.

'This one has the most excellent speed of 24 kilometres an hour,' he said.

'It would be most excellent if that was the speed we were

doing.'

The manager's smile faded, but he did obligingly put his foot down.

The catering kiosk provided two large plastic containers of dark vinegar, all they had, and I hoped and prayed it would be enough.

The faster the buggy travelled, the bumpier the ride, but after a few minutes we arrived at the labyrinth complex.

'What would you like to see first?' asked Janus. 'Perhaps the café? Perhaps the water park? Perhaps the maze? We have an employee who wears the minotaur mask for the children.'

Unfortunately, I didn't have time to be nice. I gripped his tie and pulled his face a little closer.

'Perhaps the cave system where Iapyx is stored?'

Janus swallowed and nodded. 'There is very little of the caves left,' he said, readjusting his tie. 'But I will take you there.'

'Who else knows where Iapyx is stored?' I asked.

'I am a man of honour, I assure you. I would not tell anyone that you were here.'

I gripped his tie again. 'Who else?'

'Zeus, Hera and Hephaestus.'

'Oh, great,' I sighed. 'All the big guns.'

'Wonderful, is it not?' agreed the manager.

I followed him through a wooden door in the fence surrounding the children's play area and mini-maze and along a rough, pebbled path. Parents shouted directions from a viewing platform while their children ran between stone painted barriers.

Large overgrown bushes obscured a hole in the rocky hill that formed the backdrop to the maze. Crouching low, I followed for about three metres into increasing gloom before the ceiling expanded and we were able to stand upright.

Suddenly, bright light filled the space and I realised I was in a central area with corridors of caves all around me. Janus was standing by the entrance to the one from which we had just emerged, with his fingers on the light switch.

'Through there,' he said, pointing ahead. 'I will wait here for you.'

'There are no doors down here. How do you maintain security?'

The manager shrugged. 'Who is to know? Who will come?'

I followed the direction of his finger into a corridor three or four metres long, leading into a room only slightly bigger than my bedroom at home. There was a lab bench along the right hand side and a desk with a closed laptop on the far left. Beside the desk, along the left wall, were two large, open fronted chiller cabinets, with transparent plastic draped over the front. Behind the plastic were half a dozen rows of jars and bottles with neatly printed labels in Greek. I had no idea how I was going to find what I was looking for.

The first cabinet didn't contain anything I recognised, but on the top shelf of the second cabinet I saw several small plastic crates holding glass ampoules, each about an inch in diameter and about five inches high. The left hand row of each contained a thick, clear liquid. The right hand row contained a dense, white powder.

I placed the bottles of vinegar on the desk. On the lab bench behind me, I found a box of disposable gloves and a small plastic bowl. I pulled the powder ampoules from the crates and broke the foil seals across the top, tipping the contents into the bowl. I then poured over the vinegar. The powder foamed and hissed as the vinegar made contact. I repeated the process with all the powder I could see and brought the bowl out to the central area.

'Where can I find a sink?' I asked, but Janus was gone. I tried my luck with another corridor and found a similar room, luckily with a sink, and ran cold water over the bowl.

'Well? Where is she? She has already taken the powder!'

The woman's voice was close and clearly irritated. I was not where she expected to find me.

I put down the bowl and peeled off the gloves, slowly walking towards the entrance of the room.

'You told me she would be here,' said Hera. 'Where is she now? Find her!'

Janus ran from the first room and across to another corridor. I tiptoed forward and hurried past the first room just as Hera turned around.

'She's here! Get her!'

I hurried forward, ducking my head through the entrance corridor, and retraced my steps along the path and back to the children's maze. As I ran through the gate in the fence, a man using a mobile phone turned around and spotted me.

I recognised him as the enforcer at the hotel. Looking back over my shoulder, I saw Janus already running along the pebble path. The enforcer started a slow jog towards me. I closed my eyes against the thought of what might come.

'Oh, dear God, no.'

A high pitched squeal of tyres made everyone redirect their attention as a small and nimble motorbike came to a halt between the enforcer and me.

'Quickly!' shouted Perry, holding out a crash helmet. 'Get on!'

Chapter 35

Tourists were already turning to point at the prohibited vehicle frightening their children. Perry accelerated past the onlookers, while others grabbed their children's hands and dragged them out of the way.

'We have to get Simpson to the airport,' I yelled in Perry's ear. 'My husband is waiting for us there.'

'I know,' yelled Perry. 'His bag and passport were already in the boot of the rental car. Your husband didn't go back to the house. He came to fetch me.'

We had now reached the entrance to the complex and I could see another car parked across the road from ours, also with tinted windows.

'Quick,' I yelled, dismounting. 'Get in the car.'

Once inside, Perry pulled a small leather pouch from his jacket and unwrapped a vial and a needle.

'What on earth are you going to do with that?'

'I need to give you a sample,' said Perry. 'Uncle left this with me for safe keeping. You will need his blood.' Simpson groaned and opened his eyes as the needle went in, but didn't protest.

'Why?'

'Every drug that Fireflight create is special. Each one is

somehow tied to its creator. This is how they keep their members faithful. You will need to mix the blood with liquid Iapyx to destroy it. My version does not need the powder. I will destroy it myself.'

'Why did you create your one?' I asked.

'I wanted money,' he replied. 'As much as I could get.'

'Dangerous,' whispered Simpson. 'I tried to warn you.'

'You need coffee, old man,' said Perry. 'Greek coffee, to fight the drug.'

'You may still get your wish,' I said. 'Fireflight may come to you, after all.'

'But now I have changed my mind.'

'You're a smart young man, Perry. You might change your mind, but Fireflight won't. Why not take over Perdika and let them use it as a meeting place? You said that important people ate there. You may have to persuade your mother that it's time to retire...'

Perry narrowed his eyes at me while he considered my proposal. 'How would I get in touch with you?'

'You'll have to be careful,' I said. 'But I know you're resourceful.'

Perry handed me the vial.

'How did you find me?' I said, suddenly remembering to ask.

Perry grinned and pulled what looked like a sat-nav screen from his pocket. I touched my dress and found the shiny black dot hidden in the folds.

'Here, take it. I won't need it any more. But I do need to

borrow your bike.'

I sent the car to the airport to meet Nick, and donning the helmet once more, I straddled Perry's bike. It had been a few years since I'd ridden a motorbike, but I had to pull this off, for Simpson's sake. I watched the car speed away and hoped that I could draw Hera's attention, if only for an hour.

The electric buggy shuddered to a halt at the complex entrance.

'The car!' screamed Hera. She and the enforcer ran towards the vehicle as I revved and raced away.

I followed my memory along the main roads and back towards the harbour, finally allowing myself to breath out when I saw the fort up ahead.

I parked the bike just in front of the house and risked a quick peek behind me as I fumbled for the key, hoping that Hera would stay with me and not head for the airport.

Still wearing the crash helmet, I ran up the stairs to the first floor bedroom and through the French windows to the balcony. From here I could see across the harbour, to the boats and yachts on my left, and on my right, the old city walls encircling the heart of ancient Crete; little protection against the bright lights of encroaching modernity.

The city airport was invisible from here, lost in the haze of another hot day, but a stretch of clear land gave away the location of the runway.

'Athena.'

I turned to see Hera walking across the bedroom. She suddenly laughed and pointed to my head.

'What do you think I'm going to do to you?'

I held up the small vial of blood. 'I think you're going to fight me for this.'

Hera ran forward on to the balcony and made a grab for the vial. I took a step back and swung my arm out over the railing. The poolside patio was just below.

'One more step and I'm letting go.'

Hera softened her expression and tried to look friendly. 'We're alone,' she smiled. 'Just you and me. I sent the driver back with the car and my enforcer took the bike back to the café.'

'And how are you getting home?' I asked. 'Local taxi?'

'We won't be disturbed. We can talk.'

'Well, let's talk about why you want to save this blood rather than destroy it. You know that it can destroy liquid Iapyx, so why not just get rid of it?'

'Iapyx is already being moved to a new location,' said Hera. 'The powder can be recreated.'

'So why would you want the blood?'

Hera's eyes never left the vial, but she couldn't answer.

'Because it's Daedalus's,' I said, answering my own question. I lifted the helmet up on to the back of my head and watched Hera's expression change with each new emotion. 'Each drug is connected to its creator. Now I understand. Perdix's version would suit your plans, but it would be him. You've lost Daedalus. You don't want to counteract Iapyx or create an antidote, you want to control it.'

'We don't need Daedalus, only his DNA profile. We will reclaim it.' Hera finally met my eyes. 'We reclaimed your mother's.'

'My mother worked to derail your operations. A double agent, if you like. Did you know that she was creating an antidote to Thanatos? She was not the only one.' I leant forward to whisper confidentially. 'Me too. And there are others.'

'She thought she was clever,' spat back Hera. 'Daedalus, too. But we still have sufficient information.'

'Yes,' I said wriggling the vial between my finger and thumb. 'And here it is.'

Hera screamed and lurched forward. She flung herself over me, pushing my back against the railings. We both gasped as the vial flew from my hand and spun in the air. It hit the ground with a sharp ting and bounced once, twice, flipping towards the pool. The vial stopped on the aluminium drainage grating at the pool's edge where the plastic safety cap finally cracked and the blood slowly trickled through the gaps. As the water from the pool lapped over the edge, tiny puddles of pink seeped back into the water.

Both of us were still for a moment and then we locked at each other. Hera let out a frustrated gasp before turning her anger towards me. She clutched at my throat with one hand, while the other grabbed at the helmet. I choked against her grip and fell to my knees.

'You stupid bitch!' she hissed. 'Do you have any idea what you've just done?'

‘Let me go. Hera, please...’

‘All our work, all our planning. Now we will have to find another source.’

I scratched against the inside of Hera’s wrist, but she seemed not to feel it. Wriggling my right arm, I reached up and shoved the heel of my hand against Hera’s nose. She let go with a squeal and stumbled backwards. I quickly stood and raised a hand.

‘Stop right there!’ I demanded. ‘I am a goddess and not even you have the authority to hurt me. If you lay another finger on me, I’ll have you explaining yourself to Zeus within the hour.’

Hera raised a finger to her nose and wiped away a smear of blood. She was breathing heavily and still trembling with rage. She pointed directly at my face.

‘You will pay for this. I have allies of my own. True allies. The Fireflight faithful.’ Hera backed away and was halfway into the bedroom before she turned to run down the stairs. ‘You will pay!’

I heard the front door slam and although I leant over the side of the balcony, I could not see the direction she went.

I spread my hands over the balcony railings and tried to calm my breathing. All I had wanted since this nightmare began was for everything to go back to the way it was. But I knew that was impossible. Simpson was right; as Kim I was vulnerable. Athena was my only protection.

I looked across the shimmering landscape and thought of Simpson and Daedalus and how strange it is that anyone, or perhaps all of us sometimes, can be so stupid and so brilliant.

The land seemed to respond to my thoughts as the shimmer shifted and an aeroplane pierced the haze as it rose to the sky.

Chapter 36

Two cups of strong Greek coffee later, I heard the door as Nick finally returned. I ran to hug him, but he pushed me away and pointed to the red marks on my neck.

'What the hell is this?'

'I'm fine. I've experienced worse.'

'I should have been here.'

'Nick you can't be with me constantly. You were where you needed to be. Did Simpson get a plane?'

'Yes. He's on his way to Egypt. Perry gave him coffee, which seemed to perk him up. We told the airport staff that he was unwell, but returning home. They arranged to have a doctor meet him when he lands. He'll be fine by tomorrow.'

'I didn't have the chance to return the pin.'

'Keep it. You never know when it might come in handy.'

I smiled. 'I don't intend on using it again.'

'Then I'll look after it for you.'

I slumped on to the sofa and rubbed my eyes. 'I am very tired.'

'I bet you are.' Nick sat beside me and held my hand. 'But here's some news that should make you happy.'

'Oh, yes?'

'Do you remember when I went into town to change the

flight times? I sent a personal email. I didn't want to use my iphone or the home PC.'

'I remember. What's happened?'

'DCI Little emailed me back. When you told him the account code you gave to Fireflight, he contacted a personal friend and requested an alert to be made against that number. It got a red flag.'

'So they've tried to access that money.'

'They've already moved that money.'

'What?! If the account was being watched, that should have been stopped! Are the police in on this?'

'Kim, it's not illegal to try to access your own money. The most that Little could have done is ask to be notified when someone made a withdrawal.'

'But it's illegal money! It needs to be confiscated!' I could not understand why Nick was not agreeing with me.

'They can't prove that the money was illegally acquired.' Nick stood up, frustrated. 'I thought you'd be pleased with this news. The police have something they can track.'

'That money shouldn't have been allowed to go anywhere!'

'The police can't follow something that isn't moving, Kim!'

'Moving to where? To do what? I can't bear to imagine what that money could be used for.'

'You want an answer that's going to tie everything up into a neat little bow before we go home. Well, I'm sorry. I don't have an answer to give you. The Company isn't working to any script I'm familiar with.'

'If we can't stop the money, we can't stop Fireflight's operations!'

'We? Who's we? Leave the police to get on with it. Can't we just enjoy the rest of our time here? We're going back home tomorrow.'

I didn't answer and sat in sulky silence while Nick made himself a sandwich.

'We should have a snack and then a siesta while the weather is hot,' he said. 'Let's go down to the harbour and find a little seafood restaurant this evening.'

I felt guilty holding on to a dark mood while Nick was trying to placate me, but I knew that if I didn't find some sort of resolution while in Crete, dread was going to follow me back to London.

'Nick, how did you find that Little had been in touch with you? Did you pick that up on your iphone?'

'Yes, why?'

'Here in Crete?'

Nick looked up, bewildered. 'Half an hour ago.'

'Then they'll probably know...'

'Who will know what?' Nick was starting to get annoyed again.

'The Company will know that we're tracking their money. That could be a good thing. It'll make them more cautious.'

'You're speaking in riddles again. What are you talking about?'

For a moment, I couldn't respond; I had to order my

thoughts first.

'Who takes care of the financial operations at the University?'

'The finance office. Everything has to go through them.'

'So who gets the bank statements?'

'They do. I have a departmental debit card and get sent a summary of our spending, but finance deal with the statements and accounts.'

'Exactly!'

'Kim, riddles...'

I smiled. 'I was being tested. Why would a manager of a small business, who verifies statements and has access to company accounts, need to ask someone junior for the account numbers and access codes? His authority was supposed to trump mine.'

Nick thought for a moment. 'Well, maybe he never needed to know before. You took care of that for him.'

'But why kidnap me to get that information, when all he had to do was send a request to finance?' I looked back at Nick's confused expression and answered the question for him. 'Because he wasn't working for Brownlow Print when he demanded it. He was working for Fireflight.'

'But Brownlow Print was just a cover for Fireflight, wasn't it?'

'I think Fireflight infiltrated Brownlow Print, or else they got to Tony first. Tony didn't ask me for that account code, Hermes did.'

'When we went to dinner with your father, he told you

to think of what had happened to you as a test.'

I nodded. 'Yes, and I'm still being tested. How brave am I? How do I create allies or make enemies? Tony was tested as Hermes. What would he do to get that account code? How far would he go? He complied with the kidnapping and persuasion, but baulked at my inclusion into a programme.'

'Do you think it's a coincidence that you, his finance manager, and Athena were the same person?'

'Absolutely not! I don't think anything Fireflight does is a coincidence.'

'What about you? What's happening with you?'

'I'm being treated as two separate people, Kim and Athena.' I counted the things that had happened to me on my fingers. 'Kim was kidnapped, Athena planned escape. Kim revealed account codes, Athena thought of a way to track them. Kim came to Crete, Athena fought with Hera. It was disturbingly easy to find Iapyx...'

Nick put down his sandwich and nodded while he followed my line of thinking.

'Like putting a jar of sweeties in front of a child and watching what they'll do,' he agreed. 'But if you become Athena, you'll be playing straight into their hands.'

'I vowed to stop them. This may be the only way.'

'What are you going to do?'

I looked into Nick's panic filled eyes.

'I'm going to drop a poison pill in their sweetie jar.'

Chapter 37

I didn't want a sandwich, but somehow managed to convince Nick that I'd be fine after a nap.

I waited until he was softly snoring and the sky had turned pink before I left the bedroom. I hid my phone in a kitchen drawer.

Wearing loose fitting trousers and a soft blouse, I grabbed a jacket and crept from the house, looking for the car that I was sure would be watching. About twenty yards away was a sleek Mercedes with tinted windows. The rear door opened as I approached.

'To Perdika, please.'

The car glided forward and I sat in silence until we arrived.

I was surprised to find the restaurant closed. The front door was shut and the lights outside the windows were out. I knocked tentatively and was relieved when Perry opened the door.

'Ah, you are here,' he said without any hint of surprise. 'Good. Now we can eat.'

'I've left your spare motorcycle helmet in the car.'

'Thank you for returning it.' Perry led me through the restaurant to the private rooms in the back. The welcoming smell of home was coming from the kitchen and a small table had been laid with three places.

'You were expecting me?'

'Of course. Your enforcer called me. We closed for you.'

Perry noticed the alarm in my face and laughed. 'You have no reason to worry. Your enforcer isn't here to harm you. He carries out your wishes; he is here to protect you.'

Perry indicated for me to sit.

'Mamma, our guest is here,' he called. An answer came from the kitchen and Perry rolled his eyes. 'Give her wine, give her olives,' he translated. 'Always the best for Athena.' He poured me a glass of thick, rich, red with a Burgundy aroma. 'This is very good. Try it.'

I sipped nervously. 'I came because there's a couple of things I need to ask you.'

'Yes, and you were right, of course. Hera has already visited Perdika. She says Fireflight may have a place for me. You warned me, and you were right.'

'What made you change your mind?'

'Mamma worries always about money, but who will own New Iapyx? I worry about who will control it. And me.'

'You said you were going to destroy it. Have you done that yet?'

'Not yet.'

'Perry, when Fireflight contact you again, I want you to tell them that there's a fault with New Iapyx. There doesn't have to be, but that's what I want you to tell them.'

Perry looked surprised, but nodded his agreement.

'As Athena requests.'

'How much control do you think Fireflight has here in Crete?'

'As much as they want. But this is not control of people, this is about control of power. It does not matter what the power is; medicine, oil, money. It's about who controls it and how. Mamma says that when they say they are making a better world for all of us…' Perry circled a finger over a bowl of olives, 'that does not mean a better world for all of them.' He moved his finger to circle over a dish of sweet peppers. 'The unworthy ones.'

'Your uncle's blood was destroyed, I'm afraid.'

Perry shrugged. 'Unfortunate that you could not use it, but better destroyed than in their hands. You helped Uncle escape. Mamma is grateful.'

As if on cue, Mamma came from the kitchen and carefully placed a heavy dish on the table. She sat and smiled at me as she patted my hand.

'Grateful. Efcharisto.' Signalling for my plate, she ladled on sweet smelling lamb stew.

'This is Youvetsi,' said Perry. 'You will eat it in Athens, but I think ours is better.'

'Thank you. This is lovely.' My spoon hovered while I wondered how to ask my next question.

'You worry about being part of the resistance, yes?'

I smiled at Perry's use of the wartime expression, but it seemed appropriate. 'I vowed that I would find the money they use. We've managed to track the account, but I need to find out who handles it from this end.'

Perry chewed thoughtfully. 'In the legends, Plutus is the god of abundance and wealth. He is the son of Demeter.'

I shook my head. 'Demeter is a drug. Wouldn't the son of Demeter also be a drug?'

'No, it doesn't have to be. The Company will use whatever name they need to get what they want. It could be a drug or a person.'

'How do I find out?'

'You will need to speak to your enforcer. He will find the information you need, but they may not be in Crete. And they may not be one person.'

'What do you mean?'

'In business, it is not one person who knows everything, it is many who know only a little. We are talking about money and Fireflight are careful. You must be, too.'

Mamma nodded. 'Posektikos.'

I reached for my jacket and pulled out a key. Strangely, I felt guilty. Of all items of clothing, a jacket, surely, was the most contradictory. A jacket said you were going somewhere. Yet, however comfortable, however casual, a jacket reminded you to leave.

'This is a spare for the house. Nick and I are leaving tomorrow and I don't know if there will be any sign that we were there. You may need this. Just in case.'

'You worry that they will clean away your presence? They did that in England?'

'Yes. I don't even know what happened to my

kidnappers.'

'If they disobeyed the Olympians, they will be dead. Everyone is a small part of a big machine. When they have no more use for us, we are replaced with another small part. If you hear talk of Thanatos, be wary. Thanatos means death.'

I nodded. 'I know, I've heard that before.'

Perry held out his hand to me and Mamma did the same.

'Just promise us that you will take care, and maybe you will return to Crete one day?'

I took their hands and held them tight. 'I will. I promise.'

I left Perdika just after nine, full of wine and stew. I longed for the sleep that would help me digest my dinner, but I had another date waiting for me.

Ignoring the car waiting at the kerbside, I walked towards the one parked five vehicles away. As the driver saw me approach, he manoeuvred from his space and accelerated past me. I saw a passageway to my left and ran down it, exiting into the next street. The car was held in traffic on my right. I ran towards the car, hoping that I could catch it before it made the next turning.

A local bar was doing good trade that evening and I collided with a group of tourists waiting to go in.

'Hey, watch it,' yelled an American voice, as I bumped a shoulder.

'Sorry,' I mumbled, not wanting to take my eyes off the car.

I ran to the corner, but the car turned again, this time

doubling back to pass me in the opposite direction. There was only one way I could stop it.

Stepping out into the traffic, I closed my eyes and a passing van pressed long on the horn, the wind it created ruffling the cotton of my blouse. The car in front of me stopped with a screech of brakes, its engine heat blowing warmth on the front of my legs. I let out a long breath and collapsed my shoulders as my hands came down on the front of the bonnet.

Finding my strength, I marched to the rear doors. I had plenty to say to my personal enforcer; the one who had been keeping secrets from me, the one who had been leading a double life, "protecting" me.

I yanked the door open to give my husband a rude mouthful, but the face that greeted me was not the one I was expecting.

'Now, Kimmie darling, promise you won't be cross.'

Chapter 38

'What the hell...'

Dad smiled. 'Can I give you a lift, darling?'

I climbed into the car and Dad called to the driver. 'To the house, please Henry.'

I sat with my arms folded and waited for my father to speak.

'I'm sure you must have many questions.' When I didn't respond, he continued. 'Fireflight had been watching your mother and I for many years, you already know that. When she returned to them, I offered myself as her enforcer. I still had to carry out Company wishes, but at least I could be around to protect her. We both knew how dangerous it could be, but we both thought that it was a risk worth taking. Melissa fed information back to me, which I passed on to The Network. I had hoped that when we had dinner, you'd understand the danger and stay away, but when I heard you had flown to Crete, I guessed that you'd decided to destabilise their project.'

'Who told you I was in Crete?'

'I have a contact at the airport.'

'When did you get here?'

'This morning.'

I wasn't sure I believed him.

'Have you spoken to Perry?' I asked.

'Yes. I called the restaurant earlier to warn him that you might visit. I'd seen Fireflight visit at lunchtime.'

'I didn't know that you'd been watching me.'

'I wasn't. I was watching the restaurant. Do you think you can trust this young man?'

'I don't know, I've only just recruited him. He called you "the resistance".'

Dad laughed at the term. 'We prefer to call ourselves The Network. It's less antagonistic.'

'What exactly does The Network do?'

'Everything you're doing. We attempt to discover The Company's latest plan, identify the main players and disrupt the money routes. But if you're going to be one of us, darling, you're going to have to play by our rules. You can't go firing off like a loose cannon.'

'I'm already up to my neck in this. Can you protect me?'

'My dear, I've been doing that your whole life.'

'Do I have to sign a contract? Pledge my allegiance?'

'No, not at all. And I'd advise you never to sign anything. You can't trust anyone and The Network runs on deniable operations. If you get caught, anyone will deny that they knew what you were doing.'

'All right. What do I need to know?'

'Well, first of all, if someone has a hidden identity, don't try and expose it without talking to us. I've been told that you saw the face of your driver at the Olympian's hotel.

We've managed to smuggle him out of the country, but workers not directly involved with a project don't have Company protection and won't have a god or goddess status. And nobody leaves The Company.'

'I've been hearing that a lot lately. Anything else?'

'Never record anything, copy anything or retain anything. Whatever you have in your possession can be stolen or observed and used against you. This means that to share information, you'll have to rely solely on memory. It takes some practice, but it's best to share what you've discovered as quickly as possible.'

'OK. Is that it?'

'One last thing.' Dad looked thoughtful for a moment. 'This is hard. You must always consider your own welfare first. If a friend is in danger, of course you'd want to help, but if this puts you in Fireflight's line of fire, don't do it. If they select you for assassination and withdraw your goddess status, they won't be polite enough to inform you beforehand.'

'I understand.'

Dad smiled, seemingly satisfied that I now knew the three golden rules. 'Do you have anything that you'd like to share now?'

'Only a name. Plutus, son of Demeter.'

'Let me think, Plutus... His father was Iasion. Demeter lay with him in a fallow field, thrice ploughed. Plutus was born here in Crete, so I think the best place to start looking for him is in The Valley of Messara. It's the oldest agricultural site in Crete.'

'What if I can't find him?' I asked. 'Is there another way to stop the money?'

'There is always more than one way to stop the money,' said Dad. 'Do you have a smart phone?'

Back at the house, Nick was furious.

'Where the bloody hell have you been? I've been worried sick. And I'm hungry. We were supposed to be going out to dinner.'

'Sorry I'm late back, but I ran into an old friend.'

Nick's mouth fell open when he saw my father standing behind me.

'You'd better take a seat, dear boy. We've got a story to tell.'

I found some eggs in Simpson's fridge and Nick ate an omelette while Dad and I filled him in on the evening's adventures.

'I'd love to find out what's going on at Messara,' he said. 'But we might have to delay our flight home. We're returning to London tomorrow afternoon.'

'Don't change any flight times, just yet. You never know when you might need a quick getaway.' Dad watched as I retrieved my phone. 'You'll both need to get new phones when you get home.'

'Here's The Valley of Messara,' I said. 'It's very beautiful.'

'Ignore anything about tourist holidays, tours of olive groves or vineyards,' instructed Dad. 'Most of that produce is for export, anyway. The information might be hiding in plain sight, but it won't be that obvious.'

I scrolled through my phone. 'That leaves the monastery at Agii Deka, the Minoan archaeological finds in the museum, the horse ranch in Messara and the crop fields bordering Gortys.'

'A fallow field, thrice ploughed. That could be it.'

'What does that even mean?' asked Nick.

'Many farmers still use the rotation system that their ancestors used,' explained Dad. 'You can plough and seed a field three times over, but the next year you must leave it fallow, so that the earth can rest.'

'But which one?' I turned my phone around so that Dad could see it. 'There are many.'

'Well, I would think that the corn, wheat and tomato crops would be the most prolific. Is there a farm which has all three?'

'Um, yes. I've found one.'

'Send a message to their internet page and say that Athena is coming to visit. That'll stick a spoke in their wheel!'

Nick frowned. 'Are you sure that's such a good idea? The first thing they'll do is get in touch with Fireflight.'

'That's what we want. Let's see who puts their head above the parapet.'

'I picked up a map of Crete before we came,' said Nick. He spread the sheet across the kitchen countertop and traced a line with his finger. 'There's a direct link from Heraklion to Messara via the road to Gortys. That should take about forty-five minutes. We'll have to get up early if I'm to hire a car.'

'There's no need. Athena has her own chariot.'

'What?'

'OK,' I said, interrupting them before the difficult questions came. 'Message sent. It's done.'

'Thank you, darling.' Dad took the phone from me, and then, with a force I didn't know he had, flung it against the wall, pushing aside a pastoral print of a rustic scene. Bending down slowly, he picked up the battered phone and handed it to Nick.

'You wouldn't have a microwave here, would you?' he asked.

Chapter 39

Dad looked at my startled face.

'But darling, I'll buy you another as soon as we get back.'

'Let's get some sleep,' suggested Nick. He narrowed his eyes at me. 'We can talk about communication tomorrow.'

I had trouble sleeping and spent most of the early morning packing, preparing for the flight back to London. I knew it was my intention to come to Crete, to find the source of this programme and put a stop to it. I couldn't believe I'd been so stupid. The sooner we landed in Gatwick, the better. Who was I to think that I had the means to stop an illegal international operation? In the deserted house, all I'd wanted was to go home; I should have stayed there.

It was a little after eight thirty when we left the house. Walking to the edge of the property, I saw the obligatory dark car waiting. I signalled it over and we sat in silence after I had asked for the Valley farm in Messara.

'How do they know where everything is?' hissed Nick, after a while.

'It's their job to know,' replied Dad. 'Crete is small enough for most drivers to know at least one route to somewhere.'

'Aren't their sat-nav's checked?' I asked, suddenly worried.

'Most of these cars have a sat-nav built in, but the drivers I've known rarely use them. It's possible that the car may be tracked, but you're still safer in here than in a hire car.'

Within thirty minutes, we were driving through the vineyards and olive groves. Flat open landscapes gave way to the hills three to five miles beyond. Separated squares displayed neatly laid rows of vines and bushes so straight, they could have been cut by a knife.

'We'll be coming to the farm, soon,' said Nick. 'I suggest we stay together. Let's just find this Plutus guy and have a word. And then get the hell out of here.'

We drove through a simple white gate and along a narrow driveway into a bright and very busy courtyard, where a young woman with a clipboard was trying to herd unco-operative tourists into separate groups. She stood in inappropriate high heels, pointing to the different areas of the courtyard where groups should be. Her long dark ponytail swished across her shoulders every time she moved her head.

'I think we might have come on the wrong day,' I said, as I got out of the car.

'Are you for the ceramic pottery workshop or the traditional cheese making class?' called the woman in an English accent.

'Well, actually, we're here to see the traditional corn, wheat and tomato crops,' I said.

'Oh. The farmland tour,' she replied, waving her clipboard dismissively towards the farmhouse. 'In there.'

The three of us wandered through the main door and saw a sign that promised a cooking lesson and a walk around the farm to see where the produce was grown. We followed our noses left, into the kitchen, where a cookery demonstration was already in full swing. A red-faced woman was talking rapidly; too rapidly for the tourists to follow everything she was saying. She was being assisted by a teenage girl, whose bored expression indicated she would rather be anywhere else than here. An old man rose from a battered kitchen chair with the aid of an engraved walking stick.

'This class is full,' he said, in broken English. 'But the next is in half an hour. You come then.'

'We've come to find someone...' started Nick.

'It is a pleasure to meet you,' interrupted the man, extending his hand to me.

'Let me help you.' I assisted the man back into his chair. 'I was hoping to meet someone here.'

'Everyone hopes to meet someone in Crete. It is often themselves. I am still looking.' He laughed softly at his own joke, but continued to hold my hand. 'You are strong. You already know who you are. So many changes and so many years. Once, we had so much. Many kilos of olives, many kilos of grapes. Many donkeys. People do not want our oil or wine anymore; they say they want to learn our culture.' The old man coughed and chuckled again. 'This is easy. Eat!'

I glanced around the overcrowded kitchen.

'We can browse for half an hour,' suggested Dad. He pushed us back the way we came in. 'Did you see the carvings on his cane? he whispered, 'Scenes from Greek legends, and very expensive. That certainly wasn't locally produced.'

Back outside, we turned to the right of the farmhouse and walked past open sided sheds housing ancient looking farm machinery.

'The old guy could have been Plutus,' grumbled Nick.

'That's possible,' said Dad. 'But the Company expect to use whoever they employ. If he is working for them, it's not going to be in a very active role. But his cane looked like a clue. Most of the farms here would die without the tourist visits, but his expensive cane means he's getting money from somewhere.'

'We're wasting time,' I moaned. 'How do we make contact?'

'We already have,' said Dad. 'Now we wait for them to respond.'

'How about we take a look at the stables?' I suggested.

Ahead of us and a little further from the main farm buildings, was a set of three stables. The top half of two of the doors were open and a horse had put his head out of one to sniff curiously at the approaching strangers.

'Wow, he's rare,' I said.

'How do you know?' asked Nick.

'I read about Crete before our flight. The Messara were developed by crossing native and Arabian breeds imported during the Ottoman occupation. There's now a breeding programme in place to protect them.'

'These ones are used for riding and light farm work.'

We all turned at the sound of the new voice. The girl from the kitchen was standing beside us. 'Panemorfi, here, once worked the olive press. He walked inside the wheel that worked the grinding stones.'

She stepped forward and unlocked the stable door, rubbing the horse's nose as she did so. 'Come on in and say hello.'

We were happy to step into the cool stable and pet the horse, but the girl's friendly expression changed when we were inside.

'It was stupid of you to come, Athena,' she said. 'Why are you here?'

'To meet with Plutus,' I replied, giving her a stern look of my own. 'Who might you be?'

'I am Angeliki, but my friends call me Kiki.'

'And what do you know about me?'

'Apart from the fact you are stupid?' Her pretty face gave me the incredulous eye roll that only a fifteen year old can master. 'Pappous says you are brave, but I hear that you run from England and chase shadows.'

'I knew it was the old man,' muttered Nick.

'Grandpa was the accountant, but now I help.' Kiki seemed to grow an inch with her pride. I thought back to the red-faced woman in the kitchen.

'Does your mother know how you help?'

A sudden flash of panic lit Kiki's eyes and I understood that the old man might want help with a computer, but much was still on a need-to-know basis.

My father stepped forward. 'What has your Grandpa asked you to tell us? Presumably there is a reason you followed us here?'

Kiki reached into a pocket of her jeans and held up a small flash drive, which she tossed to me.

'Good luck getting that out of Crete,' she said before walking away.

Nick looked at his watch. 'We don't have much time. Should we delay our flights?'

'No,' said Dad. 'I think we should get back to England quickly.'

'We need to get what's on this USB to DCI Little,' I nodded. 'Fireflight are watching and if we smuggle their financial information out of Crete, they will know. Our best chance of using this is to hope that the airport has an internet café.'

'Why did the old man help us?' asked Nick. 'The girl didn't seem too keen.'

'Until I can see what's on that USB, I can't be sure he has,' I said. 'There's no way for me to know if any figures on it are true. This could be another trap.'

'You'll still need to forward them on,' said Dad. 'They're the only clue you have to offer the police.'

We hurried back outside into the mid-morning sun and towards our waiting car. The tourists in the courtyard had now dispersed and the tour guide was standing in the shade of a coach, talking on a mobile phone.

'Why hasn't she walked with one of the tour groups?'

wondered Dad aloud.

'Because she's not here for them,' I replied, pushing Dad towards our car. The woman glanced over her shoulder, saw us and abruptly ended her call. 'She's here for us.'

Chapter 40

'To the house!' I yelled as soon as we were in the car.

'No, to Perdika,' called Dad. 'We will need to split up,' he said. 'Let me take the car, and you two go on to the airport.'

'No! We need to stay together.'

'Kimmie, darling, please don't argue. If what I'm thinking is correct, Fireflight will have enforcers waiting for you in Heraklion. Nick, do you still have your phone on you?'

'Yes, Tim.'

'It might be worth risking a call to your young man at the restaurant.' Nick started calling as the car sped back through the countryside. 'Ask him to pick up your luggage and passports from the house and meet you in a car at the back of the restaurant. The enforcers will follow this car back to the house.'

'You'll be alone with no-one to help you!'

'I've done this before, darling. I'll be alright. You are more important.'

'I am a goddess. I'll protect you.'

'Maybe in Athens, but not in Heraklion, my dear.'

'You can't stay behind. You can't!'

'I can stay behind,' suggested Nick, holding the phone

away from his ear. 'Draw their attention for a while.'

Dad shook his head. 'Not a good idea, dear boy. You're a person of interest.'

'A what?'

'Person of interest,' repeated Dad. 'Someone Fireflight would like to speak to. That doesn't mean that you're a threat, necessarily, or a prospect for the future, just someone they'd like to chat with.'

'That's ridiculous.'

'It's true.' Dad waggled his hand towards Nick, indicating that he should continue with his call.

'What would they want with Nick?' I whispered.

'He's married to you,' responded Dad, quietly. 'Has Nick ever had one of those silly little banking errors on the computer that stops your money for twenty-four hours and then magically rectifies itself? How about mistaken parking fines or tax mix-ups quickly resolved with a telephone call?'

'We all get those, don't we?'

Dad didn't answer and the three of us sat in uneasy silence for the rest of the journey.

When we reached Perdika I suddenly gripped Dad's jacket.

'Promise me you'll make it back to London. Promise me!'

'Of course, darling,' he smiled. 'I promise.'

Even then, as I kissed him, I think I knew he was lying. Nick reached across the seats and he and Dad shook hands. There seemed to be an unspoken communication between them.

Perry's car was waiting with the engine running. We ran towards it and Perry was driving us away the second we closed the doors. I turned in my seat to see the black car heading in the opposite direction.

'He didn't even say goodbye.'

Nick didn't speak, but gently pulled me towards him and I laid my head on his shoulder for the rest of the journey.

The airport was supposed to be fifteen minutes away, but Perry got us there in ten. I hugged him to thank him for everything he'd done for us.

'I will see you again, Athena,' he said.

We checked in our luggage and Nick looked at his watch again.

'We've only got twenty minutes before we board,' he said. 'Time to find that internet café, or risk taking the flash drive to the UK.'

We found the café not far from the entrance and public use computers facing the terminal windows.

Nick brought up his email and inserted the flash drive.

'I hope this doesn't take too long. I haven't heard from Little since he said the account had been accessed.'

'Let me see the spreadsheets. Look,' I said, pointing over Nick's shoulder. 'There's another column of figures I've not seen before. Do you remember when I said I'd drop a poison pill in Fireflight's sweetie jar? Plutus has done it for me. He's revealed hidden money. You better send this quickly.'

'There,' Nick said at last. 'Done. All spread sheets emailed over. I'd be interested to know how many of the companies that you did business with were also fronts for Fireflight.'

I looked up. 'Maybe they can tell you.'

Two smartly dressed men in business suits had just walked in through the main entrance and turned in opposite directions.

'I'll delete the files on the drive,' said Nick, 'and the history on this PC.'

'Will that be enough?'

'Probably not, but it'll take them time to recover the files.'

'We need to destroy the USB.'

Nick continued tapping the keyboard.

'Hurry!'

'OK, here.' Nick pulled the flash drive and handed it to me.

'What the hell am I supposed to do with it?'

A voice on the public address system announced that our flight was now boarding. We rushed to the departure hall as one of the men turned around and looked directly at me.

'Quick! The gates!' Nick grabbed my arm and we ran to the boarding desks. I spied a young businessman in jeans and dark glasses tapping away on a laptop, an open coffee cup placed on the floor by his chair.

I freed myself from Nick's grip and ran over to him.

'Excuse me,' I said holding up the USB. 'I think this is yours.'

The man looked at me over the top of his glasses.

'No, I don't think so,' he said.

'Are you sure?' I asked, hoping that I was giving the

enforcers enough time to see me.

'I'm sure,' said the businessman, growing irritated.

'Suit yourself,' I said and dropped the USB into his nearly full cup of cappuccino.

'Hey!'

'Thanks,' I called as I re-joined Nick at the gate. There was only one other couple in front of us and I silently begged the staff to hurry as the enforcers tried to relieve the man of his coffee. The enforcers were running towards us as we were shown through the tunnel to the plane.

I didn't allow myself to breath out until we were airborne.

Chapter 41

Back in London I waited for a call from Dad that I knew in my heart would never come.

DCI Little promised us that he was making enquiries, but I knew that if Dad was still alive, he couldn't risk making contact. If he wasn't, I'd find out soon enough. I clung to the belief that no news was good news, but here in the UK, my nervous edginess and need for order was back.

Nick had been so kind to me, he'd done everything I asked; fitted new locks, bought new shrubs for the garden, taken me anywhere I wanted to go. He was just so happy to be back home and have me there with him. But something had changed that I just couldn't put my finger on. Brownlow Print had been disbanded, and with no job to go to, I felt adrift.

In the wee hours of Saturday morning, I woke to an empty space beside me. Nick was back with his books again.

'What are you looking for, now?' I asked, stuffing my hands into my dressing gown pockets.

'An answer that isn't here,' he responded, irritably.

'An answer to what?'

'The Athena question. When we were in Crete, you were a different woman, happier and brighter. Now that we're back home, you're nervy and anxious again.'

'I'm just me, Nick.'

'Not any more. You are two women. You're Kim and Athena.'

'And you think you like Athena better, do you?'

'No, I think you like Athena better.'

I shrugged and bowed my head. Perhaps he was right. 'I don't know what I can do here. What can Kim do? I know that Fireflight will mend the damage I've caused and continue their operations. I've only managed to delay them.'

'You wanted to disrupt their money transfers. We've already passed that information on.'

I nodded, but didn't feel reassured. 'A better disruption would be if we knew something that they didn't...' I tailed off, and then looked up at Nick.

'What?'

'I just remembered something Perry said to me. He said Plutus might not be one person, it is not one person who knows everything, it is many who know only a little.'

'You think that the girl and the old man are both Plutus?'

'No,' I said, thinking. 'Kiki helped Grandpa, and he gave us what he had, but he wouldn't have had everything. We have to think of ourselves in the same way.'

'What, us?' snorted Nick. 'The dynamic duo?'

'No,' I laughed. 'More like the magnificent seven!' I counted us off on my fingers. 'You and me, Little, Simpson, Reg the Attendant, Kiki and her Grandpa.'

'But we're not even together in the same country. How

can we help each other?'

'Fireflight would also have its employees in different places,' I said. 'But we have all contributed small amounts of information. What can we learn by gathering that information in one place? We've been so anxious to find out what information they have, we've forgotten to look at what information we have.'

Nick pushed a few of his books aside and pulled a sheet of paper from his printer. He grabbed a pen and wrote 1 in the margin near the top.

'Let's start with you.'

'OK. I know the Brownlow account codes and that Fireflight were going to use that money to finance illegal drug trials.'

Nick wrote 2 in the margin. 'I know the history. The myths seem to dictate how they use what they have.'

'And, three,' I continued, 'Little had a trace put on the accounts. That means that they would have had to use other accounts to get the money they wanted.'

'Four,' said Nick, 'Kiki would have known what those values were, and five, her Grandpa would have known where that money went.'

'We must have disrupted their plans, because Perry knows they are still looking for other options. That's six.'

'But Simpson is in Egypt. He gave you a pin. That's our last clue.'

'He invented a subtle weapon,' I said. 'Athena was goddess of crafts. I need to create something.'

'What do you have in mind?'

'Well, I gave Zeus one headache when I was born. How about giving him another?'

Nick's books told me that Athena was credited with inventing many things, including the trumpet.

'Why not give the local paper first refusal on an interview with the kidnapped woman?' suggested Nick.

'There's not much point in that,' I argued. 'I couldn't tell the reporter that I was kidnapped or anything about a possible conspiracy theory. Without evidence of either, I'd just look like another crackpot.'

'So, what are you going to do?'

'Having my name in the newspaper might be enough. I'll take out an advertisement to thank all the people who have helped to bring me home. It'll be like thumbing my nose at them.'

We left the newspaper offices later that day. 'This is dangerous,' warned Nick. 'We have no idea what will come of this.' He placed a protective arm around me.

'I do,' I said. 'You were right. Athena is a different woman and her battle is only just beginning. Fireflight will respond. I don't know how, but we'll be ready.'

'So what would my goddess like to do first?'

'We have a performance to attend today.'

It was a rough, blustery afternoon and leaves were racing in circles across the tarmac of the country road.

We'd parked in a cut-in, with the wheels halfway up a grassy bank. It wasn't an ideal parking space and it certainly wasn't romantic enough to be a lover's lane, but this was the best spot to witness the demolition.

I could hardly believe that in all the time I'd spent in the house, I had never been more than fifteen minutes' drive away from home.

From our vantage point on that hillside, we had a clear view of the house below. From here, it actually looked quite pretty; the kind of place ambitious renovators would make over and sell for a profit. It seemed a little smaller than I remembered, but appeared to have some land along with it.

A small meadow, perhaps once a paddock, was just across the narrow lane and small outbuildings, now hollow shells, stood untidily against the outside hedging.

The lane, previously isolated and lonely, was now a hive of activity as workers in yellow hard hats yelled to one another and skips were loaded on to the back of trucks. A giant digger, with its claw arm raised, stood ready like an animal, awaiting the attack command.

We stood in front of the car and I pulled my thick coat a little higher up towards my ears.

'Thanks for coming with me.' I smiled at Nick. I had realised without Nick confessing that I wasn't the only person who had felt imprisoned by that house. Even though I had left its confines I still wasn't truly free from it and neither was he.

'Thanks for coming back to me,' he whispered, as he brushed aside a strand of windswept hair from my cheek.

'Sure,' I smiled.

'No,' he said firmly, suddenly grasping my face between his cool rough hands. 'I mean thanks for coming back to me.'

Then I understood. He knew. He knew what I had done, about me and Tony. I felt a heavy stone in my stomach and tears threatened to overspill.

'No,' I gasped, feeling a shiver. 'You know? How long?'

'From the beginning,' he said simply. 'I saw it in your eyes that first night. A wedge was pushed between us.' Nick looked up towards the house. A hard look had taken over his face, his mouth pulled in a firm line. 'It was Tony, wasn't it? The one you said was looking after you? I'll never forgive him.'

I realised that I had been holding on to my bitterness over Nick's encounter with his ex-girlfriend. Now we both needed to be forgiven. The house and my bitterness had created a labyrinth.

'Oh, Nick. I'm so sorry. How can you ever forgive me?' My eyes searched his face for answers but Nick only smiled.

'Oh, Kim, you dummy,' he kissed my forehead and then my nose. 'There really is nothing to forgive.'

'But I... I mean, we...'

'You did what you had to do to survive. You're here, now, alive. And you're with me. I couldn't ask for anything more. I don't want anything more.'

He kissed me. Now, that was romantic, in the freezing, bloody cold on a windy hillside.

I turned in his arms and pulled them further around my waist. Nick dipped his head and roughened my cheek with his own.

I felt the burden I had been carrying for too long, gently lift as we watched the clawed animal stumble forward and smash brick and stone into rubble.

The next KL Skinner novel - sample

The Fireflight Initiative

Chapter 1

You know that feeling you sometimes get when you think that something's missing, or you might have forgotten something? Well, that's how I felt when I heard the phone ring again.

It had rung twice last night. The first time I was out; Nick and I had been invited over to a friend's house for drinks, and the second time Nick was asleep in front of the TV and I was already upstairs getting ready for bed.

They hadn't left a message but were obviously keen to get hold of me.

I went to answer and Nick called out from the living room; 'Can you get that, babe?'

I think he was trying to be funny.

'Yep?'

'Athena, this is Gaia. I really need to see you. Can we meet?'

It had been at least ten months since anyone had called me by that name. I swallowed hard. Suddenly, I felt a little bit sick and giddy.

'Do you know the coffee shop on the corner of Connor Street?' she continued nervously. 'Meet me there tomorrow at 2 o'clock. Look, I can't really talk, I'm sure I'm being watched. Please Athena,' she begged. 'I really need you.'

I had said nothing during that call, but replaced the receiver wishing I'd been able to say no. I wished I'd been able to cry out, shout, scream, anything. But, my mouth had gone dry and my mind had raced too fast for me to get a grip on what I was thinking.

My hands were trembling as I pressed 1471. Unsurprisingly, she'd withheld her number.

I walked slowly into the living room and sat on the arm of Nicks chair and stared at the TV. He was watching the motor racing and cursing that our bloke was too slow and losing points. The image blurred before my eyes as I realised that The Company had another scheme in progress. I started to cry as I understood that I was going to get pulled back into that horrible, sordid world and that because someone needed me, I would go.

Nick's arm rested comfortably on my leg and received a light splash, making him look up and stare at me concerned.

'Kim? What is it?'

'I'm going to need a lift into town tomorrow lunchtime,' I said, but I couldn't tell him why, as emotion overcame me and I sobbed with my head buried in his shoulder.

Nick managed to get the whole story out of me before we went to bed that night and he was furious.

'Jesus, Kim!' he yelled. 'I thought we'd left that bloody mess behind. She's got a cheek phoning you and where'd she get our number from? You should've just hung up.'

'I put a notice in the local paper, remember? We did that

together to provoke a response. They've responded.'

'Well, if you're so sure you're going, I am too.'

'No, Nick!' I was suddenly afraid. If Gaia was in trouble, as she believed she was, she probably wouldn't come in to talk to me if she saw a stranger there. Although, to be honest I was a stranger too; we'd never actually met.

Nick sat on the edge of the bed with his back to me.

'I'm coming.' He said.

We didn't spoon that night.

Ten months ago I'd been sent on a simple errand by my manager and while out of the office had been kidnapped and taken to a deserted house in the country. I had been made to reveal account codes that had released huge sums of money to finance an illegal fertility drug and innocent women, believing that they had signed up for a legitimate drug trial, had their lives put at risk.

The company I'd worked for had been a front and everything I'd done for them, the professional relationships I'd formed and the dedication I had shown was wasted. It was all a lie and I'd been a fool. When I'd found out the truth, my biggest concern had been for the welfare of the female volunteers. Gaia was one.

I lay still in the dark with my eyes open. At this moment, there were only two things I could be sure of. I was definitely keeping my appointment with Gaia tomorrow and, come hell or high water, I was going to find out what The Company was up to.

The following day, I was pacing the house like a restless

tiger. I'd scrubbed the bathroom to within an inch of its life and unable to eat anything, was threatening to do the same to the kitchen cupboards. I'd been glancing at the clock every fifteen minutes and had already drunk my weight in tea when Nick returned from work at one thirty.

'Come on, then,' he shrugged, keeping his hands in his jacket pockets. 'Let's hear what she's got to say.'

The coffee shop was still busy with the lunchtime trade when we arrived. Harassed office workers ordered extra strong espresso and calorific snacks to take away while those who could afford to spare a whole hour, lounged in leather chairs and pretended to look important as they read the newspapers or browsed their phones.

I chose a low table with a sofa facing the door so that I could people watch. I had no idea how I'd recognise Gaia when I saw her.

I bit my nails and ignored a fast cooling cappuccino as Nick sipped black coffee until a quiet voice said, 'hello Athena.'

She was slightly older than I expected; early to mid-forties with shoulder length light brown hair and blue eyes. She was pushing a modern looking pram with a baby boy, about two months old, who was wearing clothes that looked more expensive than what she was wearing herself. His serious dark eyes observed me curiously. There was no mistaking who his father was. I would have known Hephaestus' child anywhere.

I involuntarily shivered as I remembered that

psychopathic drug developer. He had tried to attack me and enrol me into their plans. I had been lucky to escape him. I wasn't sure I wanted to know what had happened to Gaia.

Gaia sat down opposite me, leaving the pram near Nick who offered the boy his keys to slobber over.

She smiled at me and looked relieved.

'You came. I'm so glad. I read your notice in the paper.'

'I've been waiting for a response.'

'But that was months ago,' said Nick. 'Why wait so long?'

Gaia glanced at the windows. 'Who's watching us? Eyes are everywhere.' She sat down opposite me. 'I was released about the same time you were.' She smiled at Eric. 'At least I was able to have my baby at home.'

'Who released you?'

'Hermes. When I read "Athena wishes to thank," it gave me hope that there was a life outside the clinic. I was surprised you hadn't left the area.'

Nick and I had briefly considered it, but I decided I was going to brazen it out. It was my crazy way of sticking two fingers up at everyone. If we were going to move house, it would be because we wanted to, not because we thought we had to.

I quickly glanced at Nick, wondering if I should introduce him, but Gaia pre-empted me.

'I'm glad you came too, Nick. This will involve both of you.'

I was immediately suspicious. 'How do know who Nick is?'

'The Company has files on everyone. I used my home computer to find you. They probably know that by now.' She glanced at her watch nervously. 'I'm fairly sure I'm being watched, so I'll get straight to the point.' Gaia leaned forward with her elbows on her knees to talk confidentially, but I could see Nick was having trouble taking this seriously.

I wasn't sure if all this cloak and dagger was necessary either. If The Company had wanted us dead, we'd be dead already.

'I'm pretty sure that I'll be sacrificed in the next Company project and I want to know if you'll agree to care for Eric and raise him as your own.'

There was a moments silence as Nick and I glanced at each other before staring back at Gaia.

'Sacrificed,' Nick snorted. 'Don't you think that's being a bit melodramatic?'

I didn't think so. At one point, not so long ago, I thought I was going to be sacrificed too. I threw Nick a shut-up-and-listen look and hoped that Gaia would continue. She fiddled with the packets of sugar and sweetener on the table, arranging them in order.

'After Hephaestus's mistakes became known, we had to move to a different location. We were bussed for miles during the night. When we arrived, I saw that the place we'd been brought to was an abandoned hospital. It wasn't as nice as the clinic, but it was clean. It had obviously been prepared in advance.'

I was unsurprised. The first clinic probably looked lovely,

to project a professional image. The hospital was on standby.

'I asked what was to become of me and they said I was a heroine, my baby was destined for great things and I wasn't to worry, they'd take care of me.' She looked towards the pram and I saw a tear overspill, but Gaia quickly brushed it away and glanced up towards the other customers, embarrassed.

'Later, I was told that if I wanted to keep my baby, I had to work to earn the things he'd need. I thought that they meant prostitution, but when they found out that I used to be a lab assistant, they had another idea.' She'd finished with the sugar and was now neatening the serviettes in the tray. 'I examined ovarian tissue for its suitability for cryogenic preservation.'

I reached over and gripped her hand to stop her and the touch seemed to startle her, as if physical human contact was strange and unexpected.

'What are they doing, Gaia?'

I hadn't meant for my voice to sound as harsh and demanding as it did. Gaia looked like a rabbit caught in headlights and I could clearly feel her pulse throbbing in her wrist.

'I'm not sure,' she whispered. 'We didn't know where the tissue had come from or where it was going to and we didn't ask.'

'How many samples are there?'

Gaia closed her eyes and dropped her chin onto her chest. 'Thousands.'

KL Skinner

Karen has always loved reading and has been writing short stories since she was at school. Karen has always had a particular interest in reading about the darker side of life, but found that a lot of what she was reading didn't have much emotional drama and so started to write for herself.

Karen has been a member of the Hertford Writers' circle for the last 12 years and contributed to their anthologies as well as other short stories online. This is her first novel, part of a series. The next instalment is already in progress and due for completion next year.

Karen is married and lives in Essex.

KL Skinner

Select Bibliography

The Hellenistic World
- MM Austin, 1981, Cambridge University Press

The Greek Myths
- Robin Waterfield, 2011, Quercus Editions Ltd

Laws, by Plato
- Benjamin Jowett, 2012, Digital Edition

The History of Assassination
- Brian McConnell, 2015, Endeavour Press Ltd

World Mythology
- Mark Daniels, 2016, Michael O'Mara Books

Beyond Reasonable Doubt
- Veronique Greenwood, July 2016, National Geographic Magazine

Greece, Gods and the Beyond
- Caroline Alexander, July 2016, National Geographic Magazine